The Urbana Free Library

To renew: call **217-367-4057**
or go to **urbanafreelibrary.org**
and select **My Account**

UNTIL WE HAVE FACES

STORIES

by Michael Nye

TURNER PUBLISHING COMPANY

"The Time We Lost Our Way" first appeared in *Epoch*; "Beauty in the Age of Chaos and Savagery" in *Kenyon Review*; "The Sins of Man" first appeared in *Pleiades*; "The Photograph" first appeared in *American Literary Review*; "Who Are You Wearing?" first appeared in *The Normal School*; "The Good Shepherd" first appeared in *Hunger Mountain*; and "Reunion" in *Notre Dame Review*.

Turner Publishing Company
Nashville, Tennessee

www.turnerpublishing.com

Until We Have Faces

Cover design: Tree Abraham
Book design: Tim Holtz

Library of Congress Cataloging-in-Publication Data

Names: Nye, Michael, 1978- author.
Title: Until we have faces : short stories / Michael Nye.
Description: Nashville : Turner Publishing Company, 2020. | Summary: "In a
  style reminiscent of John Cheever and Alice Munro, Michael Nye's second
  collection of stories, Until We Have Faces, contend with transfixing
  themes: marital and familial estrangement, ways of trespass, the
  intractable mysteries and frights of modern life, the uncertainty of
  knowledge and truth, the gulfs between people and the technology we use,
  the frailty of our economic lives-while underlining throughout the
  persistency of love"-- Provided by publisher.
Identifiers: LCCN 2019035622 (print) | LCCN 2019035623 (ebook) | ISBN
  9781684425051 (paperback) | ISBN 9781684425068 (hardcover) | ISBN
  9781684425075 (ebook)
Subjects: LCSH: Life--Fiction. | Short stories, American.
Classification: LCC PS3614.Y43 A6 2020 (print) | LCC PS3614.Y43 (ebook) |
  DDC 813/.6--dc23
LC record available at https://lccn.loc.gov/2019035622
LC ebook record available at https://lccn.loc.gov/2019035623

Printed in the United States of America
17 18 19 20 10 9 8 7 6 5 4 3 2 1

For Elizabeth

TABLE OF CONTENTS

THE TIME WE LOST OUR WAY

I

In 1998, the winter before they were to start ninth grade, swearing that as freshmen they would be the varsity starting backcourt for the St. Xavier Bombers, Ronnie and Quentin did everything they could to find a game. They were seen everywhere: over on the courts in Highland Terrace, down at Washington Park in Over-the-Rhine with its crowds of homeless veterans and ex-athletes turned junkies, up at the Sportsplex on that weird rubbery court—back when the Sportsplex still had basketball, before they shut it down and put in an indoor soccer field because too many ballers started fights, pushing and throwing punches and calling each other *motherfuckers*, screaming so loud it scared the soccer moms all the way on the other side of the building. Even at age thirteen, well before he would hit his growth spurt, Quentin—shaved head, baggy shorts, long arms— glided, walked up to the chain-link fences with such ease, as if he was saving all his energy for the court, which he was, but once he stepped on the court he switched gears, cradled the ball like it was an extension of his body, as if it was under his command, before lasering no-look passes, crossing dudes over with a vicious shake, launching up a silky baseline jumper. In time, when he grew into the man-child that would get recruited by North Carolina, Syracuse, Michigan State and other top schools, Quentin would thunder through the lane, rising, a skywalker, and throw it down on the horses in the low post.

But that was later. At the time, they were an odd pair: Ronnie was white and Quentin was black. In 1998, Ronnie was taller than Quentin, just a notch under six feet. Ronnie was freckled, pink as a scraped cheek, with bushy dark red hair and shoulders wide enough for his parents to sign him up for JV football. On their eighth grade team, they jogged through the double doors together, shoulder to shoulder, leading their team to the layup line, and when the cheering and clapping settled to sporadic shouts as the bassline blared through the speakers, Ronnie had already stopped hearing it, because he was feeling the leather in his palms and studying the way the rock spun off the glass and dropped through the rim.

Sometimes, the parabola of Ronnie's jumper was a shooting star streaking across the gym, settling into the bottom of the net as if disappearing into a black hole, and even the other team knew they had no chance. This mystery—*the zone*, ballers called it—thrilled him. He shot the first jumper and just watched the rim and waited for the ball to disappear into it; if he was a little off that night, he wanted to see whether it rattled off the front or the back of the rim. And the next one. And the next one. Then he wasn't watching the rim anymore but simply playing the game.

Now, under the sun of an unseasonably warm February day that brought everyone out to the playground, ballers surrounded the court, waiting. Ronnie sucked on his water bottle. His team had just won four straight games, scoring the most points on his squad in all four games, a fact he knew had surprised the onlookers waiting for their chance to get a run. Q—no one called the kid Quentin, he was simply Q—had the next run. Ronnie sprang to his feet. He'd hit the last two shots, both on crossovers that the kid guarding him, a senior at a local high school, all muscles and oversized feet, simply didn't believe a skinny white boy could do: break his ankles and pull up on a dime to drop a pair of eighteen footers on him.

"Ready?" Ronnie yelled.

Q nodded, his eyes far away, pretending to be disinterested.

The teams gathered on the court. Someone's ball came from under the basket, and Ronnie cupped it, spun it behind his back, and flipped it underhanded to Q. He caught it with both hands. Q held the ball for a moment, gentle, as if it was a prayer offering, a thin suppressed smile on his lips. Adrenalin surged through Ronnie's chest.

"Ready?" Q said softly.

In the summer of 1998, on the rare times when Ronnie came home and found his father both there and awake, the old man was usually in the living room looking at his coins. His albums of coins were slim leather books that were strategically displayed next to his mother's expensive shiny coffee table books. They continued to hold his father's attention even when Ronnie banged into the room. He wondered when his father had last rotated them—he seemed to swap out his display albums with the ones stored in his basement workshop at least once a month. Neither Ronnie nor his mother understood this obsession, but they did understand the angry, satisfied look chiseled on his father's face. This was the side of his father—distant, quiet—that Ronnie most feared.

"How was basketball?" His father remained hunched over his coins.

"Good." It didn't matter if he prattled on for ten minutes or gave a one word answer: his father wasn't really listening. "Working on my left hand. You know. New stuff."

His father hummed in agreement, turned a page.

"Mom home?"

The smile vanished. "Of course not. How does tuna casserole sound for dinner?"

"That's cool." His father's love of tuna was yet another mystery. "Mom coming home?"

"We might eat in front of the television tonight. Is that okay with you?"

He shrugged even though his father wasn't looking at him. His father gnashed his teeth, tipped up his jaw, and ran a palm down the length of his neck. He had been a three-sport athlete in high school, and his arms retained a ropy muscularity; his calf muscles bulged over his socks from his days as a long-distance runner. But shirts, no matter how small, draped off his torso, and when they used to take beach vacations, Ronnie always marveled at his father's pale, concave chest. His father had a receding hairline but thick hair, unremarkable glasses, and the glazed expression of a man who had found life to be perpetually disappointing.

By contrast, his mother's fairness, her skin almost porcelain, made her seem otherworldly. She was a woman that always wore dresses with her toenails painted, her makeup minimal and flawless. When Ronnie was a child, she always seemed to be there: basketball games, school plays, Cub Scouts. But lately, like his father, she had become prone to staring off into space, unblinking and unhearing, and she would let the cigarette at the end of her fingers burn itself down to a sliver of ash.

Ronnie couldn't remember anything that had actually happened between his parents, just a gradual sense that they were unhappy. Every word they spoke to each other was tinged with a hidden, hateful meaning. When all of them were home, his parents managed to never be in the same room together, let alone on the same floor. In 1998, even though they had lived there for three years, Ronnie still thought of it as the New House. It was too big for them; it had four bedrooms even though Ronnie didn't have any siblings. His parents found ways to not be home in the evenings: his father started working out at the local gym, spent Friday nights playing poker with his coworkers, took up golf, went to movies by himself; his mother, who once had never worked, kept busy with substitute teaching, book clubs, an over-thirty women's soccer team, PTA meetings, volunteering at the library, until all these activities weren't enough. Last year, she landed an entry-level position with Provident Bank.

Ronnie and Q had been friends since kindergarten. Their desks were paired together, and since neither boy's parents had provided them with the complete list of new materials for their school years, they shared pencils, markers, erasers, glue sticks, scissors—they even used the same three-ring binder. During the second week of school, a group of first graders, both black and white, surrounded Q on the playground, towering over him and jabbing at him with their fingers, mocking his voice. It had too many strange inflections to be white, but there were hints of something musical, something foreign. All the kids knew was that Q didn't sound black, didn't sound like a white kid either, and what was up with that? Where you from? What's wrong with you? They jabbed at him until tears ran down his cheeks, and when Ronnie saw Q surrounded by three bigger kids and his chin lowered and shoulders slumped under their taunts, he was enraged. Ronnie raced out from the middle of a game of four square and, asking no questions, grabbed the nearest bully by the shoulder and flew forward with a fist, cracking the kid in the nose, and he proceeded to throw punches, blooding noses, scraping elbows and knees, until they were all on the ground grabbing and clawing at each other, which landed all five of them in the principal's office. Ronnie and Q had been inseparable ever since. So in sixth grade when Ronnie's family moved into the split level house across the street from Q, after basketball had become The Thing for both boys thanks to an undefeated fourth grade season, they considered themselves far more than just lucky.

Until 1998, it remained this way—seemingly perfect—for Ronnie, as long as it was outside his home. On the cusp of high school, growing into his body, able to pick his own clothes and his own music, playing ball in different gyms and on different playgrounds, gaining respect and admiration from kids who knew him as a guy that had game, the world Ronnie lived in expanded. But, in his parents' house, everything seemed to be closing in on him.

One day in late June of '98, Ronnie stretched his legs across the carpet of the enclosed porch and folded his arms back over his head. He was watching his tapes. He recorded every NBA game with a good point guard, replaying the games over and over again, studying how they created space, how they got in the lane, how they read the defense. He had five seasons of complete playoffs and scatterings of regular season games, and organized his recordings around the point guard rather than the team or the year. The ceiling fan clicked over his head, and he was about to sit up and look for a tape of Gary Payton games when he heard a noise from the front of the house. It was the distinct groan of the front door opening, his mother coming in from a job interview. From the way her bags hit the floor, he knew his mother didn't have good news. Ronnie turned the volume up and pretended he didn't know she was home.

When she wasn't interviewing, she spent her time at the kitchen table teaching herself about the stock market. She kept copies of charts for high-dividend yielding companies and sometimes invited Ronnie to study for a lecture on the risks associated with foreign municipal bonds. "Save all the money you can, and put it in a private account. And don't tell anyone," she warned. "The markets are irrational. People are too. Particularly your spouse. You never know what they're going to do with what you tell them."

Ronnie popped the tab off of his soda can and put it with the recycling under the sink.

"In fact," she said. "It's better to just not get married."

Through the window over the kitchen sink, Ronnie watched the tree branches. No wind. Good day for outside shooting. He prayed his mother would just stop talking.

On the night they celebrated her being hired as a junior loan officer, his mother suggested they sit down together for dinner. She even set out the beers she normally forbid his father from drinking during a meal for fear he'd turn Ronnie into an alcoholic. Despite the fact that they both now worked the same full-time hours, they still managed to never be around one another. On those nights, if Ronnie was not at Quentin's, his father joined him on the living room couch to watch TV. Ronnie ate popcorn and slurped sodas while his father drank bourbon. His mother never seemed to be home on Saturday nights; when he asked his father where she was, he ignored the question. His father had long suffered from insomnia and Ronnie would often wake in the middle of the night and hear him shuffling around downstairs. But this year, it seemed to grow worse. His father's sense of reality had become permanently addled: he was always half-asleep, half-dreaming, surfing waves of mental exhaustion that turned him absentminded, an effect enhanced by the alcohol.

"Your mother should have married the black guy," Ronnie's father said one night after his fifth or sixth beer, and Ronnie was unsure whether he meant an actual black man or just the possibility of one. They were sitting on the screened in back patio, television on, neither one really paying attention. His father knew that

7

Ronnie and Q were best friends, have been for years, and Ronnie wondered why the fuck his father would say some shit like that. Cigar smoke plumed around his father's head, almost as if it was steam from his own anger rather than the tobacco, and after five minutes of not speaking, Ronnie stood up and went back inside.

St. Xavier High School was an all-boys prep school in western Cincinnati best known for its football team, which regularly competed for state titles. The basketball team was good, not great, not known the way Elder or Turpin or Moeller or Taft or Withrow or Walnut Hills or Summit Country Day have been known for decades, for generations morphing from Chuck Taylors to Reebok Pumps to Air Jordans to Hyperfuses. Ronnie and Q could have gone to any of those schools, any of them would have been happy to have them as their backcourt. But St. X was in their neighborhood, just south down Winton Road and then one left turn followed by a fork in the road, perhaps a mile at the most, and there was the school. In their neighborhood. Where it, and they, belonged.

One night in late July, his mother found Ronnie in the living room watching an old Clint Eastwood movie. It was a western. She watched the movie silently for a long time.

"Did I tell you the about the time a gun was pointed at me?"

Ronnie shook his head. He lowered his eyes, staring at the speakers at the bottom of the television.

"When your father was failing out of college," she said. "I got a job at the front desk of a hotel. I worked nights. Your father did, too. I was already getting my masters by this point. And this guy walks in with pantyhose over his head and sticks a revolver in my face. It took a good ten seconds before I could even process what was going on. All I could tell the police later was that he had a mustache. He got away with a couple hundred dollars. He didn't hurt me. Just took the cash and left."

Ronnie's heart echoed in his ears. All he wanted was his parents to stop talking to him like this: in cryptic memories spoken as justification of who they were now.

"It was summer," she continued. "Hot, like this."

Through the cracked windows, they could hear the slushy drone of traffic in the distance, a neighbor's door slam shut. Around his parents this summer, Ronnie had been faking being asleep so long that he often wondered if his parents' stories were real or dreamed.

She ran her fingers through her hair, a cloud of black and silence.

"Your father made me keep working there. He said if I didn't I'd never be able to walk back into a hotel again. For months after that I had nightmares of being shot, bullets ripping through my skull. In some of the dreams, I'd still be alive, and see my own blood and bones splattered around me. Over and over again. And your father never even finished college. Isn't that remarkable?" She stopped, and they continued watching the movie in silence.

Along with these unprovoked soliloquies, Ronnie walked into arguments that didn't make any sense. Incoherent. He often wondered if his parents were talking about the same thing, as if their words were stripped from entirely different movies.

"Great," Ronnie's mother snapped. "Can you at least clean up your messes?"

"You're a selfish human being," his father said, his face in profile to them. "An attorney. You should have been an attorney."

"These messes, these messes. They're like pits of lava, all around our feet. You're responsible for all of this!" She waved her hand at what, to Ronnie, was a spotless living room.

His father stuck his head deep into the refrigerator and came out with a jar of pickles and a can of Schlitz. As he ducked past again, she screamed, "You're Nero. Nero! Go fucking fiddle some-where else!"

Ronnie grabbed his Walkman and zipped out the front door. Across the street, Q was mowing the lawn, and when he saw Ron-nie, he released the clutch so they could do an elaborate handshake greeting. Q went inside, grabbed two cans of Coke, and Ronnie sat down on the porch, headphones on, waiting for Q to hurry up and finish so they could go get a run in. He followed Q to the backyard and flopped down in one of their lawn chairs, the Walkman snapping as it automatically flipped from side A to side B, Das EFX thumping into his ears. Q moved in steady continuous strips up and down the lawn, and Ronnie blinked, watching nothing, hearing nothing.

Q's family were the most normal people Ronnie had ever met. Q had an older sister who went to Smith College, which appar-ently was a big deal, but all Ronnie knew was that they didn't have a basketball team worth shit. Q's father had a trim graying beard, and his mother had the patience of an elementary school teacher, which she was. When Q wanted to raze them, he called them Mr. and Mrs. Cosby. Everything about their home was warm and inviting, the kind of place where Ronnie wished he could wake up on Christmas morning. Q's father was from London, his mother was Dominican, and they had lived in the Midwest for over twenty years, their voices a concoction of inflections that confused Cincin-natians. All Ronnie knew for sure about Q's parents was that they loved each other: they spoke without anger, touched each other on the hand or elbow when they walked by, and could spend time in a room together without arguing.

Sitting in the shade of Q's house, watching his friend mow the lawn, Ronnie thought of something he had seen earlier in the week. Before dinner, his mother had pulled a glass from the dishwasher and discovered that it was cracked. But rather than throw it away, she held it closer to her face and stared at it. Her gaze reminded him of the time she caught him taking five dollars from his father's wallet. It was disappointment as much as anger, disappointment in her son, disappointment in the world, disappointment that life was always this way. His mother stared at the glass as if willing it to say something, do something, knit the long crack fissuring its lip back together.

The police came on a Tuesday afternoon. Ronnie was sitting on the floor of the back porch, shirtless, his leg stretched out in front of him, still dripping from the heat, too hot to take a shower. He and Q had won five straight after lunch, but in the late afternoon, the older kids showed up, and they had a way of using their bodies—subtle shoves, thick legs that clung to the ground like magnets—and Ronnie and Q found themselves coming in and out of games, waiting for a run. On the screen was a Lee Marvin movie; Ronnie had rented three of them from Picture Show Video that week. At the knock, Ronnie slipped a clean shirt over his head, and walked to the front door, puzzled to see two middle-aged men wearing ugly ties, holding in their hands both badges and a folded piece of blue paper. Ronnie would understand later that this was the search warrant.

"Is your mother home, Ron?" one of the cops asked him.

"Ronnie?" his mother called.

He turned. For years after this, he would think about the way his mother said his name. *Ronnie?* It wasn't just a question. It was barely contained panic. As an adult, Ronnie would cling to this memory. Whatever anger, maybe even hatred, that had built up between his parents over the course of their marriage, there remained something that seemed inconceivable to Ronnie, both then and now—his mother's fear of a life without his father.

"Mrs. Wagner," the cop said. "Is your husband home?"

"Go to your room," she said to Ronnie. "Right now."

Upstairs, he closed the door, the soft click of it latching shut, and pressed his hand against the wood. He listened but couldn't hear anything distinguishing downstairs. He crossed the room, and stood on his desk to look out the window. In the driveway were four unmarked cars, and two more at the curb. All up and down the street there was nothing, not a kid on his bike nor a person walking the dog, as if the entire area had somehow become poisonous.

No one came upstairs. No one explained anything. He sat on the edge of his bed and started rocking, eyeing the door, waiting for it to open, waiting for someone to come through and explain what was happening. He glanced at his alarm clock. Sixteen minutes. Thirty eight. Sixty two. None of this made any sense.

Then, with a knock, his door opened, and his mother came in the room, carrying her purse. Her color was ashen, her eyes red and unfocused.

"We're going to the movies."

"What's going on?"

"I'll explain in the car."

But she didn't. In silence, they headed toward the city, driving to the new Showcase Cinemas with the chairs that tilted backwards. He stood on the pavement in front of the doors and watched his mother stand alone in front of a group of pay phones to call her father in New York. She kept her back to him, gesturing frantically with her left hand. Once, for just a moment, she turned her face toward the theater, and Ronnie could see her frantic eyes, her face streaked with tears, and her mouth moving rapid and mechanical like a puppet.

In the lobby, she bought him a large popcorn and soda. They watched *Jurassic Park*, which Ronnie had already seen two times, without comment. After, they walked outside and stood on the long, wide concrete pavilion, and now, at age thirteen, taller than his mother, he had to dip his chin downward to watch her scan the parking lot for their car, her eyes flipping from row to row, seeking something she clearly was in no rush to find. They stood there for a long time, and then she lead them to the curb, sat down, and stretched her legs out in front of her. Ronnie pulled his knees to his chin.

He leaned into her as she stroked his hair. He remained cradled against her shoulder for a long time, taking in the strawberry scent of her shampoo. How long he wanted to be this close to his parents. How much more alone it actually made him feel.

And then she started explaining. How his father was a thief. Despite having a career as a lab chemist, he had been breaking into homes. He broke in and took their cash, jewelry, credit cards, electronics, and then tore their homes apart, slicing open their couches and chairs and mattress, spray painting their walls, shattering all their glasses and dishes on the kitchen floor. He terrorized people, and had been doing so for years. Since college, according to the police. In the affectless voice of a victim still in shock, she explained to Ronnie how she had no idea, had never known, and how she couldn't understand how she had lived the last fifteen years without really knowing the man she called her husband.

"Those coins," Ronnie said. "The ones he leaves out in the living room. He stole all those?"

She lowered her chin, lips trembling. She closed her eyes, her shoulders rising and falling in a quiet rhythm.

"Who would do something like that?"

His mother couldn't think of anything to say. He never actually remembered standing up and getting in the car. When they arrived home, she parked the car in the driveway and they got out and took in the emptiness: all the boxy police sedans were gone and not a single light was on in the house. The lawn was littered with cigarette butts, sitting along the top of the grass like dead fish. Inside, things were gone: a television, a computer, several lamps, and the refrigerator. They took the stairs to the basement and found that their old fridge was now jammed with all the food from upstairs. At least, his mother said, they didn't let it rot. In his room, his stereo was gone; so too were his autographed baseballs, and for the rest of his life, whenever Ronnie signed an autograph, he would think of the absence of those names—Johnny Bench, Pete Rose, and George Foster—that sat on the top shelf of his bedroom bookcase, and his face would harden into a mask of annoyance as he scrawled his name on ticket stubs, scraps of paper, basketball cards, cementing Ronnie Wagner's reputation as a malcontent.

His father didn't leave them a note. There was nothing from the police. They had no idea where he had gone, how to get a hold of him, what to do next. Ronnie's mother sent him upstairs to sleep, and he lay down atop his sheets, his hands curled into fists, and he listened through his cracked bedroom door as his mother called the police to find out where his father was being held and what the bail process involved, calling one of her friends and sobbing her way through the evening's events. The click of her lighter, over and over again as she ignored her own rules about not smoking in the house, interrupted her words. The absence of any feelings confused him, and waiting for all of this to make sense, he listened to his mother's voice until he fell into a tenuous sleep.

In the morning, Ronnie came downstairs already wearing his basketball gear and found his mother making a breakfast of eggs, sausage, and toast, while across the room, sitting by himself at the kitchen table was the man Ronnie recognized as his grandfather.

He wore a suit that Ronnie somehow knew was expensive, his gray hair was immaculately parted, and while not a large man, his presence seemed to entirely fill the kitchen chair. He hadn't seen his grandfather in five years—for reasons he didn't know. He knew only that it was a subject not to be broached, that his father was terrified of this man. His grandfather's hands were steepled together on the table. His mouth smiled; his eyes didn't.

"Good morning," his mother said. "Why don't you sit down and eat something?"

Ronnie sat. The *Enquirer* sat in the middle of the table. He pawed it open, looking for the Sports page. The paper was still perfectly creased, but something was wrong.

"Where's the Metro section?" Ronnie said. He flipped the corners again: sections A through E, but D wasn't there. He wasn't even sure why he asked. He never read the Metro section. He looked up. His mother's eyes were lowered, but his grandfather was looking at him.

"We've had," his grandfather said, "an unfortunate situation here. Did you sleep okay?"

Ronnie shrugged.

"You're like me. No matter how bad my day was, I always slept at night. It shows good character, I think." He flipped his palm upward and glanced at the ceiling. "Especially in a place like this."

"A place like what?"

"I believe in being direct with people, Ronnie. I don't like to dance around a subject. So. I've talked it over with your mother, and we agreed. How would you feel about coming to stay with me and your grandmother for a little while?"

"In New York?"

"That's right."

Ronnie looked over his grandfather's shoulders at his mother. Her eyes remained focused on smearing jelly onto toast.

"I'd rather stay here," Ronnie said.

"Just for the summer," his grandfather said. "Until school starts. Until things return to normal."

"I gotta stay here and play ball. Me and Q are trying to start varsity."

"You mean 'Quentin and I', not 'me and Q.' Speak properly." He sighed and spread his hands flat on the table. "Your mother has told me how important basketball is to you. And your friend. I believe I can find a coach for you in the city, someone who can do some extra work on your basketball skills. Further, your uncles have a restaurant in Manhattan, and they could use your help. It would be a really good experience for a young man. How does that sound?"

"Mom?"

"Ronald." His grandfather did not blink. "You and I are talking."

His mother seemed so young then, unmoving and porcelain. She wasn't going to help him. He turned his chin back toward his grandfather.

"I'm not going to New York."

"I understand why you would feel that way right now. But your father? He's in a lot of trouble. I'm going to post his bail today, and then he'll be at home until his trial starts. It might be better if you weren't around to witness these next few weeks."

"To 'witness' it? Is he being executed in the town square?"

Without taking his eyes off Ronnie, he said, "Does he talk this way all the time?"

"Dad, take it easy on him."

"I don't know what's going on," Ronnie said. He stared at the newspaper, knowing full well why the local section had been removed. "Where's the Metro?"

"If basketball is what you care about, your grandmother and I can hire a basketball coach for you. Someone to work on your shooting and other skills. An excellent coach. You'll come back here in great shape for the new school year."

"My friends are here."

"You'll make new friends."

"Is he serious?"

His grandfather's hand shot out, grabbed his wrist, and squeezed.

"You need to learn that when you're talking to an elder, you are talking to an elder, not to someone standing behind him."

The grip was painful and shockingly strong. Ronnie squirmed, his mouth open in surprise. His mother raced over, but as if her father was a hot stove, she kept her hands to herself. Her eyes wet with tears, she pleaded, "Dad! You're hurting him."

Ronnie snatched the newspaper and cracked his grandfather hard across the face. His arm was free. He bolted for the garage, ignored his mother screaming for him to come back, hopped on his bike, and raced down the driveway and up the street. Convinced they would follow him in a car, he veered up a lawn and raced up between two houses and through two backyards, zipped across the parallel street, up and through another two more backyards, and then veered south, heading for Wyoming, knowing Fleming Road was downhill all the way to Springfield Pike, putting miles between him and home. On the Pike, he pedaled behind a church and dropped down onto the concrete, braced himself against a brick wall, and—legs shaking from exhaustion, adrenaline finally slowing down—cried until his chest ached.

When he was emptied, he pressed his head against the wall, the brick grinding into his skull. Legs sprawled in front of him, his laces were loose, and he retied them, then pulled his knees up to his chest and rested his chin against them. He sat curled like that for a long time, trying to figure out how long he should sit there if—and this was a big if—his mother had come looking for him. He doubted it. Across the parking lot, birds hopped in and around a dumpster, picking at the crumbs around its base, and squirrels dipped into the garbage bags, disappearing for several minutes, then reappearing with something small and inconsequential between its paws, gnawing on it in bursts before skittering away into the trees. Ronnie sat watching this for hours, the distant whirl of cars a background noise he learned to ignore.

Finally he stood up. He knew not to go to Q's house. He guessed Hartwell, which was the park where they had their regular run during the summer and the easiest bike ride from here. Legs stiff and tight, he eased onto his bike, let the blood return to his muscles, turned south toward the city, pedaled down the sidewalk, and before he crossed the street into the park, he spied Q sitting on the bench waiting for the next game. Ronnie chained his bike, came onto the courts, and sat down next to his friend.

"Got five?" he asked, even though there was no one there but them.

"Hey, what's up?" Q said. "No, you're with me. We'll have to pick up. It's quiet today."

Ronnie nodded. Above, the sky was cloudless and gray. Rain, maybe. On the court, the ball skipped around the perimeter, worked inside, back out again. These were a group of kids that played in a church league together: fundamental, polite, lost most of their games. The other team was full of gunners. Ronnie expected this one to be over soon.

"Score?" he asked.

"Think it's, like 16-10 or something. Going to 21 since there wasn't anybody here but me. Won't be long now."

Ronnie nodded. They watched the game silently for five possessions, and then Q asked, "You okay?"

With his eyes on the court, Ronnie said. "I guess."

"I saw all those cars in front of your house, and I thought maybe your mom was having a Tupperware party."

"Really?"

Q shrugged. "I don't know. Seemed weird."

"Metro section of the paper was missing from my house."

"I read it today."

Shards of yellow and blue light swam before Ronnie's eyes. "What it say?"

They watched one team clank a jumper, grab the rebound, kick it back out, and clank another jumper before the ball bounced off knees and ankles and skipped out of bounds.

"Paper said," Q began, "that he didn't fit the profile. They were looking for a high school dropout, not a college-educated chemist. They said that what broke the case was that your dad sold a bunch of rare coins at a mall store. Said something like that, something so sloppy, was almost like he was trying to get caught."

My dad never graduated from college, Ronnie thought. Which was something his mother frequently reminded them about, how his father couldn't pass French. How not buckling down and studying a foreign language prevented his father from a degree, from going to medical school, and having a life he knew he deserved.

"Said he'd been breaking into people's houses for decades. Said they're trying to connect him to robberies in cities he claimed to be in for business trips. Kansas City. Houston. Shit like that."

"He's coming home. My grandpa is posting bail today."

Q spun a basketball in his hands. They still hadn't looked at each other.

"You gonna see him?" Q asked.

19

Ronnie wanted to say that it didn't matter: he was going to New York. His grandfather was going to get him a shooting coach, and his mother's brothers were going to have him bus tables in their restaurant. He wanted to say that he was absolutely terrified of his father, that he had been, he realized then, scared of him for a very long time. He wanted Q to know how scared he was, not just of his father, but of everything: his mother, his grandfather, of not having any idea what was happening or why. Most of all, he wanted Q to know this without having to tell him, without having to say aloud the words *I'm scared*.

"I don't know," Ronnie said.

"My parents said you can stay with us for a while. You know, if you want to. They already called your mom this morning. Said she'd talk it over with your grandpa."

Don't cry, Ronnie thought, *don't cry*. "Thanks," he chirped.

Q finally turned his head and looked at him. Ronnie could feel his friend's eyes drilling into the side of his face.

"Yeah, man," Q said. "Whatever you need."

"What I need is to play some ball. How long is this game gonna take?"

Q laughed and leaned back against the chain-link fence. "Forever. These guys are killing me."

"What's going to happen?" Ronnie asked.

Q dribbled the ball between his legs, the soot of the blacktop all over his fingers. He palmed the ball with his left hand and cocked it against his hip. His eyes were up, looking out across the parking lot. Ronnie lowered his chin, determined not to cry, and focused on a soda cap near the edge of the lot. All the anxiety of the last few months was really the anxiety of the last few years, the years in the past, what was coming next year, all of which now seemed to be uncertain and impossible. He thought of everything he hadn't been able to say to his mother, his father, his grandfather.

"I'm really fucking scared," he said.

Q turned his head. His mouth was a thin line, his eyes wide and pooling.

"Yeah, man," he said. "I would be too."

Now Ronnie looked up and away. The tears that came silently down his cheeks shamed him. Q clapped him hard on the back of the neck and left his hand there. He gave Ronnie a shake.

"I'm your best friend," Q said.

And for the rest of his life, every memory of the summer his father was arrested came back to this: Q's firm hand gripping his neck. It is what Ronnie remembered when, later in the day, his mother called Q's parents and agreed that it might be good if Ronnie stayed with them for a little while. It is what he remembered when, eight weeks later, his father was sentenced to twelve years upstate in Chillicothe Correctional Institution. It is what he remembered when his mother went to New York for the summer and came back only to put their house up for sale, what he remembered when Q's parents started referring to his older sister's bedroom as "Ronnie's bedroom." All of it came back to this moment, right then, right here. And he thought again of when he and Q stood at the back of the layup line in the first game of the season for the St. Xavier Bombers varsity team. A home game, Q right next to him. He gave Ronnie a hard, solid clap on the back of the neck and left his hand there. Even though he couldn't see his friend's face, Ronnie knew they were both looking into the stands, seeking out Q's parents.

But just to see them, not to wave. Can't be seen waving to your parents.

Gotta be cool.

Ronnie had never played in front of such a large crowd: the bleachers on both sides of the gym were filled, a collage of coats and hats and faces that he didn't know, all here to see his team play. His heart roared like they had already won the game because he and Q had done it—freshman, starting backcourt for the St. Xavier Bombers, opening night in December, just before Christmas. Just like they always said they would.

Everything seemed to shake from the music blasting out of the loudspeakers, and each step on the wooden bleachers seemed to reverberate in Ronnie's ears. He scanned the crowd for his mother, who said she could take time off from her new job in New York and fly in for his game, spend the weekend together. He didn't see here anywhere. *I'll try to make it,* she had lied. *I'll try to make it.* He refused to think of her. She and his father were in the past. They were gone. Always look forward, he thought. Forward.

II

What a beautiful stereotype: white boy shooting guard from the Midwest gets a scholarship offer to Indiana University. Forget the fact that Bob Knight was gone, that a young African American Mike Davis, all his emotions naked on his face, all indignation and determination and effort, was the new head coach, and the person who actually recruited Ronnie in the first place. Undersized white shooting guard equaled Indiana University. Or, Duke, but even Ronnie thought, you know, fuck that shit.

This was 2002, two full seasons removed from Bob Knight's departure. Mike Davis would resign in 2006, but Ronnie wouldn't be around for that, and besides, he always knew he wasn't long for Indiana. His high school senior season, the state title run, the growth of his body, all of this told him that the NBA was reachable.

Bloomington wasn't what he expected. He imagined corn fields. He imagined tractors and farmers and overalls. Even on his campus visit, when two seniors showed him the facilities of the athletic department (which were equally good at every campus and made no impression on Ronnie other than the schools were spending a lot of money on ball, which he already knew), he figured that Bloomington would reveal itself to be the land-grant college that it was, and the halls would be filled with farm-strong boys and girls with sturdy bodies beneath sturdy clothes. He figured wrong. IU was known for attracting international students—like a symphony, there were a number of languages around him every day: Chinese, Swahili, Russian, Spanish, Farsi, Portuguese, the unfamiliar vowels and annunciations a reminder of just how small Ronnie's world had once been.

He learned quickly what he was to the Hoosiers. He could see the angle on this one: he would be their honor student, the one they could point to that lifted the GPA of all fifteen guys on the team who were reading at a fifth grade level and had the tutors type all their assignments for them. Not that they didn't try to let Ronnie be just one of the guys: they filled out his first semester of classes with remedial math, intro to business, intro to sports management, and a football coaching class that met once a week and was taught by the head coach who hadn't had a winning season in three years. He stared at the class schedule handed to him, then looked up at the graduate assistant who created it. She gave him a curious look; it was almost as if she was surprised Ronnie could read.

"Here's what I would like," he said, passing her a list he knew she wouldn't accept: calculus, advanced Latin, intro to existentialism, and an honors course in African American literature.

She shook her head. "Ronnie, you need to be an honors student to take this course. You know that, right?"

"I am an honors student. You know that, right?"

She frowned at him as if he wasn't quite in focus. Ronnie leaned back in his chair and folded his arms. She lowered her eyes, twirled her pencil, and began to erase Ronnie's preferences.

"We still need to keep you eligible," she said. "The first semester is overwhelming for every freshman. I would suggest we search for a middle ground."

"You would suggest or you're telling?"

"Ronnie—"

"Do you see me with chaw in my mouth and juice dribbling down my chin? How fucking stupid do you think I am?"

The grad student leaned away and looked at some point over Ronnie's shoulder. He bit his tongue—his anger seemed to be less controllable each year, something that would rise up like unexpected nausea. A chair scratched on the linoleum, followed by the heavy sounds of athletic trainers squeaking across the room. Ronnie smelled the assistant coach's Old Spice before he spoke.

"There a problem?" the coach asked.

She simply looked at Ronnie, leaning away from the table, her eyes clinical, boring down on him with sadistic pleasure. She seemed to be the type of person who enjoyed when athletes "got in trouble."

"I'm just trying to sign up for classes, coach."

"Is that right?" He came around the table and into Ronnie's view. John Treloar was not the assistant coach that had recruited him. Treloar was a power forward, and the width that was once in his chest and shoulders was now in his butt and stomach, his movements a lurching gait from arthritic knees and chronic soreness in all his joints. Ronnie liked Coach Treloar tremendously; he carried himself like an old warrior at rest from the battles he had won and where his life ended up, and there was something peaceful in that. But right now, Ronnie didn't want to see him. Treloar had a job to do, and it involved keeping kids like Ronnie eligible and obedient.

"These look pretty advanced, Wagner. You sure about this?"

"Sure as I am about the corner three."

Treloar grinned. "You fucking with me, Wagner?"

"No, sir. Just don't sign me up for Intro to Knitting, that's all."

"Uh-huh." He lifted Ronnie's course requests, holding the paper between fingers that were long, crooked, and oddly beautiful. On his left hand was a gold wedding ring; on the right, a championship ring from his time in the Association. "You actually gonna go to these classes, Wagner?"

"I love to learn."

"Can't tell with the way you defend that high screen." Treloar turned and nodded at someone. Another grad student—grad assistant, tutor, high school teacher, who the fuck knew who all these handlers were?—crossed the room and was next to Treloar in a breath. He looked down at the two sheets, the tutor's recommendations and Ronnie's requests, that Treloar now held down low by his waist, as if the pages somehow smelled rancid.

"What do you think?" Treloar asked. "Make this work?"

This student—a boyish man in expensive glasses and a knit tie—looked at Ronnie and seemed to recognize him. The other one, the woman, scooted from the table and walked away. Ronnie crossed his arms and watched the guy shrug an affirmation.

Q left messages but never seemed to talk on the phone. The time zone difference between Indiana and Oregon was just enough so that their lives didn't match up: Ronnie was off to class before Q was awake; Ronnie was coming back from practice when Q's was just starting. Everything Ronnie did was just a little bit ahead of

Q., as if he was an apparition that filled the memory of Ronnie's presence. All of Ronnie's phone calls to his friend ended up with a voice mail; whoever Q's roommate was, Ronnie had never spoken to him.

On the other hand, Ronnie would occasionally get messages from his roommate. These would be scrawled on the back of fast food receipts and left on the stack of *Maxim* and *ESPN The Magazine* on their coffee table. The athletic department had snitches everywhere, a bunch of narrow-shouldered kids who had never played ball and never would, compensated with nothing but a false belief they were significant, all of them willing to drop a dime if, heaven forbid, you didn't go to class. Forget not doing the schoolwork—tutors surrounded athletes like locusts (and still, Ronnie thought, motherfuckers managed to fail classes that weren't much more than addition and subtraction)—Ronnie wasn't allowed to sleep in on a Thursday like any other college student. All Ronnie had to do was go to class, and still, he resented it.

He even liked class. Being an honors student simply meant the classes were smaller, and that was okay with Ronnie. When he was there, watching the calculus formula fill one of six chalkboards that could be raised and lowered like a window shade or listening to how access to a warm water seaport drove the decisions of Russian monarchs for centuries, his mind was on the subject, scribbling notes, highlighting passages in the text, as if calculus or Russian history or African literature or cognitive psychology was the most important thing in the world. Between classes, when Ronnie didn't have time to do much else other than wolf down a bratwurst from the vendors parked at all the right spots on campus during the day, he read the assigned texts, plopped down on one of the ubiquitous benches sprinkled throughout the quad, and then he hurried off to the next class.

But, off-campus, he had no interest in studying. His concentration was gone. Tapping his pen against the tabletops, his fingers jittering to a subconscious rhythm, he pictured a game, a fastbreak, an offensive set, and he stood up and pushed aside the books and found something else to do. Studying required the self-control Ronnie did not possess.

The first year was nice, a year of adjustments. It was a year of being told where to go and what to do at every waking hour of his day. His school schedule was set, and there were "friends" of the program who would rat you out if you didn't go to class. The schedule, though, also told him when to practice, lift weights, eat, walk across campus, attend Indiana charity events—visiting kids in a cancer ward or serving lemonade at a university fundraiser or wearing a suit and tie and clapping at the right times for some old timers he didn't know—and when, exhausted and spent, it was okay to sleep. No one, not even the other players, told him before he came to college to play basketball that his life would no longer be his own.

On the court was where he had the most freedom. Ronnie earned the job as the sixth man, subbing in at point or shooting guard around the twelve minute mark, and doing what was needed: clean entry passes, rotate and help on defense, knocking down open shots. He was a bit deferential, and he knew it, but he was a freshman that scouts were interested in (six foot one, 175 pounds, there was a chance, just maybe, that Ronnie could run the point in the pros), and that didn't necessarily endear him to his teammates. Freshmen needed to know their place, and even if Ronnie knew his was above the upperclassmen, he certainly couldn't act that way. He knew how these things worked and needed to be worked. He was permitted to move out of the dorms his freshman year, as long as he bunked with Jackson, an upperclassman, a power forward with few friends and lots of enemies, a no talent enforcer who called everyone "motherfucker." Ronnie figured it was better than the dorms and signed the lease.

His freshman year went fast; the Hoosiers made the tournament, and it reminded Ronnie of his high school games, only bigger and more artificial. Nothing special. He had a cool detachment from everything he did in Bloomington; it made him an effective player who didn't brood on mistakes and learned fast. It also made him seem cold and indifferent to the people around him, which, if Ronnie was honest, he was. Even after an entire year of classes and basketball and being told he would be the starting point guard his sophomore year, he didn't have any idea what he was doing there.

So he did what any college kid displaced in the world, pissed off at his parents and their demons, reasonably smart, with a healthy dose of ego would do: he started drinking. Heavily. Being an IU player, it didn't matter how old he was, he could walk into any bar in town, the bouncer giving him a pound and hug (*What's up, boy, when are they going to take the reins off you?*), and once inside, any number of narrow chested boys with backwards baseball caps would scream "Wagner!" and start buying the drinks. Cheap beer didn't do much to him. He needed to drink a lot of it to really start feeling loose, start feeling that sleepy dream quality that his life was no longer real. So he switched to shots, vodka, which someone told him has less calories than beer, as if he gave a fuck about calories. Did they know how many sprints coach made them run? Did they know that Ronnie could run forever, could sweat that hangover out, could puke two, three, even four times, and that still wouldn't stop him from running?

He drank whiskey and cases of beer. He liked walking to the counter with a case and a bottle, as if, somehow, Jameson canceled out Natty Light. There were several stores he visited, making sure he never appeared at the same one more than once every two weeks, and this system, however loose he held it in his mind, made him feel in control. This system is what got him through his sophomore season.

Ronnie missed the playground. There, although you were always trying to win, if you did lose, you just sat down, caught your wind, and got the next run. The game never ended. The game continued. He missed this sense that failure wasn't failure but a momentary pause in the action, nothing more or less. When he thought this way, he took a bottle with him to an outdoor court near his apartments. On these nights when the moonlight gave him all the light he needed to see the hoop, Ronnie placed the bottle at the top of the key, the base of the whiskey as close to the white line as possible without touching it, and just like when he was a kid, he'd imagine every shot he took was a gamewinner, and with each made basket all the pressure in the world slid off his shoulders. Narrating the play, imagining different broadcasters calling the last play for a Big Ten championship, an NCAA championship, an NBA championship, Ronnie Wagner, Jr. would be the one hitting the buzzer-beating shot. Over and over again. At least until the bottle was empty and his legs were jelly and his eyes were heavy and then it was time to head home, trudge back through the park, climb the steps to his apartment, struggle to get the key in the door, and do everything he could to get his shoes off before he fell into a drunken sleep.

Ronnie and Q never played against each other in college. During their junior year, there was one opportunity, when Indiana and Oregon were in the same early season "tournaments," one of those corporate pre-Christmas cash grabs that showcased eight teams, usually two very good ones and six disappointing mid-level squads.

This was in San Francisco during the Thanksgiving weekend, and they had five days in the city, the first two to see the sights under some kind of student-athlete, cultural experience bullshit, followed by three days of basketball games during which the coaches, for reasons no one could understand, dressed in outlandish seventies garb, striding the sidelines in loud suits with open collars and fake medallions dangling around their necks. The entire event was cosponsored by an insurance conglomerate and an internet company that specialized in cheap web hosting.

Being on the West Coast fucked with Ronnie's sleep schedule. According to the clock radio, it was four in the morning. His roommate snored, then farted. After tossing and turning for a while, Ronnie figured, fuck this shit, threw on some workout clothes, and headed out the door. Team breakfast was at nine a.m., and though he had no idea what he would do in the meantime, as long as he was back in time for the meal, he wouldn't have any problems.

The elevator dinged and Ronnie was in the lobby. He frowned— didn't San Francisco get cold at night? He figured he had enough on that he'd be warm. He crossed the atrium, eyeing the lobby windows to see if he could tell what the weather was like in the dark of early morning, and there, in a club chair, feet up, reading the newspaper, was Q.

"Hey," Ronnie said. "What are you doing up?"

A look of surprise and delight crossed Q's face. He tossed the paper aside and they slapped five.

"I should ask you the same thing," Q said. "I don't know, man, I'm just awake. I've gotten used to entertaining myself when I'm up early. But I left my PlayStation in Eugene, so here I am. East Coast papers come early at hotels."

"That's yesterday's paper."

Q frowned at the date. "Oh, man, I didn't even notice. And here I thought I was all smart and shit."

Ronnie pointed to the doors. "Wanna see what we can see?"

"Yeah, man, fuck it, let's go."

The two friends headed out the door. The city was disturbingly quiet—no cars from diners and clubgoers on the streets—and it was still just a bit too early for deliveries or garbage trucks. Still, there was a steady hum in the air, the whole city electrified, as if all these inanimate objects were somehow anticipating the next day. Streetlights showcased the homeless slumped against the buildings, huddled in stairways, and yet like everything about San Francisco, this seemed normal and nonthreatening. Every block possessed an art gallery, and while Ronnie didn't know the first fucking thing about painting, it was cool to see something other than strip malls or shoe stores or any of that other same old shit he saw in every neighborhood in Cincinnati. And the air! The hint of saltwater, of the beach, drifted through the streets, and when Ronnie inhaled, his lungs expanded like sails in the wind. Though his hands were jammed in his pockets, his head was high and his chest up, as if the city was gently pushing his body from the inside out.

From the Hilton they headed east toward the harbor. Neither of them spoke. They were in no hurry. This—the company of others unfilled by mindless jabbering—was an adult experience, and Ronnie found that he enjoyed both the silence and the companionship. When he first got to college, he had been nervous around other people, which surprised him given how effortless making friends in high school had been. There, he didn't have to search for something to say, but in Indiana, around strangers, sweat raced down his ribs and he would pray for a familiar face to walk by and fill the awkward silence. But with Q, he felt more and more relaxed until all the tension eased out of his shoulders, and comfortable, Ronnie walked with ease as the sidewalk carried them down toward the sea. Across the bay, the hillside, California was dotted with a smattering of lights. Others were waking up, or had never slept, and this knowledge pleased Ronnie.

"First day of practice at Oregon," Q said. "There's a senior, this mean motherfucker, all muscle no brains, he's eyeballing me the whole time. We're sprinting, then some drills, nothing all that complex, but something comes up where I need to speak. Something about who shoots in what order or something. And then, every chance he gets, he starts talking shit. All this 'Why you talk white?' and this other bullshit I used to get when I was kid. I mean, I've heard that stuff for my entire life. No big deal, right?"

Ronnie nodded.

"But, you know how it is. Freshman on the team, I had to prove myself all over again. So when we scrimmage, any time this guy is between me and the rim, I dunk on him. And after this happened a couple of times, he doesn't even try to hide the fact that he's just slamming his forearm into my ribs. He might as well be punching me, you know? I look at the coaches, and they see the whole thing, but they want to know how I'll carry it so they don't say or do anything. Up to us to sort it all out.

"So, next position, I want the ball on the block. I want to tussle against this guy. We move on our offense, and I run baseline and switch and switch until this dude's on me. And I hold my ground, and he's bigger than me, but he lets me catch it, lets me know, 'Okay, you and me.' Ball comes into the post and I pivot to face up. But when I do I make sure it's elbows up, and I spin hard, and absolutely blast this motherfucker, full in the face, with my elbow. I mean, blood sprayed from his nose like in the movies or something. He drops to the floor, howling, clutching his nose, and I'm just standing over him, ball in my hands, looking down at him, and my heart is jacked, like pounding through my chest, you know, what if I killed this guy or something, but I'm trying to keep this fierce 'Don't fuck with me!' look on my face." Q laughed. "Crazy."

"What happened?"

"Nothing. Ball boy mops up the court, dude goes to the locker room, we continue like nothing happened. Coaches never said shit to me, neither did the seniors. But nobody hit me in the air again after that."

"You throwing elbows, huh? That shit wouldn't play at Indiana. I'd get a whole lecture on doing things the 'right way' and all that other bullshit."

"There's no history out west. Everyone is still writing their own rules. You know what I thought? I thought there would be a bigger mafia presence or something out there."

"In Oregon? Didn't you watch *LA Confidential*? Or *Menace II Society*?"

"Yeah, I know, it was dumb. I just thought . . . I dunno, there's that whole part of the world out there that, far as America goes, is relatively young."

The incline steepened, and the boys walked hard, planting their heels into the pavement and leaning back as they crept toward the harbor. In the dark, the bay remained an opaque mass beyond the buildings. Every few steps they saw a homeless person curled up and asleep somewhere on the San Francisco sidewalks and alleys. Soon, they reached the waterfront and stood on the docks of the east harbor. Across the water, dots of light sprinkled the otherwise dark mass of land.

"How 'bout this, huh?"

"Beautiful," Q agreed.

"I wish we had something to drink, something to toast this view with."

"Little early in the morning for drinking," Q laughed.

"Not really."

Q closed his mouth, and his smile slowly vanished. His eyes dropped in concentration as if a thought that he didn't yet understand began to grow in his mind. He threw a curious glance at Ronnie, who sniffed, spit a loogie, and gazed around him, shifting his weight from foot to foot.

"You nervous about today?" Q asked.

"Nervous for what?"

Q shrugged.

"I'm cool," Ronnie said. "Ain't nothing to be nervous about. All I'm saying is that this seems like the type of thing you raise a glass of champagne to, chug it down in one swig, and then throw the flute down on the pavement, like, boom!"

"I guess so."

Ronnie looked over his shoulder. He could feel Q's eyes boring into the side of his face.

"What we really need," Ronnie said, "is food. My stomach is growling. Did you see a diner on the way in? I feel like this city should have a bunch of twenty-four-hour diners."

"Let's find out." And they turned and headed back toward their hotel, and Ronnie recognized that he would need to be careful, even around Q.

In the game that ended Ronnie's college career, the opposing point guard was a Purdue junior named August Harper, a white boy with shaggy blonde hair and a deliberate air of money and entitlement. There wasn't a time that Ronnie had the ball when Harper didn't have his hands on Ronnie: he grabbed the hip, his off-forearm, and shorts, hand-checking his lower back if Ronnie got around him, placing an elbow in his chest if he was off the ball. Leaning too hard, he sent Ronnie sprawling to the floor twice, and neither drew a whistle from the ref, who refused to make eye contact with Ronnie or Indiana's assistant coaches when they hollered for the call.

They were in Chicago for the first round of the Big Ten conference tournament. The beginning of the end came at the end of the first quarter. A series of rotations and cuts got Harper off Ronnie, who moved to the corner and waited. A back screen got Ronnie free to cut baseline to the rim. The high post sent a rocket through the lane; Ronnie dribbled once and rose up, ball high above his head, ready to thunder down an easy deuce. Harper slid over, and rather than jump and challenge the shot, he ducked at the waist, and bumped Ronnie's legs in midair. Defenseless, Ronnie lost his balance and landed hard on his back. He was up before the whistle even blew.

"Motherfucker!" he screamed. "You piece of shit!"

Three players were between the two of them, and Harper turned away and smirked at his bench. The refs separated the teams, Ronnie's face was beet red, and saliva flew from his mouth as he screamed, spraying fury.

"Take out my legs! What the fuck is wrong with you?!"

Someone pushed, and then all ten on the court were ready to fight, all of them pushing but no one throwing a punch. The Indiana coaches raced onto the court and pulled their players away from the Boilermakers, and Coach Davis shepherded his men toward the bench, telling them to relax, be cool, relax, be cool. The crowd was on its feet, and the bleachers shuddered as everyone anticipated this becoming a brawl.

"Coach, did you see what he did?" Ronnie said. "He took out my fucking legs!"

"I saw it. It's over, all right? We need you to keep your head."

"Piece of shit!"

"Wagner, you need to calm down."

"Goddamn, Coach, did you see what he did?"

"Ronnie. Easy."

Ronnie put his hands on his hips and blew out a deep breath. And the anger seemed to go then just as fast as it came. He even laughed ruefully. He shook his head. He thought of that long ago February game against Q and how all the kids expected Ronnie to get his ass kicked.

With hands on his hips, Ronnie walked to the free throw line to shoot his technicals, his eyes up, looking at the top row of seats. It was a trick Q taught him; you keep your head up but you never make eye contact with any fans. Fans are like vampires, he said, sucking the soul right out of you.

Through your eyes? Ronnie had asked.

The shit's a metaphor. Don't think so much.

Who's thinking?

He was an eighty-nine percent free throw shooter. Ronnie drilled both free throws. At this time in the game, Ronnie had four points, one assist. On the next possesion, Ronnie popped out on a pin down, caught the pass at the top of the key, turned— his footwork perfect, feet shoulder-width beneath him—and sank a long three pointer. The Hoosiers got a stop, the outlet came to Ronnie, and he knew he was getting to the rim before he turned up court. Bucket, foul, and one—he was in double digits. Then he ran Harper off a baseline screen and sank a corner three, turning and glaring at the benchwarmers who had screamed "HEY!" on the catch. His jumper created space, and he whipped two passes from the free throw line to the big on the block for dunks. Soon it wasn't just the small IU crowd roaring for him. Ronnie went into halftime with eighteen points, two rebounds, three assists, and a steal.

On the first possession of the second half, Ronnie caught a pass at the free throw extended, Harper guarding him too loosely. What came next was Q's favorite move: a hard jab to the side then a strong dribble the other way, almost straight ahead. The sliding door, Q called it. Harper bit on the fake. Ronnie blew past him. With two dribbles, he rose up and, with one hand, tomahawked the ball through the rim. He hung on, swung under the rim, slapped the other side of the backboard with his left hand, and howled as he dropped to the floor. The referees were too stunned to give him a tech. The entire crowd stood, screaming with bug-eyed disbelief.

Ronnie finished the game with forty-two points, and if Coach hadn't pulled him with five minutes to play, it would have been fifty. It was the kind of scoring night that reconfigured draft boards and made scouts evangelical. August Harper was three inches taller than Ronnie, and a prospect. That night, scouts saw that maybe, just maybe, Ronnie Wagner had a real future in the pros.

Ronnie, and his coaches, saw it too. They made a decision: move Ronnie off the point, go with a smaller backcourt, and unleash him as a two-guard for the remainder of the tournament. Ronnie did as he was told—score, wherever, however—and hit for 32, 29, and 35 points in the next three games, winning the conference tournament for the Hoosiers and, after a shaky 17-12 season, earning a seeding in the Big Dance.

"Listen," Q said. "You're just lucky you're not playing in our region. I'd shut that bullshit down in no time. Only way you're lighting it up is because it's a bunch of short motherfuckers with these little T. rex arms that can't block your shot."

Ronnie held the phone with one hand and cracked a beer with the other. It was a Monday, the day after the Big Ten tournament and the announcement that Indiana's season would continue. *SportsCenter* flashed on the muted TV screen.

"Who's your first game?" Ronnie asked.

"South Dakota State. They're not bad."

Since they left St. Xavier, Q had grown an additional three inches, and was now a six-foot-seven swingman who some scouts thought could be the next Scottie Pippen. Oregon was a number three seed out west; Indiana had slid into the tournament as a nine seed in the South region.

"Be happy I even got a hold of you. My phone has been ringing off the hook."

"Agents? How's your grumpy-ass roommate like that?"

Ronnie shrugged and set his Miller Lite on the coffee table. It was ten a.m., and he had just finished practice. He had class in one hour.

"He isn't here," Ronnie said. "He's been staying at some girl's place. That guy really fucking hates me. Even at practice he doesn't look at me."

"He doesn't play anyway. When do you guys go?"

"We fly out Wednesday night. Hey, how do you handle the agents?"

"I tell them to call my dad. My roommate and I have this note-card taped to the wall right above the phone. We just read that aloud."

"Seriously?"

"Yeah, man. No matter what they say, no matter what the question, we read off the card and say, 'I appreciate your interest in Quentin Daniels. Due to NCAA regulations, at this time, I have no comment about Quentin Daniels's future plans. Please direct any questions and all future contact to his father, Frederick Daniels, of Cincinnati, Ohio, by way of London, England.' Which is really hard to say without breaking into a big shit-eating grin."

Ronnie laughed. "That works?"

"I guess. I mean, really, I don't even listen. This phone rings all the time. My voice mail has been filled for weeks."

"Your dad doesn't mind?"

"Not really. We've already got it narrowed down to three agents anyway, and we're gonna talk to them after the season's over. I mean, they can't really hustle my dad, you know? Plus, once they hear his British accent, they get totally confused and shit."

Ronnie belched and opened his second beer. "Yeah, I probably shouldn't fuck this up. I figure I'll just ask Coach who I should talk to."

"Are you thinking about coming out?"

"I don't know. I'd always thought I had to do four years, but if I can keep shooting like this, maybe I can leave after this year."

Q sniffed. "Is that a good idea?"

Neither of them every really acknowledged what had become crystal clear over the last three years: though both were four-year starters at a Division I high school in Ohio, winning state their last two years, their points and rebounds and assists comparable, only Q was considered an NBA prospect. Q was a lottery candidate by his junior year thanks to a growth spurt and a pterodactyl's wingspan, considered an elite talent, a gamechanger, not just a guy but a Guy. Guards like Ronnie were a dime a dozen in college. Guards like Q had shoe companies name their next product after them.

Ronnie said, "I don't know. Things here? I mean, Indiana's been all right. I don't know."

"Call my dad. He's been getting all my calls. He knows a little bit about it, and he'd be happy to ask these guys about your prospects."

"Yeah?"

"We're family. Course he won't mind."

With his right foot, he reached out and touched his toes to the lip of an empty beer can. He got it to lean just a little bit, coming a bit off its base, before easing it back down. He received a birthday card from his father every year, usually two or three weeks late, with an odd message inside. Always his father wrote about his strange dreams. His father dreamed he was Jean-Luc Picard on *Star Trek*. Or that a shadowy figure was pouring poison into the ventilation system, killing him softly. Or he's working in a mill, sending log after log of thick pine through the teeth of the machinery, and when a fellow miller's hands gets sliced off, all the men continue working, ignoring the man's screaming. All the logs were covered in blood, his father wrote, isn't that weird? Happy Birthday, Son!

After they hung up, Ronnie tried to write down the same prompt that Q used for the agents. But he couldn't remember the words. The phrasing didn't seem quite right. He gave up, setting the pen down with great formality next to the grocery receipt he had scrawled upon. He yanked a Gatorade from the fridge, drank half of it to get the taste and smell of beer off his breath, popped gum in his mouth, and headed to practice.

Practice was sharp. Everyone was focused and intense until the whistle blew, and then it was all laughs, all except Jackson, who was now a fifth-year senior. At the far end of the court, as removed from his teammates as he possibly could be, Jackson shot free throws. His face, pulled tight, was exactly what people meant when they said "sourpuss." Ronnie dribbled a ball between his legs, slow, fast, working his way over to his roommate.

"Hey," Ronnie said. "Ready to go to Memphis?"

Jackson responded by pounding the ball twice, then shooting a free throw. His body was muscular and tattooed. His gray jersey, soaked with sweat, clung to his skin, and when he bent to shoot, his knees bent stiffly and his arms extended robotically, like he was shot-putting the ball. Jackson—a decent free thrower shooter, regardless of the mechanics—rebounded his made shot and palmed the ball in his large hands, spinning it around his waist, and taking his place again at the line.

Ronnie watched Jackson sink three free throws without acknowledging his presence.

"Did I do something to piss you off?" Ronnie asked. "I mean, if you need me to clean the kitchen or some shit, I can do that."

Jackson palmed the ball. He held at his waist and stared off into space. "I can smell it on you."

"What?"

"I said, I can smell it on you."

Despite the tumbling feeling in his stomach, Ronnie laughed. "What do you smell?"

Jackson lowered his eyes and spun the ball in his hands.

"You can't hide it," he continued, "with bubble gum or a breath mint. It comes out of your pores."

"Fuck are you talking about?"

Jackson took another free throw, the shot rattling around the rim before falling through the net. Ronnie waited until he was sure that nothing more was going to be said and then dribbled away. He looked around, making sure no one had been close enough to hear Jackson, then glanced back at his roommate, whose eyes remained focused on his free throws. Fresh sweat poured down Ronnie's ribcage, waiting for more, another accusation, thinking up excuses, conjuring lies. But Jackson said nothing more, just kept shooting, and finally, Ronnie bounced the ball hard just once, turned his back, and strutted toward the locker room as if he was the hardest man alive.

Years later, Ronnie often thought about how Jackson's words had shamed him and how he had remained sober—not a single drink, not a sip, not even the slightest urge—during those next ten days in the tournament. Those next ten days of practice, of anticipation, of travel, three games stretching into the second weekend of the tournament. For the first two games, they were in Memphis—a reasonable drive from Bloomington—a city with a deep love of college hoops, the kind of people that would watch all four opening day games and actually know what they were witnessing.

What they were witnessing was the Ronnie Wagner coming out party. What they were witnessing was Ronnie Wagner showcasing what made basketball so beloved: a guard, a "small guy," an "underdog," flashing the kind of pizzazz and joy that makes people practice their moves, makes these fabulous athletes seem human, seem real.

All that pressure and not once during those ten days did Ronnie need a drink.

The anticipation by the national media was intoxicating enough. Could Ronnie Wagner keep this run going? Could he shine in the NCAA tournament? He made a simple decision in the first game: free throws. Get fouled, get to the line, and shoot the easy ones. Ronnie sank ten of ten in the first game, driving to the rim, holding off the smaller Davidson guards with ease, his strength and size allowing him to keep those narrow-shoulder white boys on his hip. Shooting free throws didn't take any thought. He found it easier to shoot them in games rather than in practice, where his mind often wandered, trying to still his thoughts as he focused on bend, release, follow through, bend, release, follow through, over and over again.

Efficiency wasn't yet the phrase on the tongues of NBA scouts, but it's hard not to notice a kid who scores twenty-seven points on just eight shots—all those free throws, a couple of corner threes ("RW moves well without the ball, instinct is to find the best shot.

Hits corner three from both sides of floor"). And, perhaps more importantly than all the numbers, Ronnie looked cool. It looked smooth, the treacherous made effortless, his expression serene and confident as he jogged up and down the court, a young man expecting to win.

The next game, the Saturday night primetime game, had the Hoosiers up against a much better team with a long-armed wing player whose size, Ronnie figured, might give him trouble. But for all his size and length, Ronnie's first step was lightning quick, and he regularly beat the kid off the bounce. His footwork, never a strength, was impeccable, his feet underneath his torso on every catch, ready to spring and snap his jumper from anywhere on the court, giving his defender fits.

With the help coming to rotate, Ronnie found passing lanes for his teammates, and along with another night of crisp shooting, he had twenty-six points and nine assists to lead the Indiana Hoosiers—a bubble team just a week ago—to the third round of the NCAA tournament.

They flew home for three days of classes. Nobody in Bloomington got any work done. Just the presence of a Hoosier basketball player stopped any and all discussion that was unrelated to the tournament. Practices were quick, spirited, fierce; three days later, they boarded a plane to Atlanta. Making the Final Four was a real, true possibility. And Ronnie did everything he could, hitting for thirty-four points, five rebounds, and six assists in what was ultimately a losing effort.

"I mean, I played great," Ronnie said.

"Still lost, though," Q said. This was the Tuesday after the third round, when both Indiana and Oregon had lost.

"Whatever. We weren't supposed to even be in the tournament. It's not my fault we couldn't rebound."

"Yeah, but you were close. Man, we were so close. Those last two minutes. I mean . . ." Q's voice trailed off. His Oregon Ducks made it to the Elite Eight, only to have a three-point lead slip away as the ball never found its way to Q and Syracuse hit a pair of threes. "I keep seeing it all in my head. Over and over. The details. I cannot get over the details."

Ronnie held the phone against his shoulder and tipped more whiskey into his Coke.

"Look," he finally said. "What does it matter now? We're leaving college. None of this matters."

"You sure you're going?"

"Aren't you?"

"Yeah, but I'm a lottery pick. Maybe. Probably not top five, but I'm going in the first round. What did my dad tell you? Agents will say anything to get you to sign."

"Haven't talked to him yet. Don't matter. I'm just done with college, with Indiana, all of this shit. I gotta get out of here."

"You sure about that?"

"Fuck yeah, I'm sure. Aren't you? I mean, what if we get drafted by the same team? What if we're a starting backcourt all over again? Take the league by storm!"

Q laughed. "Boy, how much you been drinking?"

Just for a moment, he thought Q was serious. He held his breath, trying to still the sound of ice cubes and the carbonation of his drink. Ronnie looked down at the cans and bottles littering his back deck. *I've been drinking lots*, he thought. *And you don't know it.* Above, it was a clear, cool night in Indiana. His rental was a house west of downtown, and on the shaded back deck a mile from campus, his only thought of Bloomington was a place he would never have to return to, with no memories or thoughts of good times his freshman or sophomore years. He simply wanted to leave, to turn his back on it all and not consider the shallowness of his relationships, the mundane nature of life in a college town. Away, away, away.

III

Two simultaneous and equally striking thoughts hit Ronnie at the same time: he couldn't believe how beautiful Ireland was, and he had never felt so miserable and alone. He lifted the can of Mickey's to his lips, slurping loudly. Stumbling through Dublin, making his way down brick sidewalks, dodging the commuters on their way to work, he found his way to the waterfront. He staggered down to the docks, the rich scent of the ocean churning his stomach, every step sending a shockwave of pain rattling through his bones. He was thirty-one years old and had just been cut by a second-rate Irish basketball team. As if Irish basketball wasn't second-rate enough.

Ronnie sat down on a park bench and gazed into the sea. He had played for the Dublin Crusaders for less than six months; he failed a medical exam, or a drug exam, or a medical exam and a drug exam—Ronnie's memory was hazy on this detail. All he knew is that the Crusaders refused to re-sign him. Over the last eighteen hours, with the help of a large amount of alcohol and methadone, he had come to the conclusion that he didn't need the game, particularly this international bullshit they called ball. Maybe it was time to go home. Maybe he could catch on with a D-League or independent league, show the scouts that Ronnie Wagner still had something to prove. Over the last seven years, he had played professionally in Italy, Turkey, China twice, Israel, and Germany, and with scouting international now, certainly, there had to be NBA scouts who knew he was still out there, still able to be a gamechanger. Or at least a contributor. Or something.

He pulled out his cell phone and panned through the list of contacts. All his phone held, all the names, some capitalized, some not, some a mixture of letters and symbols, lacked surnames: Frankie D., roni T, jacqui M, austin, Mr. Choo, Susie Redhead, dont answer, 7 Spark, Yuri Russian, Z-Bass, Dieter. They were a list of people Ronnie used to know as carriers of pills and powders, club goers, hangers-on, like the groupies back in the States that seemed to know where the ballers were at all times, staking out the hotels and restaurants and clubs like femme fatales from bad noir, always on the prowl, always a step ahead. Not a single person in his phone could be called a friend. No one that missed him or even thought about him now and again. It's like he never existed at all.

Tiny yellow lights along the waterfront of the city flickered on as the sun rose across the Irish Sea, the light shimmering like broken glass off the dark choppy waters. An ache rippled through his jaw. The realization anchored in his chest: he was out of a job, out of basketball. His life, everything he worked for, was over. He reached into his left pocket and fingered open a plastic bag and reached in for one pill. It didn't really matter which one it was. He popped it in his mouth. From his right pocket, he pulled out a bottle of whiskey, a brand so cheap and disgusting he didn't even recognize the name. The can of Mickey's sat next to him on the bench and Ronnie couldn't remember if he had finished it or not. Whatever. He tossed the whiskey cap onto the ground and washed down the pill. He took out another pill and swallowed. With a flick of his wrist he fired his phone into the sea, disappointed he never heard it hit the water. Pill, sip; pill sip; pill sip. His jaw continued to ache, the popping when he moved his mouth growing louder. He wanted to stand; standing was too much effort. Slouching into the hard wooden bench, Ronnie pulled a fistful of pills from his pocket and stuffed them in his mouth. The last thing he remembered seeing was those tiny pills bouncing off the bench, off the pavement, small and insignificant, rolling to a complete stop.

Florescent lights, covered by textured plastic. He had never really looked closely at these before, and he wondered if all the plastic covers were exactly the same, if there was one company that made all these covers, one company that shipped them all over the world. It is, after all, always two long tubes of lighting covered by the same clear foggy plastic sheath. Isn't it? Ronnie considered this for a long time, too long, before he became aware of how dry his mouth was, and the steady ache that ran through his shoulders and neck. Once, in China, he had been in a car accident that killed the driver but spared him and one of his teammates, and the sensation was like this—a steady, acute pain rippling through his bones like electricity. But that had been years ago. He blinked and started to consider where he was and why he was here.

He raised his head and fresh pain rippled through his shoulders. He set his head back down and faced left. In a chair by a window with its vertical blinds angled open to let in light but not the sun was Q, a pair of reading glasses perched at the end of his nose, his finger hovering over an iPad.

"What are you reading?"

Q didn't look up. "Comps on a restaurant I'm thinking about buying."

"Where?"

"Cincinnati."

"Where am I?"

"A hospital in Dublin."

Q closed his iPad and set it on the windowsill. He stood up and gazed out the window and seemed to consciously slow his breathing. Then he twirled his wrists and dragged the chair over to the bedside. He wore a trim goatee and his hair in a close-cut fade, and his shoulders were broad and defined; he wore a platinum wedding ring and tailored clothes, and everything about him screamed success. Even though he had pulled the chair close, when he sat down he leaned away, his fingers folded in his lap, as if there was a stench to Ronnie he didn't want to get near his skin.

"Gotta say," Q continued. "I'm missing a pretty fucking cool Fourth of July party. Can't even tell you how many people I invited. I'm supposed to be working the grill. I guess I should be happy that you put me down as an emergency contact on your paperwork with your last two teams. You know, flattered and shit that you remembered my number. But I don't know, man, even though I'm glad you're alive, I'm super fucking pissed off at you right now."

Ronnie waited for a feeling—sorrow, grief—to hit him to be able to truly apologize, and instead, all he felt was a self-indulgent misery. It was pathetic. He didn't want to say he was sorry, but it was what people should say in moments like this. Instead, the thought that entered his mind was *I am so tired*. Q leaned on the bedrail and stared down at him, and the intensity and anger in his gaze made Ronnie begin to cry. And once the hot tears began, he couldn't make them stop. The noises he made were deep and guttural and continued until his throat was dry and his stomach ached. He turned on his side, wiping his face on the pillow.

Q reached out. He placed the palm of his hand against Ronnie's face. His touch was cool and electric, and Ronnie was too ashamed to look at him. They sat like that for what felt like a long time, the hand placating him, stilling him, until Q finally said, "I'm going to bring you home."

No one expected Ronnie to say anything in the first meeting. It was exactly what he expected: the basement of a Catholic church, entered through a back stairwell; folding metal chairs set in a circle; a table with donuts and coffee; a range of addicts, like himself, in nondescript clothes. It was a room of hopeful sorrow. Back when he was in the league, Ronnie hated wearing suits, and one of the small nice things about losing everything was that he now wore sweatshirts and basketball shorts all the time. He took a cup of coffee to have something to do with his hands and sat down.

"I'm Cheryl," a woman said, "and I'm an alcoholic."

In chorus, everyone intoned, "Hi, Cheryl." Ronnie kept silent. Fuck that shit.

After his release from the hospital in Dublin, Q and Ronnie boarded a plane and flew back to Cincinnati. Four days later, Ronnie went to a nearby detox facility in Kentucky where he was without outside contact for three months. Next was a three-month stint at the Dalton House, a twenty-four-bed residential program housed in a Victorian manor in Lexington. Now he was back in Cincinnati, sober for one hundred and ninety-one days. Each morning, the new tabulation of his sobriety chimed in his head like a clear, sonorous dinner bell calling him from a long day of work. One nine one. One nine one.

He wasn't really listening today. He looked at Cheryl without seeing her, then at the next speaker, a man who was still in the throes of self-loathing. Ronnie could hear the guilt, shame, and resentment in the man's voice; he recognized that place, one that he left behind in Kentucky sometime over the last one hundred ninety-one days. When the meeting was over, Ronnie helped the group leader, a man named Chet, clean up, folding the chairs and stacking them in the corner, sweeping the floor, collecting the garbage.

"Need a ride?" Chet asked.

"My dad is coming. Thanks, though." They shook hands and stood on the curb, not speaking. Chet lit a cigarette. Ronnie could feel Chet appraising him, considering if Ronnie was to be trusted, if his sobriety was firm yet, if he had completely bought into the ethos of addiction and recovery and how they were always one step away from falling. But Ronnie knew the ledge. He knew how easy it was to slide off the cliff. He'd fallen too many times, and he knew he wasn't sliding again.

The silver Audi pulled up, the engine purring, and Ronnie thought of that first car he bought when he signed his first pro contract. A Mercedes C240. Two door. Beautiful ride. He tried to tell himself he didn't miss that car, that life.

"That's your dad?" Chet asked.

"That's what he keeps telling me. I'll see you next week."

Chet was still laughing when Ronnie shut the door. "Hey, Freddie."

"Hey, yourself." Q's father put the car in gear. "How did it go?"

"Fine. Nice group of people."

"Hungry? Saved a plate for you at home."

"Sure." The truth was he wasn't hungry at all. He ate his meals in the kitchen with the Danielses out of politeness. Since returning to the States he was rarely hungry, preferring water most of the time, and wishing to avoid people as much as possible. He approached time around people with the same discipline he once used to play ball: the process was more important than the results. Being back in his old neighborhood was unnerving. Even though his parents had moved away long ago and there was no need to actually drive or walk on his old street, just being within a few blocks brought back that deep sense of loneliness, of being invisible, that he had felt for years and years.

Despite Q's success, the Daniels' home hadn't changed at all. The photographs were different, of course, and now that Q was married, pictures of Q's wife Adriana and their son, the young-est Daniels—Malik Kristofer Daniels, a boy Ronnie had never met—were plastered on every conceivable wall of the home. Since he had come back to the States, Ronnie hadn't actually spoken to Q. Text messages, a long e-mail, but he hadn't actually seen his old friend, and he wondered, with the same suspicious fear of the morning after a long night of drinking when great gaps of time had vanished, if there was something essential that now permanently divided him from Q, and regardless of what this thing was, it was something that Ronnie couldn't see or touch.

When he first came out of rehab, the Danielses had offered Ronnie his old bedroom, and he refused. He didn't want to be upstairs, to be in his old room, the space given to him when his parents had let him go. Downstairs was where he felt most at peace. At night, in the basement on the couch, Ronnie gazed up through the window wells into the backyard, his arm folded behind his chest, mind racing like he was on a fastbreak, taking it all in, seeing all the angles, the players, the defense, the whole game slowing down into a single frame, a snapshot, a Polaroid image of the game. He never thought he would miss it. He never thought it would slip away from him, even though he always knew he wouldn't play ball forever. Now what was he? Now what did he have left?

Ronnie pulled away the blankets and tugged on a pair of basketball shorts from the floor. He rolled off the couch, placing his hands and knees on the carpet, and while on all fours, he looked over at the cabinets and saw rows of VHS tapes. The labels were in his own handwriting: Jason Kidd, Penny Hardaway, Warriors Playoffs 1991–92, D. Harper, Rockets '95 Run, and dozens more. He pulled the tapes off the shelf one at a time, pulling back the box to see whether the tape was fully rewound or at a random halfway point. For no reason, he selected "Stackhouse Mix," slipped it in the VCR, and leaned against the coffee table.

As a kid, Ronnie had made these tapes by setting the VCR to record all the games, then using the second VCR to make a copy of a copy to skip over the games, players, sets, whatever he was working on that he didn't need. He stood up and took the stairs quietly. The entire house lay in shadows. In the Danielses' white room, the carpet thick and soft under his bare feet, he crept from photograph to photograph, the Danielses smiling from behind unmarked glass, framed in gold. Ronnie sat softly onto the nearest couch. He didn't think of them much, but he wondered now where his parents were.

Amendment nine: make amends to people whenever possible. Did he owe them the apology, or was it the other way around? He vaguely recalled calling his mother sometime in the last year. Or maybe it was the year before. He wasn't sure. Time melted into a Dalí nightmare over the last few years, and he wasn't quite certain where his memories accurately began and ended, what was real and what wasn't. Did they know if he was back in the country? Would it matter?

Here's what he knew: his father, after serving all twelve years of his sentence in a state penitentiary, had gotten out and moved west. Arizona or New Mexico, Ronnie honestly didn't know which. Maybe Utah. His mother never spoke to him. She had left Ohio, moved to Delaware (who moves to Delaware?), and remarried to a man Ronnie had never met. He might have a stepbrother or two. He didn't know. It was amazing, actually, the more he thought about it, how much he did not know about the people who raised him, both when he lived in their home and in the years after his father's arrest. His biological parents were complete strangers.

Nothing brought his parents back into his life. Not being in the *Enquirer* sports page with Q, not winning the state championship and being on the front page. Not signing with Indiana. Not his big moment in the NCAA tournament. Not getting drafted by the Seattle Sonics in the second round. Nothing. Other than their birthday cards, their continued silence made him stubborn, made him refuse to look them up or even give the task to a hanger-on—hey, find my parents' numbers for me, will ya?—because, right? Fuck them, I'm their son, I'm the one who needed them, it was their job, their duty, to raise me, and who abandons their only child? I wasn't so bad. I was a good kid. Why should I call them? Where the fuck were they?

Blaming my parents, he mumbled. What a fucking cliché. He made fists with his toes on the carpet, the plush feel soothing, and he dropped to his hands and knees, then slowly rolled over, flat on his back, and stared up at the ceiling. Like he didn't know he was fucking up in college, in the NBA, in China, in Israel. Like there was ever any doubt that this, all of this, was on him.

Ronnie kept his hands at ten and two, steering the Audi like his hands were holding the reins of a horse. Everything in his wallet was new: the single debit card, the business card with the name and number of his sponsor, and the driver's license that he finally renewed. He couldn't remember the last time he drove an automobile, and now he was driving Dr. Freddie Daniels' car north to Indianapolis, the dentist in the back seat and his wife riding shotgun.

"I have a lot of leg room," Freddie said. "I didn't know the back was so spacious."

"Why would you ever sit in the back?" his wife asked.

"I do not know. Read the paper, maybe?"

"In the back seat of your car?"

"Why not? It's my car."

"Not the way Ronnie is driving it, it's not."

"Ronnie, you stealing this car?"

"This is a kidnapping," Ronnie said. "Don't you two know that?"

It was Christmas Day, and for reasons Ronnie didn't fully understand, Freddie and Clara had asked him to drive the car to Q's 2:30 game in Indianapolis. Ronnie was happy to go, intrigued even, because the truth was, he had never seen an NBA game in person, in the stands, as a fan. The idea that he had to buy a ticket just like any other regular person was both a relief and an insult. Still, he would see Q for the first time since this summer. He had thought, more than once, that it was a miracle that his old friend appeared; in rehab, he had asked people, his sponsors and doctors and Freddie and Clara, if Q had really shown up, if he hadn't just hallucinated the bedside visit. Everyone insisted that it had really happened. No doubt about it. Why, then, Ronnie wondered, had Q not returned a single phone call or text message or e-mail in the six months since?

The seats were good, a few rows off the floor, high enough to see the sets unfold and close enough to see the sweat splatter down faces, jaws, and necks. He was recognized—he had been famous long enough to be aware when people were looking at him with recognition, a point or a nod or a "Yo, is that him?"—but because he was famous for being a failure, and a drug addict at that, no one approached him. Any fear he had of being recognized evaporated among the crowd of Indianans who were too polite to bother him for an autograph, a picture, or to just ask "What happened to you?"

Q played great. They were facing the Knicks, a reliable rivalry the league trotted out on major holidays like a show pony, and there was the appropriate number of hard fouls, extra elbows, and technicals. His old friend was the best player on the court, and it showed. Q wasn't a superstar, not an elite, but there was no shame in being really good, and in a game like this, he showed off the whole arsenal: three-point range, coolness at the free throw line, sharp passing to open shooters, a willingness to grab rebounds against men forty pounds heavier than him. It was a slow, plodding game, and Ronnie kept picturing those summer days when he and Q would just sprint toward the rim, the ball barely under control, dreaming of the Next

Big Thing. Now look at him: a tall, proud, full-grown man, playing in the NBA, endorsing shoes, all of it. He was happy for his friend, and his happiness made him feel as remote and distant from the game as if he was from the bottom of the ocean.

After the Pacers won, his phone vibrated with a text from Q: "Wanna come down?" Ronnie simply wrote back no. He had no interest in going into the bowels of the fieldhouse, getting hand-shake-hugs from guys who didn't give a fuck about him, the coaches and the trainers eyeing him with contempt for wasting his gifts. Q responded with, "meet you at Adriana's."

Christmas at the home of Adriana's parents, their house decorated in a tasteful and expensive style reminding them of their childhood in Spain, passed at a glacial pace. The names of parents and siblings and their children vanished from Ronnie's memory as soon as they were spoken, and around a dozen people he didn't know, buzzed, mixing their English and Spanish, bits and pieces of which he could surprisingly recognize from his time overseas, making him still, quiet, the most dangerous side of himself. All this family, all these people and their love and their energy and their unity isolated Ronnie, and their attempts to bring him closer—an arm around the shoulders, a cold soda pressed into his hands—only made him feel farther away.

The wine and beer and vodka circled around the room like fireflies on a muggy summer night. His old bottle of whiskey sat perched at the top of the key, watching Ronnie shoot jumpers well into the night, still and patient and waiting to be picked up and brought to his lips like a sacrament.

More than once, Freddie clapped a big paw on Ronnie's shoulder and whispered, "You all right, son?" He always gave him an affirmative nod and an unconvincing smile, which neither of them believed, but for now, in front of everyone, they both pretended to buy it. Ronnie was grateful to even be asked; it forced him stop and assess his feelings, rather than wallow in panic, and remember that he was all right. When the night was over and they were caravanning back to Q's house, Ronnie fell asleep in the back seat of the car before they had even pulled out of the driveway.

When he opened his eyes again he was on a queen-size bed in a nondescript room. His shoes were off. He raised up, joints popping in his neck and shoulder, rolled over, and stared at the unmoving ceiling fan above him. For a moment, he feared the worst, but as he took slow inventory of his body, none of the pain of waking up trashed rippled through his body. He hadn't gotten high. He hadn't drunk anything. Stepping through his memory of the last few hours, he realized he must have woken up in the car and entered the house and said good night to everyone and walked up the stairs and found his room and kicked off his shoes and collapsed face first into the mattress. That must have been it. What frightened him was that these blackouts didn't seem to stop even though he was going on six months of sobriety. Even after six months he could still lose long passages of time.

Out in the hallway, the entire house was still. He slipped barefoot down the hallway, took the stairs down a floor, and stood in a great room that he had no memory of ever seeing. How did he get upstairs last night? Ronnie waited for his eyes to adjust and for the shadows and scrims of light falling through the windows to differentiate themselves, and then searched through the house for the room he knew existed.

But it still wasn't what he expected to find. He thought that, outside, he might find a court with timer-controlled lights he could flip on for a few minutes. Maybe he'd find a set of double doors along an outer wall of the house leading into a dark gym, his eyes tracking up off the floor into the rafters. Instead, Ronnie faced a wall of glass. He was in some sort of an atrium, surrounded by tele-visions and speakers and video game cables, and he stepped around four club chairs and a circular coffee table and walked straight to the glass wall. Though it was dark below, he knew he was looking down at Q's gym.

This was some kind of eagle's nest, and something about the darkness, even in the shadows of a house dimmed for the night, wasn't right. Ronnie took the winding stairs to his right down to the gym floor and then stood on the edge, convinced his eyes deceived him. He placed one bare foot on the gym floor and rubbed.

Whatever synthetic it was, he had never felt a gym floor like this. He dropped to his knees and ran his hands over the surface. His eyes adjusted. The floor was blue. As if they existed only because he thought of them, white lines appeared, stretching the length of the court into squares and rectangles. A tennis court. Thinner dashed lines outlined a three point line. Above, two bas-ketball backboards hung from the ceiling.

"Kinda weird, isn't it?"

Ronnie looked back over his shoulder. Q stood with his hands in his pockets, tube socks pulled up to his knees. He walked over and crouched down next to Ronnie and ran his palm over the sur-face of the court.

"You wouldn't believe," Q said. "How many options there are in court surfaces. Officially, there are four types—grass, clay, hard, and synthetic. But there's quite a bit of variety in each of those to get the effect you want, and when you get into synthetics, well, get your chemistry set out."

"You don't play tennis."

"Fuck no, I don't. But my wife does. And if I'm not home eight months out of the year, this can't be just a basketball court."

Both men stood. Q continued, gesturing with his hands.

"So we needed something multipurpose. The tennis net comes out from a hideaway at midcourt, backboards come down from the roof, padded walls all around. That was pretty easy. The surface, though? You know what's in there?"

Ronnie shook his head.

"Sand. Teeny tiny particles of sand, so small you can hardly see it."

"No way."

"Yeah, man, swear. Blew my mind when the contractor told me about it. See, the nice thing with a synthetic is that you can have a greater consistency of the bounce, especially indoors, where you can control the climate. But you can also decide what kind of bounce. You can vary the speeds. It's all physics and chemistry. The quantity of sand added to the paint can change the speed of the ball. Different paint, different speed. How hard you want the surface not only changes the ball speed, but also the pounding on your back and knees. More sand means a slower bounce. Also, you can use larger sand particles. You can even fuck with the amount of friction. That magnifies the topspin, which my wife likes."

"Why blue?"

Q shrugged. "It looks like the ocean."

A sharp memory warmed Ronnie's mind: the San Francisco harbor, the sound and smell of the sea.

"How bad does she beat you?"

"Dude. Adriana was an alternate for the Spanish Olympic team. She whups my ass."

Q turned and walked to the wall. A loud series of clicks announced the blast of klieg lights before they shone down on the court. Q picked up a basketball from against the wall and threw a bounce pass to Ronnie, which he caught with one hand. He looked down at his bare feet and wiggled his toes.

"Just to shoot," Q said. "Not one-on-one."

"What are you doing up?"

"Watching game tape. I couldn't sleep. Remember how I couldn't sleep in college? It got worse in the pros. The weird thing is that I don't get tired anymore. I seem to be fine on four or five hours now. Doctors said it was nothing to worry about so I'm not going to worry about it."

Ronnie looked down at the ball as if it would bite him. He hadn't touched a basketball since Ireland. At some point in his life that he couldn't yet identify, basketball had morphed from an escape from the world into a burden stealing him away from having fun, from partying, from forgetting about everything else. Basketball had become a job. Sliding his fingers over the pebbled grooves, each dimple like a dot matrix, he thought of pointillism, those beautiful compilations of dots that became an image when you could step back and let your eyes be deceived, and always in his memory these were beach scenes, picnics, something where people were gathered in a festive atmosphere. Never were there people alone, never were there broken down ex-athlete junkies who were simultaneously told they were in control of their addiction and that they were not in control of their addiction, leaving them in the limbo of always needing their sponsor, the meetings, the cheap coffee and hard metal chairs and church basements. One addiction replacing another. He wrapped one dribble around his back, then another, his hips and knees dipping in a familiar dance. At the free throw line, he fired up a jumper. It rattled around the rim and fell through. Q rebounded and flipped it out to Ronnie. He launched another jumper, long, and banked it in.

"Want shoes?" Q said. "I have a couple in the locker room."

"Locker room?"

Q jabbed a thumb over his shoulder. "Yeah, hold on. Size fourteen, right?"

In a moment, Ronnie had his sockless feet in a pair of new Nikes. Spongy and responsive, they felt like the factory direct ones the shoe companies used to send to the locker room, not the pair he had to buy for himself from the stores in Europe and Asia. He shot, hitting most, missing a few, and every time, Q rebounded and fired it back to Ronnie, never taking any shots himself. Ronnie didn't consider why. He just kept shooting, some short jumpers, some from three feet behind the line, shooting and shooting until sweat poured off his body and the mindless joy of shooting baskets fully returned. Finally, he caught a pass from Q, ball faked, then took two hard dribbles to the rim and rose up.

Even before he jumped, Ronnie knew he couldn't throw it down. He last dunked in a basketball game years ago, in China, on a breakaway with no one around him, and he took three steps then, hammered the ball home with one hand. Too many years of junk in his blood took away something from his muscles and bones that, though scrubbed clean, would never fully come back. Those days were long over. He just wanted to see how close he could get, how truly far away was the past.

And it was close. He pulled the ball to his hip, leapt off his left foot, cocked the ball behind his head, rising, and as he gripped the rock behind his head, knew with an instinct he couldn't explain that he couldn't finish. Rather than spring-loading his arm, he twisted his palm 180 degrees and flipped the ball up, laying it softly into the net, his fingertips just grazing the rim. He landed and kept his eyes facing away from the ball, away from Q, unwilling to acknowledge what they had both witnessed: a recognition of limits.

Ronnie sat down along the padded wall and stretched his legs out. From somewhere, Q pulled out a red Gatorade, and Ronnie drank half of it in one long gulp. Q slid down the wall next to him.

"What are you gonna do now?" Q asked.

"Breakfast, I guess."

"No, I mean, what's next for you, when you get back to Cincy."

"Oh, that 'what now.' Yeah, man, I don't know. One day at a time, I guess. I've talked to a few kids at high schools about substance abuse. I like doing that. Just, you know, when you and I were sitting in the bleachers, if some old timer came through and talked about that shit when we were sixteen years old, would we have listened?"

"We didn't have problems when we were that age."

"You didn't."

Q said nothing.

"I mean, technically," Ronnie continued, "I didn't start doing shit until I went to Bloomington. But my problems, the things that got me using, started way before then. Way before. Just, at some point, basketball wasn't enough to keep my mind off things. The game became just one more thing I didn't know how to handle."

"You didn't have to call them? You know, part of the rehab process, apologizing to who you hurt and all that."

"I called you. I called your parents. Called my agent, couple of girlfriends. I mean, I don't even know how to get a hold of my parents."

Q remained silent.

"Those people are gone. Some people just aren't meant to be parents. Or together, or with me, or something."

He sensed Q studying him, and Ronnie kept his gaze focused on the length of the court.

"You aren't damaged," Q said. "You aren't a bad person. You know that, right?"

Even though Ronnie was supposed to be long past this sticking point, thanks to meetings and detox and all that, the truth, which he had confessed to more than once, was that he often felt

61

like a bad person. No, worse than that: he felt like a person who was undeserving of kindness, a person that was neither bad nor good but simply forgettable, a person who would drift through the lives of others like a fog and dissipate. Tears pressed behind his eyes. He blinked rapidly, sniffed, and turned his chin away from his friend.

"I know that," he lied.

"You know why you called my parents, right?"

"To apologize."

"You called them," Q said. "Because they are your parents. We are your family."

Ronnie clenched his teeth and closed his eyes. Q placed a hand on the back of his neck.

"You aren't alone, Ronnie. You never were."

Back to that game in 1998, that warm February day, when two boys, Ronnie Wagner and Quentin Daniels, a pair of eighth graders that had taken over the park at Winton Woods, putting on a show for players and spectators alike. It's a game. There are no ties. One boy wins, one boy loses. That's just the way it has to be.

Q spent the first few possessions jogging around the perimeter. When Ronnie sensed he was ready to cut, he took a step back and Q stopped moving alltogether, waited for the pass, threw it right back. Six possessions, one up, before Q even tried to make a move.

He caught the ball and exploded, moving forward: hard dribble into the lane, using his left forearm to keep Ronnie at bay. Moving his feet, his left hand ready, Ronnie was prepared to slap at the ball, leaning left—just like Q wanted. Cupping the rock, Q spun away from Ronnie's pressure, and even though he could have attacked the rim, Q rose up, cocked the ball to the side of his head, and shot a textbook jumper—elbow in and wrist snapped and arm fully extended—and held it out in front of him like a salute until the ball nestled through the rim.

Hoots and hollers sounded from the bleachers, and coming up the court, everyone seemed to know that Ronnie had to take the next shot, had to find a way to score, to even up the showdown that everyone was waiting for. So when he took the inbounds and raced up the left sideline, dribbling with his left hand just to show that he could, everyone knew what was coming before Ronnie did: crossover to the lane, dribble behind his back to the left, skate the baseline, step back, and float a twelve footer just over Q's outstretched fingertips.

The game was tied, two up.

Q caught the ball, jab stepped, then shot a long jumper that rattled in—three to two now. Ronnie needed to show something. He swung the ball to his left and cut down the middle hard, gravel squirting out from under his feet, he cut along the baseline, hands up. The pass came, perfect, at his chest, and he spun and leaned away as he shot the ball, just getting it above Q's outstretched arm, and it shuddered off the left side of the rim before falling through the net. Three to three.

After the release, Q took off. He already had two steps on Ronnie, but he raced after him anyway, and the pass, a little long, was still in Q's grasp. He caught it with his right hand, and dribbled twice, crossing midcourt. Ronnie couldn't catch him, and knew it, so he slowed down, thinking he might get a quick pass back—there was one guy ahead of Q, probably dogging it a bit, but he was at least there, a defender. And Ronnie knew this would be something to see.

Q stuttered, the ball in his right hand, and got the big man moving back on his heels. Q was going to the rim. Ronnie knew it; everyone knew it. No way was Q going to pull up and shoot an open jumper. He lowered his shoulder and drove left, and the defender put his right arm up, ready to slap away the layup. Q cradled the ball, took one step, then spun to a jump stop, spinning against the defender, back into the lane, and looked ready to scoop it up with his right hand. The big man jumped. Q jumped, too, holding the ball high in the air like a torch, and just when you knew the shot was going to be blocked, just when everyone knew this shot wasn't going to make it, Q pulled the ball down, wrapped it around his back, switched it into his left hand, and just before his feet came back to the pavement, hefted up a soft left-handed shot that dipped over the rim and into the net, soft, hushed, like a whisper.

Everyone went nuts.

Ronnie caught the pass on the wing. Q came slow around the pick. Ronnie dribbled left, just around Q's outstretched arm. He took one more dribble, and there was Q, on his right hip. With a forearm, Ronnie gave Q an imperceptible shove, making space, and leaped back to square his body. Ronnie had an open look. He raised up, leaned left, and arced his shot a little extra, getting it just over Q's hand, and the ball spun perfectly as it soared through the air, seemed to stop for just a moment, then fell and fell and dropped through the net without touching the rim.

The game was to eleven, win by two. Soon Ronnie's team was up ten to nine. They weren't guarding each other. Q caught the ball on the wing, stepped back, and fired a long two that rattled out. The rebounder kicked it to Ronnie, and with a teammate, they raced up the court, only one defender backpedaling, a two-on-one, and to the left of the key, Ronnie gave a hesitation dribble, thought about trying to shake the kid, not one single move in mind, just the knowledge that he was going to take the last shot. The defender, bigger than him, a good ballplayer, knew it too, and for the first time all game, this kid really bent his knees, got down in his stance, prepared to make an effort to play defense. Ronnie dribbled left, skipped back, and leaned forward, ready to embarrass this kid.

Q jogged back and crossed midcourt.

Nothing happened the way one might hope from a moment like this: Ronnie didn't beat the kid one-on-one, Q didn't block Ronnie's shot, Q didn't get the stop and then score three straight points. There wasn't an argument about fouls ending in a fistfight with the two boys standing side by side, bloodied knuckles raised, mouths sneeringly defiant.

Instead, right before Ronnie prepared to make his first move, from the corner of his eye, he spotted one of his teammates sprint past Q, heading down the middle of the lane. Ronnie didn't think. He simply pulled the ball to his waist as if preparing to shoot a jumper, and when the defender leaned forward, Ronnie rocketed a bounce pass by him and into the waiting hands of his teammate, who caught the rock, jumped, and dropped in an easy layup to win and end the game.

So why do both boys think of this moment, this day, as so important?

Ronnie and Q walked to the sidelines, the former announcing he's done. Q took his place, and his team won four straight while Ronnie watched on the sidelines. When Q had also decided he'd had enough, when the sun started to dip behind the clouds, they stood up, slapped five, and headed toward their bikes. They yanked on discarded hoodies, draped their bags with their shoes and basketballs and empty Gatorade bottles over their shoulders, and pedaled single file down the Winton Road sidewalk back to Q's house. Strange weather like this never lasted, and the boys knew that the temperature would drop and though there would be no snow, it was supposed to be windy with freezing rain. The sooner they were home and out of this crazy warm day, the better.

Rain already slickened the streets, making their tires skid treacherously, before they even reached their neighborhood. Windy and overcast, the race home made the boys giddy despite several games of basketball, and the rain spit down hard when they were three blocks from home. Water sprayed from their tires as they screeched to a halt under the awning above Q's garage. They raced around back, entered through the garage door, and in the laundry room, stripped off their shoes and socks, standing on the suddenly cold linoleum, talking loud and trying to not curse the way they'd learned to on the courts. Q's mother hollered from the adjacent kitchen, telling the boys to put on the fresh sweats, which were clean and warm, stacked on top of the dryer, straight from the dryer less than an hour ago.

"Ronald," Q's mother said. "Why don't you call your mother and ask if you can stay for dinner?"

"Can Ronnie sleep over?"

"*May* Ronnie sleep over." Her hard gaze softened when it shifted from Q to Ronnie. "If it's okay with your mother."

When Ronnie called home it was his father who answered. He said, Mom isn't here. Where is she, Ronnie asked. But, yeah, sure, his father said not acknowledging the question, stay over there. I'll watch the game, I suppose. As if they spent any time together. Ronnie pictured his father shrugging as he spoke. Same as you guys, his father continued, except I'll be by myself.

His father hung up. Ronnie held the receiver in his hand and a flash of anger that Q had seen in his face for years—the anger that led Ronnie to beat up those kids that were teasing Q all those years ago and had formed their friendship—zipped across Ronnie's eyes, and then it was gone. Q learned that when Ronnie was like this, quiet and distant like his pops, it was best to leave him alone for a few minutes and let that shit settle, bury it wherever Ronnie would bury it. Only when Q was an adult and Ronnie was looking for a basketball team overseas did Q finally understand all the damage rendered by this suppression.

The boys begged Q's parents for pizza for dinner. At the door, handing the driver cash, the sky now darkly gray and the clouds whirling, Q was grateful to be indoors and warm, a memory he would later learn to recognize as love and safety. He left the veggie pizza in the kitchen for his parents and banged down the basement stairs with the breadsticks, mozzarella sticks, and Meat Lover's pizza. The game was on—Bulls versus Pacers—and the boys hunched over the coffee table to inhale their food, and then leaned back into the couch, sated, while the wind outside continued to howl.

Q glanced at the window well. He couldn't see anything other than darkness, and he wondered how sixty and sunny could become thirty and freezing in a matter of hours. Wind couldn't be seen, of course, just its effect on the world, people huddling into their coats, scarfs and hats hiding their faces, leaning forward; strong enough, wind could rip down trees, power lines, form a tornado. But didn't a tornado need heat, some mixture of hot and cold in atmospheric pressure?

He considered this for a few minutes before a roar from the Chicago crowd brought him back to the game and its third quarter. The players' footwork always captivated him: they never seemed to be off balance, always in control, jabbing just outside their shoulder to get the defender on his heels, and then they zip the other way. Control, always under control. His thoughts turned back to the day's game: Had he been in control? Of himself, or the game? He replayed the games in his head, who had the ball, where on the court they were, what movement happened off the ball, whose head was turned the wrong way. He remembered everything, and only when he got to the third game was it clear to him how odd this was. Pippen scored three straight for the Bulls. Q frowned at some point below the TV screen.

Ronnie said something about the game, and Q grunted agreement. But he wasn't listening. Instead, his mind was on his afternoon game, and how he didn't make enough space coming off a baseline curl. It didn't really matter, he knew—the guy with the ball wasn't looking his direction at all, juking and dribbling nowhere until he bricked up a jumper—but somehow, still, this poor cut bothered Q. He could have made it a ninety degree cut, kicking out to behind the arc for a shot, or coming 180 back toward the rim for a lob. He couldn't quite dunk, but he could get close enough to the rim to tip the ball in, lay it in really, with control, and even a little bit of flair. But what he had done was curl lazily, like cursive handwriting, and then linger for a beat, indecisive, standing in concrete space. What was that? What good did that do if there wasn't a real decision made?

He pressed paper napkins into a ball and looked at his hands. They were huge, too big for his arms; his father called them "puppy paws" and didn't seem to get upset at how often Q was knocking things over the last few months. Water glasses, picture frames, dropping pens and shoes, like his hands didn't belong to him. You're just growing, his father said. Q didn't acknowledge him; though he didn't really know why, the idea was embarrassing.

After the game, they watched *SportsCenter*, then *Saturday Night Live*, and at some point, Ronnie fell asleep. When he realized Ronnie had tapped out, Q turned the volume lower. He was sprawled on the couch beneath the windows, horizontal on the couch, his feet stretched out across its length, arms behind his head, the cable box resting on his stomach as he tapped the buttons, seeking something late night to hold his attention. But he wasn't really watching. His mind was on what he could have done better today, what advantages he had given away, as if his palm was upturned and all that was valuable to him was lifted into the breeze, gone. He pictured the kid who ran by him for the winning bucket. The kid was neither good nor bad, just a guy, just a dude getting in a run, and Q let him run by. Q wasn't tired. He just wasn't all there in that moment, and this kid, this nobody, took advantage of him. That was all it took. Just a blink and then, boom, over: he was off the court and on the sidelines.

He crossed the room and examined the VHS tapes. On the shelf was one of Ronnie's tapes that he had loaned to Q a few weeks ago, an Allen Iverson mix. Q had never actually watched it. He meant to. He removed the tape from its sleeve, popped it in the VCR, muted the sound, and sat down cross-legged in front of the television.

This was a game in which AI scored forty-two points. The entire offense was constructed to get him the ball. That's what Q had read, at least, but he hadn't really thought about how that would work, what it would look like, and watching it now—the screens set, the curl AI came around, his hands up waiting for the ball— the discipline of the entire team became clear. AI was off-balance on most of his shots, whether he was driving or shooting, leaning in or leaning back, and Q didn't see anything he could learn. So why had Ronnie taped it?

He rewound two plays, knowing what would be run, and watched carefully. AI came around two baseline screens, baggy shorts parachuting like a cape, and curled wide but back toward the ball. AI caught the pass at the free throw extended; the point guard set a pindown screen to the shooting guard in the opposite corner, who raced up for the pass from AI that everyone—AI, his defender, everyone in the arena—knew wouldn't be made. The first screener, too, was open, turning and sealing his defender on his hip. AI ignored all of them; he caught the ball, swinging it low, jab stepped to get the defender back, and then fired up a terrible fadeaway jumper that rattled in. Q rewound it, watched it again. And again. He watched the defense the third time: Where are their eyes, where are their feet?

Why was Ronnie watching this?

With the remote in his hand, Q watched the rest of the tape, fast forwarding and rewinding depending on what he saw, what he wanted to study, nodding to himself at how Stackhouse created space with a slight push-off with a forearm. He watched the whole tape, unaware of the time. When he was finished, he thought again about everything he hadn't done today, how unprepared he was, how that dude just jogged by him for the game-winning layup while Q was just hanging back, acting like it was easy, acting cool.

Pretending. Pretending to be someone or something he wasn't. Hey, we are all that way, right? He'd heard that: teenagers are always trying to figure out who they are, always insecure, growing, learning, figuring out boundaries. His father was saying that word to him like a mantra: teenager, teenager, teenager. Sure, Pops. Keep talking like you know what I'm going through, like you know what this all means to me.

But there was a part of Q's mind that recognized that in fact his father did know. He just didn't recognize factually that his father had at one time been his age, but felt, like a hand pressed against his chest, that everyone always thinks their situation is unique and special and his father did know, did understand. Q grasped something just then, something his father had stressed, something that Ronnie wasn't quite seeing.

He cannot take the game for granted. He has to work at the game. It won't ever come easy to him, or anyone else, no matter how gifted. Q tapped the remote against his chin in a staccato rhythm. In interviews, for the rest of his life, he would talk about this moment, this realization after a day of ball and watching a Bulls game on TV and how prepared Michael Jordan was and how his dad always stressed hard work. It was a good story, a reassuring story, a true story.

But it was incomplete. Q always knew this. Q always knew that he omitted Ronnie from the story, that he didn't talk about how his oldest friend, his brother, was on the team that beat him, or how Ronnie was asleep on the couch as Q stayed up all night. He never mentioned how he watched Ronnie, remembering the anger that crossed his face when he was on the phone with his dad, and how he knew, always, that something in his friend would soon explode. It was a guilty, horrible thing to acknowledge: he saw Ronnie's addiction and demons long before anyone else did and he told no one. Lying on the couch that night, well into the morning, the remote resting on his chest, Q didn't have the vocabulary or understanding to tell anyone about Ronnie.

However, here, in his house, on his blue gym floor, with Ronnie's chin turned away from him, and his hand resting on his old friend's shoulder, he did have the words. He did not, however, need to say anything. He just needed to keep his hand here, for as long as it took, for as long as it took to be acknowledged that, yes, I'm still here, and you, Ronnie, you are one of us.

BEAUTY IN THE AGE OF CHAOS AND SAVAGERY

Denny Birdwell was thirty-nine years old and retired from the National Football League for almost four years when he was arrested in the produce section of a Schnucks grocery store in St. Louis, his hands covered in the remaining pulp and mush of the fruit he had spent the last twelve minutes smashing. Later, he insisted that he had no memory of it. The last thing he did remember, he told the police, was driving into the parking lot. It had been a hot September day, and he had the windows of his pickup truck rolled all the way down so that he could feel the breeze as he cruised around the city. He vaguely recalled getting out of the truck and finding a shopping cart.

"And that's it?" the officer asked.

Birdy nodded. His massive forearms rested on his thighs, and he studied his hands as if they held a book and the explanation for his behavior was written in clear, periodic sentences. Flipping his hands flat, he curled his fingers into his palms, feeling the arthritic tug on his knuckles. Maybe when he started, he had been thinking of the white envelopes.

"Gave us a good scare," the officer said. "We were thinking about shooting you."

Birdy laughed.

"I'm dead fucking serious."

"What about a Taser?"

"A guy your size? Covered in mashed fruit and screaming at the top of his lungs?"

Birdy tried to imagine it. As an ex-lineman, he knew that his enormous size made rooms feel smaller, ceilings seem lower, and when he was not smiling, his expression was one of ferocious intensity. He was the type of man who scared people when he ate in restaurants. So while no one knew what he smashed first, when he lifted a watermelon over his head like a sacrificial offering to God, then slammed it down, spraying the yawningly suburban shoppers with seeds and pulp, they saw him as a thing of enormous size to be feared. At that time, according to the statements of five witnesses, Birdy's face was already covered with mashed bananas.

"I'm sorry," Birdy said. "I get these headaches."

"Yeah, you've already said that. Lucky that you passed out. You just stopped moving and then collapsed."

"I hit my head," Birdy said, more to himself than anything. On cue, the lump forming behind his ear began to throb. What would Natalie think of this? "I'm really free to go?"

"You posted bail. Toxicology is clean. Schnucks isn't pressing charges. Store manager is a Mizzou grad. But the district attorney still might bring charges against you. If you don't have a lawyer, I suggest you get one."

The last lawyer Birdy had spoken to was his divorce attorney, a man named Oberschmidt who seemed more interested in funding local nightclubs and marginally talented musicians than practicing law. Birdy hoped he still had his number.

"Mind if I call a cab?

"Phone's right there," the officer nodded. "By the way. Can I trouble you for an autograph? My son plays football. Right tackle. He's a huge fan of yours."

Birdy smiled. Of course he'd sign an autograph for one of the cops who arrested him. Absolutely! Forever, he would be the ex-athlete. And twenty years of being an athlete reinforced this one fact: the public would tolerate anything. After he retired from the NFL, Birdy had been a realtor at House of Brokers, where he was on a "team" with two other realtors, who didn't entirely resent him because the name recognition of Dennis Birdwell— All-American at Missouri; Pro Bowler with the Rams—brought business into their offices, even when the clients quickly discovered that Birdy was there mostly to shake hands and pose for pictures. His real estate signs showed Birdy with a football tucked under his left arm and his right arm extended, the Heisman pose, all while wearing a dark gray suit, clean white shirt, and black tie, his face beaming in an "aw shucks" smile. Waiting for clients at the curb of some house, he always stood studying this ridiculous sign, his new life distant and unrecognizable. After just nine months, he quit.

He signed out of the police station and directed the cab to the Schnucks parking lot. It was night, dark and muggy, and his body creaked as he exited the cab. He stared at his pickup truck, and the idea of driving was exhausting. He wished he could have Natalie pick him up, but of course, she was twelve years old. Not much help there. He climbed into his truck and turned the ignition, the bones in his neck and shoulders rattling like dice.

At one in the morning, his street was laconic: no barking dogs, no children playing, every porch light off, all the houses and yards as still as gravestones. Natalie would have gone to bed hours ago. Perhaps her father would have answered—a tall, serious-looking man whose face always seemed to be in shadows. Birdy had never spoken to him. He pressed his thumb against his right ear until he heard the cartilage pop. The idea of explaining himself to Natalie's father sent a fresh wave of nausea up his throat. He opened his front door, sat down on his couch, and promptly fell asleep.

"What do you have to eat?" Natalie asked.

Birdy blinked and sat up. There she was, just inside his front door. Tall with midnight dark hair and impossibly blue eyes, a smattering of freckles across the bridge of her nose like a cluster of distant stars. Even at her height and the curves in her hips and chest beginning to show, she seemed impossibly young. Her expression was wry and knowing, and she leaned against the door frame as if she had seen this scene a thousand times before. Perhaps she had.

"I don't know. Whatever's in the fridge."

"Can we order pizza?"

"Are pizza orders in the fridge?"

She folded her arms and stared down at him.

"Why did you sleep in your clothes?"

"I got arrested."

"For what?"

"Mashing fruit."

"You're funny," she said without humor. She stood straight and tall and eyed the kitchen. "So, you have nothing to eat?"

She turned her head so that he couldn't see her expression as she took in the bareness of his living room: two black leather couches and a matching recliner, a big screen HDTV along the far wall, a wide and low glass coffee table, carpeting that was both new and bland, and white walls decorated with two paintings of generic landscapes Birdy had picked up at a yard sale after his wife left him. The blinds were half-drawn, and through the windows, the outside world looked so much more inviting and secure than his home. His headache was muted, manageable, but he couldn't remember what day of the week it was. Thursday? Tuesday?

He ended up ordering a large pizza, breadsticks, and a couple of two-liters, and sat at the table on the smooth slab patio in his backyard. Birdy remembered how at one time he liked to eat an entire extra-large pizza, with the works, and drink a six-pack of beer all by himself. The small yard was surrounded by a six-foot-high cedar fence; he had planted three trees a uniform distance from each other across the back of the property. Everything about the scene in front of him appeared posed and unreal.

Birdy listened as Natalie told him about school: algebra and how its linear construction actually made quite a bit of sense to her; Western civilization class and the French kings; French class and verb construction, smoothly leading into her saying words Birdy couldn't understand (*"Monsieur Birdwell, comprenez-vous ce que vous faites en ce moment?"*). He placed his third slice of pizza on the plate, the pepperoni and mushrooms sliding off the cheese. His fingers trembled. Birdy turned up his palm, curious at the source of this sudden tremor, as if there might be something at the end of his now numb fingertips. A surge of heat ran through both his arms. He leaned back in his chair; sweat poured down his rib cage.

"Birdy, are you okay?"

Her voice sounded far away, like a distant echo in the woods. He blinked, then again, then rapidly. He stood, shoving the metal chair back; the clatter of metal on concrete reverberated in his legs.

"I'm certain," Birdy said, "that Grover Cleveland was the twenty-second president."

Above, clouds rippled across the sky, and Birdy's voice was an indecipherable roar in his ears. Everything went dark. When he opened his eyes again, a face looked down at him. His mouth was heavy and dry, the distinct texture of grass tingled against his calves, arms, the back of his neck. A hand moved across his chest. Birdy gripped it.

"Jesus," Natalie said, "are you alive?"

"I'm alive." Her face came into focus—her pretty eyes first, then her entire face—and he'd be damned if there was anything more beautiful in the world to him than this girl. Her name came to him then. Natalie. He stared at her as if she could save him. "What happened?"

"You passed out. You're okay, Birdy. You're lying down right now. You're in your backyard. You know where that is?"

"St. Louis. Overland. 2733 Ridgewood Court."

"Can you sit up?"

"Yes. But not yet."

Birdy relaxed, his head easing into the ground like burying his head into a pillow on a Sunday morning. He could feel blood pulsing through his arms and legs as if a faucet had been turned open, and he closed his eyes, waiting for the spinning to stop.

"What happened?" she asked.

"Don't know. But that happens sometimes."

"You say shit about presidents?"

This was a moment to be strong, to be the kind of man to plow forward even if he sees stars in front of his face and has no memory of the last ten minutes. Birdy opened his eyes, rolled to his right, and pushed himself to his feet.

"Want to see something?"

"Should you be standing right now?"

"Come inside." He headed toward his house without waiting for her, the pins-and-needles sensation shooting through his legs and back just like a goal-line stand. He pushed the sliding door aside, lumbered to the front room, and flipped through stacks of caseless DVDs. The couch sighed, the leather puckering.

"Want me to call a doctor?" she asked.

"Want to show you something." He lifted the disc he had been looking for up to the ceiling, peering at it like a miner making sure he held true gold in his fingertips. Then he popped it into the DVD player and sat down on the couch across from Natalie. He sensed she was looking at the side of his face, not the television, and he continued to stare at the screen until she turned her head and followed his gaze. "That's me," he said, pointing. "Number seventy-six. This is my sophomore year."

"You were all Big Twelve that year."

Birdy nodded in confirmation, newly aware that she had, at some point, memorized his biography. He scanned ahead to the third quarter, his Missouri Tigers down by three points against Texas Tech. He found the play. It was a Power O, Birdy kicking out and sweeping behind the center and right guard, firing into the line, and seeking out the linebacker. Perfect footwork, dancing behind the line with those feet that rose and fell with the speed of a piston, Birdy following the fullback's block into the crease, seeking to crack the first defender that made the mistake of attacking the gap—usually a linebacker. Birdy rocked him, slamming his forearms and helmet right into the 'backer's numbers, blasting him out of the play. It was execution with the kind of military precision that made line coaches assistant coaches, assistant coaches head coaches, and the head coaches—whose faces were always demanding, unsatisfied, and angry—shine with malevolent delight.

This play always amazed Birdy. He can hardly be seen: the camera was centered on the running back, a kid named Worthington, who was at this point in the secondary on his way to a forty-seven-yard touchdown. Birdy was barely in the frame. His man, the linebacker, was defeated, back on his heels, out of the play, and in frustration, he swung his left arm and batted Birdy upside his head. It wasn't much of a hit. Birdy got hit harder on almost every play from scrimmage. In football, this was almost like a love tap.

Even though he now knew concussions are often this way—the last of a series of repetitive slams to the head—something about this seemed wrong. Maybe it was the way he saw it, on a television monitor, because the last thing he actually remembered about this play was seeing Worthington juking a cornerback. Then there was a series of scattered memories of vomiting in the locker room, bright lights shining down on him as he lay horizontal, the mechanical hum of the sliding doors of a hospital. Only two days later with his then girlfriend sitting next to him did the headaches and dizziness begin to make any sense.

On film, Birdy stumbled forward, his legs turning to jelly, his knees collapsing, and then he fell, his arms still and defenseless against his body as he tumbled to God's green grass. He dropped like a man who had nothing inside him: no organs, no muscles, no bones.

He was out of the picture. There was no footage of what happened to him next. The running back, the touchdown, the obligatory shot of the crowd roaring with delight, painted faces screaming, fists pumping the air, joy all around. It is like Denny Birdwell never existed at all.

"Do you see that?" he asked Natalie. "Do you see?"

The next day, they were in the backyard. With the football clutched between her long slim hands, she pointed at Birdy. Laces turned skyward, her bony knees bent, right foot slightly in front of the left so that when Birdy screamed "Hike!" she was already in perfect position to pivot and explode out of the crouch, spinning and pushing off her feet, arms extended as if to hand the ball off. Then she pulled the ball back to her body, crouching at the waist to sell the fake, and she sprinted out to her right, head and eyes high, both hands on the football until she pulled her right arm back and—still in a dead sprint—fired a perfect spiral, her hand turning in and the thumb down, the throw laser straight as it jetted the length of Birdy's yard and ricocheted right between the "8" and the "4" he had painted on the center of the plywood. The wood shuddered, rocking the homemade scarecrow back, the football bouncing off and hanging in the air for just a moment, then falling into the yellow grass, skipping once, twice, three times before rolling to a soft, silent rest.

She puffed out her cheeks, her freckles more visible then, and trotted back to the pile of footballs. Her upper body was all bones, and more than once, Birdy marveled at how such undefined muscles could rifle a football through the air like a pro. Her legs were, perhaps, the key: her quads and calves bulged with the ropy muscles of a soccer player. For weeks now, Birdy had been training Natalie to be a quarterback, and it seemed no one noticed or cared that a thirty-nine-year-old ex-football player was spending all his free time with a twelve-year-old girl. Why she had asked him to tutor her he didn't know, or couldn't remember: this relationship was a mystery he preferred not to solve. He glanced across the yard, waiting for a ripple of movement from the windows or door that he knew he would never see. Her father's name suddenly came to him: Oliver. He couldn't recall her mother's name. What did it matter? Her parents were never home.

Overhead, the sunlight slipped in and out of fast moving clouds. Birdy's head ached, but it wasn't the kind of ache he had recently learned to fear. This was the ache of standing on his surgically repaired knees for too long. He thought of the white envelopes.

When they were done, Birdy lifted the plastic garbage can and carried it to the scarecrow. He and Natalie filled it with footballs, and Birdy carried it to his garage and put it up against the far wall.

"Plans tonight?" he asked her.

She shrugged. "A bunch of us are going over to my friend Mallory's. We have a soccer game early tomorrow morning."

"Make sure you get your rest."

"I will, Birdy."

"I know I partied too hard when I was playing ball. Did I tell you about when I played hungover in college and had vomit down my jersey the whole time?"

She made that face that teenage girls made at teenage boys: a pleasant combination of being grossed out and intrigued by what was just said.

"I promise I won't vomit on myself."

"Good deal."

She placed her hands on her hips. "You should come. Game's at nine thirty in Clayton. It's not far from here."

"Maybe." He always said maybe. "We'll see."

He watched her run out across his yard and up to her house, pull the sliding door open, and disappear. This was a neighborhood of ranch houses, and though Birdy had never been inside her house, he assumed that the layouts of the two places were exactly the same. He wondered if her house had the same college-dorm-room smell. Inside, his answering machine blinked. Birdy tapped Play and listened as an associate of Oberschmidt's introduced himself, said he was proud to represent Dennis Birdwell, give him a call, let's make an appointment, etc. He listened to it three more times, waiting for some sort of feeling about his legal problems. When none came, he walked to the fridge, opened it, and stared at the empty Brita pitcher and the milk and the baking soda that wasn't doing a particular good job of concealing the smell emanating from the fridge he hadn't cleaned in months. He closed the door and got a drink of water from the tap; he guzzled it down, twice, then leaned against the counter with his big forearms folded across his chest.

Birdy made a pot of coffee and took a mug to the kitchen table. He considered his kitchen and what a bad selling point it would be: a small room with barely enough space for the rectangular table he was sitting at, wallpaper of yellow flowers on the walls, appliances that were twenty years old, no counter space, something he had once considered important only to housewives. He flipped on the radio and listened to the Cardinals game. All the lights in his house were off. Birdy sat sipping coffee, listening to baseball, then the post-game, then the late-night sports show, drinking his calorie-free and non-alcoholic beverage, looking at his massive hands as they raised the mug to and from his lips, the fingers gnarled and swollen. He thought of Natalie throwing a football, a quarterback trapped in a girl's body, and wondered if he'd be alive this time next year.

Birdy drove his pickup truck to a house he was renovating in the Shaw neighborhood of St. Louis. Tower Grove North was not quite dangerous but not quite safe either, an area ripe for buying low and a place where Birdy could work by himself, at his pace, and when the work was done, he could sell the house himself, no rush, no worry, no uptight yuppies asking him about square footage or heating bills or the school districts or any other shit that Birdy couldn't care less about. Still. There were times he regretted quitting his last job. He had tried. He really did. But he couldn't remember when to come into the office. He couldn't remember when to show up for an open house. He couldn't remain smiling and patient for six hours at a time. After years of football and being told what to do and where to go, every minute of his life scheduled by coaches who were more tyrants than teachers, it was nice to choose not to do something. But there was always a reminder that he did eventually need to finish and sell every rehab: the white envelopes holding the letters from the NFL denying his disability claim and the early pension he desperately needed.

Just thinking about those white envelopes from the league infuriated him, the way the logo was so prominent and perfect in the upper left corner, fonts with his name and address all immaculate. Even the quality of the white envelopes seemed extraordinary in their brightness and durability. Each time he would hold one in his hands for a beat too long because maybe this was the time they would read all the medical forms and finally admit that, yes, Dennis Birdwell's medical condition was unquestionably due to fourteen years playing in the National Football League, only to open the envelope and once again be denied disability coverage.

He parked at the curb, and as he climbed out of the truck, something clicked in his mind, almost audibly, and he realized he left his tools at home. His lunch, too. He set his eyes on the ground and let the anger drift over him. He slammed his hand on the roof of the cab and felt a shock of delight at hitting something. Pain followed, trembling through his arms, and he set his forehead against the truck, fighting the urge to start punching something else.

Thirty minutes later, he pulled back into his driveway to find Natalie sitting with her backpack on his front porch. Her expression was open and observant, hunched down behind her legs with her chin tilted to the side and her cheek pressed against her knees. Her fingers batted at her shoelaces. Birdy opened the door, his body groaning and popping as he slid out of his truck and walked with his slow gait—bone on bone in his left knee, the ache shivering up

his spine—until he was standing in front of the girl, his shadow covering her face.

"Hey, Birdy."

"Don't hey me. It's Wednesday. Why aren't you at school?"

"Holiday."

"Yeah? Which one?"

"Harry S. Truman Appreciation Day."

"Why are you really not in school?"

Her mouth smiled but her eyes didn't. She stared at her house with the burned-out look of adulthood.

"Why are you home?" she asked.

"I forgot my tools. Were you going to sit here all day?"

Natalie answered by shrugging her eyebrows and staring off into the distance, as if this somehow conveyed she was deep in thought. Birdy shuffled his keys in his hand, the arthritis making them jingle more than he wanted. His fingertips were numb. He looked over his shoulder, up and down the street, to see if anyone was watching him.

"You can come in for a second," he said. "But I'm just grabbing my things and heading back out."

With the nimbleness he so admired, she shot up, spinning on her toes, and turned and waited for him to step up and unlock the door. When he did, he held the screen door back so she could walk in first, her head high and shoulders back, like a queen, and not for the first time, her ability to shape-shift from forlorn to entitled surprised him.

Inside, Natalie took only enough steps to be out of Birdy's straight path to the kitchen. "Want a soda?" he asked.

She shook her head and sat down on the nearest couch. She pushed through the pile of items on the coffee table: old newspapers, pizza boxes, empty containers of beer or Gatorade.

"At least you don't smoke," she said.

Birdy lumbered to the kitchen. His cooler was in plain sight on the kitchen counter. He wrapped his hand around the handle, then hesitated—had this been normal forgetting, or was this from the headaches?

Cooler in hand, he focused on the hour he needed, and just lost, to lay new flooring in the rehab. He clomped to the living room. Natalie had flipped on the television, becoming absorbed in a soap opera, reclining into the arm of the couch. She wore sandals, and her toes were painted dark pink.

"I gotta go," he said.

"Can I come with you? I want to see the house you're renovating."

"I've got work to do, Nat."

"I won't bother you. C'mon, I forgot my key, and I can't get in my house."

"Forgot your key? Really?"

Natalie swung her feet to the ground to face him. "Please," she asked. "Please?" And he told himself there was nothing wrong with this. Nothing wrong with having someone sit on the porch while he worked. Nothing wrong with having his protégé hang around and learn that football—hell, anything in athletics—will soon be over, sooner than you think, and that you'll have to find work, real work, that the people who never have to work again like Dan Marino and Deion Sanders are an elaborate lie, an illusion that the League takes care of its own and that all its ex-players don't, in fact, suffer from debilitating pain and injury that leaves most guys dead before they're sixty. Guys that blow their brains out with shotguns, guys that intentionally drive the wrong way into highway traffic, guys that drink antifreeze, guys that will find anyway to die and end all the pain.

"Birdy?"

He blinked. Natalie was standing in front of him.

"I'm fine," he said. "Sure, you can come. Let's go."

In the truck, they drove with the windows down. It was October now and one of the last warm days of the year. His body told him autumn was coming: the ache in the screws inserted in his left ankle, the arthritis that shivered in his hips and spine, the way his elbows and knees could harden into stone. They drove in silence, Natalie tapping her phone the whole way, her thumb skipping around the screen like a bug.

He parked at the curb and led Natalie into the house. To the left were the stairs to the second floor; to the right was the living room and dining room, each with a pair of stained glass windows high up along the eastern wall. Straight ahead was a small bathroom that Birdy had recently finished, then the kitchen that was in some halfway stage of functionality.

"I'm putting down a new floor in the kitchen," Birdy said. "Can't have you in there."

"I'll do my homework on the porch."

"So you're skipping school to do homework?"

"Harry S. Truman Appreciation Day," she smiled. "Not my fault."

She turned away. She spun her phone in her palm, the device spinning like a top, and turned on her coltish legs, and bounced out of the room. Good god, he thought. Don't grow up. Don't get older. Stay like this forever. She walked out and the aluminum screen door banged shut loud and uneven into the frame.

The hours passed. The kitchen was stripped to its bones, all the old cabinets and counters and broken appliances visible atop the large dumpster at the edge of the backyard. When the ache in his body became too much, he stood, his body popping like it was carbonated. He looked out across the overgrown weeds, imagining all the things he might find out there—bottles and cans, cigarette butts, used condoms, fast-food wrappers, odd bits of clothing—if he ever bothered to walk into the backyard. He preferred it uninviting.

The headaches were never gone, just lying dormant like a volcano, the pressure building at the base of his skull or behind the eyes, and then came a great emptiness of time that could last hours or even days, and Birdy would wake up on the floor somewhere and not have any memory of the pain and confusion he had just gone through. And not remembering only made it more terrifying.

He stepped out onto the porch. Natalie was sitting cross-legged on the concrete, a history book open on her lap. She looked up at him with blank curiosity.

"Did I ever tell you about when I almost drowned?" he asked.

She shook her head. He eased his body down onto the steps, his hips popping loudly, an electric snap of pain running from his skull to his ribs. He closed his eyes, clenched his jaw.

"Birdy?"

He brushed invisible crumbs from his thighs. "We were in Chicago. November. Rainy and real fucking cold. You know how you see linemen on TV and we aren't wearing sleeves? We really are cold. I don't care what anybody says, how tough they pretend they are. We're cold."

Natalie closed her book.

"So there was this fumble," he continued. "Ball hit the ground and you could actually hear it plop, like throwing a big rock in a small lake. The field looked like shit, like a pig pen. Dead grass and mud and it was rainy and foggy. Nobody could see anything.

"Anyway, so the ball is loose and I get to it first. Pile-ons are the worst goddamn thing in football. Just fucking miserable. Guys are punching and grabbing fingers and wrists and twisting. If you get a hand in someone's mask, you try to gouge his eyes and bend his nose. You get a hand in your mask, you bite that son of a bitch. I'm serious. Take the flesh off if you have to.

"Since I got to the ball first, I get buried at the bottom of the pile. And my face was all the way into a puddle. I couldn't breathe. I was snorting water, couldn't even scream. I opened my eyes and all I could see was black. I kicked and pushed with all I had. Nobody moved. When I tried to raise my head this pain ran through my neck like a nail had been driven through it. I lived, obviously. But I fucked something up in my neck and they took me out of the game. I played the next week, though."

Natalie lowered her chin. Finally, she said, "I hate the water. I can't even swim. My mom used to swim."

He thought, *Please remember me when I'm gone.* But he was terrified to say this aloud, to admit that he was scared. And that he needed her, his only friend, to make sense of his days.

Instead, all he said was, "I don't think I've met her."

"Really?"

"Neighbors often don't know each other."

"My mom isn't home much anymore."

He wrapped his fingers over his knees. "Marriage is hard. I was never good at it. My first wife remarried. Has two kids. My second wife was more of a party girl. We don't talk anymore."

"Sounds lonely."

He chewed on that word like it was flavorless gum. The street was empty of cars and Birdy looked up at the smoky sky. Was there really any difference between *lonely* and *alone*?

It was Halloween. This year, the holiday fell on a Saturday, and Birdy could sit at home watching movies, rocking up and out of his recliner when the doorbell rang. Kids appeared in a wide range of costumes, from ghosts to superheroes to princesses to Harry Potters to the occasional kid who didn't wear any costume, just showed up with a pillowcase looking for candy. Birdy didn't mind this. At the door, Birdy smiled at the kids terrified of his size. Way out, far away, at the edge of his dark lawn, parents stood on the sidewalk, hands in their pockets, wearing stocking caps. He wasn't sure if they were smiling or not.

Shortly after eight, he dumped all the remaining Milky Ways equally between two kids, then stood with his hands in his pockets on his plain concrete slab of a front porch. All down the street, porch lights illuminated the decorations in the front yards: dry ice in plastic cauldrons, scarecrows thrown back into lawn chairs, cobwebs on lamp posts and windows and gardens, cheap signs reading "Happy Halloween!" Behind the shades of living room windows, neighbors that he did not know settled in for the evening. Inside his house was nothing he wanted: an empty kitchen, a bathroom filled with various pain meds shipped from foreign countries, and littered all throughout, those white envelopes from the league, all saying the same thing over and over again: denied, denied, denied.

On the other side of his driveway, appearing almost like a ghost, was Natalie's dad, Oliver. He nodded. Hands in his pockets, Birdy crossed the driveway and stood on the interstitial strip of their lawns. Oliver wore a barn coat and jeans and looked cold.

"What did Natalie go as this year?"

"I don't know. She and Missy moved out."

All the air left his lungs. The neighborhood seemed eerily still. "What?"

"Two days ago. My wife bolted in the middle of the week. You didn't notice?"

Birdy stared at his shoes. How long had it been since he saw Natalie? After he took her to the house in Tower Grove, she hadn't come around again, but when was that? Trying to count days and weeks made his neck ache.

"I saw her just the other day. I think. Shit, Oliver, I'm really sorry."

Oliver looked at him with a mixture of curiosity and pity. He sniffed and then spit into the grass. "You really didn't notice my daughter was gone?"

Birdy raised his head and focused on some distant point over his neighbor's left shoulder. He could hear the threat, the low snarl in Oliver's words, the same tone that coaches used: barely masked disdain.

"I get these headaches," Birdy said. His eyes glassed over and his breathing echoed in his ears. "I can get through the day, you know, the little things. But big picture stuff? Sometimes, I just lose track."

Oliver nodded, and his squint soon relaxed into something like indifference. They stood quietly like that for a long time. Then he asked, "How many surgeries have you had?"

"Thirty-four."

"That's a lot of time under the knife."

"Some were minor, some were major. No big deal."

"I played safety in high school. Wasn't any good, though. I always seemed to fuck up the timing of the pass. Always way early or way late." Oliver laughed. "Whatever. You want to come in, watch the late game?"

Only after Birdy accepted and started to follow Oliver into the house did he realize how strange this was, this sudden show of friendship. But he recognized loneliness. Inside, the warmth of the house reminded him that, yes, it really was after sundown, almost November, and it was actually quite cold.

Though this house was a ranch with a chain-link fence, just like Birdy's, he recognized that Oliver had an immaculate home. The hardwood floors shined, its surface unscratched and gleaming. There was crown molding and artwork Birdy didn't understand but knew was tasteful, expensive furniture, and a fireplace that probably worked. The kitchen, Birdy knew, would make his old clients salivate: granite countertops, custom cabinetry, stainless steel appliances.

"Beautiful home," Birdy murmured.

"You sound surprised."

"I guess I just figured it would be like mine."

Oliver didn't comment on this, and for that, Birdy was grateful. They sat down on the couch, and on the massive flat-screen in front of them was a college football game. It was just the first quarter. They could be here for a while. Oliver offered a beer. Birdy accepted, and they watched the game in silence. Occasionally Oliver would ask a question and Birdy would explain what was happening on the line, blocking schemes, where the mistakes were made, point of attack.

"Sounds like the army, doesn't it?" Birdy said.

"Exactly the same."

Birdy nodded. He had thought more than once that his coaches would have been better off fighting wars. Tear men down, build men up. Nothing ever good enough.

The second quarter started. A crossing pattern on the left side led to the flanker was lit up by the outside linebacker, and after several first downs, something about Oliver's words seeped into Birdy's mind, making him turn and look at Oliver's profile.

"What war were you in?" he asked.

"Desert Storm."

"No shit."

Oliver nodded, never turning his eyes on Birdy. All of a sudden, as if by magic, Birdy could see the crow's feet around his eyes, the subtle sagging of skin around his jaw. Oliver was older than he realized.

"Armored division," Oliver said. "Tanks. Frontline stuff."

Birdy nodded. Somehow, in a way he recognized but could not understand, he knew that this was not something he could ask Oliver about.

"What do you do now?" Birdy tried.

"I'm a dentist."

Birdy laughed. Oliver grinned.

"Sorry, man," Birdy said. "Sorry. That's just funny to me. Why a dentist?"

"I don't know. Why not, I guess. It's actually pretty solitary. You don't deal with people much, and you get paid well."

"I didn't know that."

"Which part?"

"All of it." Birdy's vision flickered, and he gazed at some point above the television. "Did you know the state can have up to a year to prosecute you for a crime? Missouri's statute of limitations is a full year. Can you imagine having something like that hang over your head for a year?"

"No, I can't."

Birdy could feel Oliver's gaze drilling into the side of his head.

"I tore up a grocery store. I didn't hurt anybody. I mean, that's what the cops said. I don't really remember it."

"You get headaches."

"I've never laid a hand on anyone. I mean, since I left football."

"I know that. I always knew that." Birdy's breathing came hard, and he sensed that Oliver knew something, some kind of secret, a secret that could only be told in a language Birdy couldn't understand.

Oliver asked, "What do you do now? For work."

"Real estate. It sucks."

Oliver pointed at the television screen with his beer bottle. "Better than that shit, though, isn't it?"

On screen, it was a third and two. USC, on offense, called an inside handoff. They might have made it. While the officials came out to measure, the replay was shown, again and again, from various angles: the Skycam high above, then from both sidelines, even a view so inside the play it seemed there must be a player literally wearing a camera. Every shot showed young men, eyes aflame with adrenaline and testosterone, and then they hit, and their bodies shook and their faces disappeared behind helmets and pads and piles of bodies. Birdy clenched his teeth together.

"Goddamn, I miss it," he said.

"It's hard not to, isn't it?"

Birdy pictured Natalie. He pictured her running in full sprint, both her small hands on the football, her eyes up, her face compressed into this look of total concentration. It was really beautiful. He couldn't help feeling the beauty of that moment. Yet even in the reverie of such a beautiful thing that he had helped to nurture, it saddened him that he didn't have his own daughter to think of, that he didn't think of his own family, that he couldn't picture anything other than football. Now he looked away from the television at the screen door, open and letting in the cool air, and all the darkness out in the backyard. He thought about things he could not see. About darkness. About being face down at the bottom of a pile of men paid to tear each other apart, down beneath all those slabs of muscle and bone, down, sinking into the earth.

THE SINS OF MAN

Connectivity was the type of company that called all its locations a "campus," but when Kane looked around, he saw it for what it was: a former regional airport fifty miles south of his home in St. Louis that had been converted into the main delivery hub for a consumer goods company. The old runways were now a massive parking lot surrounded by fences and security checkpoints more appropriate for Homeland Security. Beyond the fence line was a small forest of red maples, their bright branches the first hints of the Ozarks to the south. After exiting his truck, Kane often rested his forearms on its roof and stared into the forest, trying to find the exact spot where, if he walked into the tree line, he could no longer be seen. He wondered if this same thought was what his ex-wife Alice was thinking during those last months of their marriage, when she often stood by the back of the house and stared into the yard: Where and how will I disappear completely?

He locked the door, trying to mentally leave Alice in the cab of his truck where, under the front seat, he had been driving to and from work with his loaded Beretta. He was an ex-military man, always on time for his shift, never permitting himself to linger too long on the woods. He entered the makeshift lobby, stepping out of the oppressive Missouri heat and into the climate controlled airplane hangar that Connectivity had converted into a clean, sterile work space the length of a football field. The only sound was the steady and unlocateable hum of electronics. On this end, there were a dozen Eagle's Nests, each the size and shape of a shipping container. Kane strode to Nest #6, took the three wooden steps to the entry, keyed in, waited for the light over the keypad to change from red to green, and pulled the door open.

"What's the word?" Kane asked. Schroeder, his Eagle's Nest partner, turned from the monitors. He too was ex-military, with the ruddy complexion of a man who had lived too hard for too long. For ten hours, they shared this windowless box lit almost entirely by the glow of computer and television monitors on all of the four surrounding walls. The floors made of vulcanized rubber hushed their footsteps, and up in the corner opposite the doorway, a Febreze car vent clip worked its magic, filling the room with the chemical "fresh citrus" smell of overripe fruit. Schroeder tilted his chair back.

"Ozarks have been quiet today," Schroeder said. "All week, actually. Control thinks the militia might have another attack planned."

"An organized one?"

"That's the rumor."

"An attack on the planes, or on us?"

"Honest, buddy?" Schroder said. "No one knows."

"I thought we took this job to avoid that shit."

"I took this job for the donuts. Got some pretty good donuts here."

This was not hyperbole. Outside, on the hangar floor near the restrooms, there was a long series of banquet tables covered by thick white tablecloths, stocked solely with donuts and coffee. Sugar and caffeine: the guys loved it. Kane's favorite was the s'mores, a donut filled with gooey marshmallow, topped with chocolate icing, and sprinkled with finely powdered graham crackers. Best goddamn donut he'd ever had.

"Manifest?" Kane asked.

"Thirty-six singles," Schroeder said, passing a clipboard to Kane. "Then a whole bunch in Oklahoma. Here's to continued good luck."

Kane took his ergonomic chair, slipped headphones over his ears, and adjusted the slim microphone to a place just below his chin, out of his line of vision, keeping the six monitors in front of him visible. His first drop mission was in Mississippi. Pretty easy. He checked his monitors, verifying fuel levels, drone weight, merchandise integrity, FAA schedule, weather forecast, and the last maintenance test (logged at 16:34 yesterday). Then, clearing all flight security and safety checks, Kane used the flight stick to ease his drone onto the runway. He was eighth in line. From inside his Nest, he couldn't hear or see the drone take off, only what the screens told him. The drones, which Connectivity called Griffins, soared to the unowned airspace between skyscrapers and the FAA that Connectivity had purchased in Missouri, Arkansas, Kentucky, Tennessee, Mississippi, Alabama, Louisiana, Texas, Oklahoma, and Kansas. They were allowed to base a command center in Florida but not actually permitted to send Griffins into the Sunshine State. New territories took time to pass state legislatures, a fact that Kane had learned quickly in his two years with the company.

It was the middle of the day, and a short flight down to Oxford. Kane checked the manifest: in forty-seven minutes, he would be delivering a KitchenAid Super Capacity Three-Door Stainless Steel LG EX700 refrigerator to one Ruth Anne Warren of Oxford, Mississippi. According to satellite maps of her yard, which she provided to Connectivity upon purchase and her request for Griffin Expedition, the driveway was 114.5 feet long, swept left into a three-car garage, and terminated in front of a carriage house. Kane had already decided he'd need the full driveway to land, given the weight of the package. He could easily bank his way toward Warren's back door and unload the refrigerator at the foot of the steps. Paperwork indicated that Ruth Anne Warren had not purchased Connectivity Helpers to move her purchase from the foot of the steps into her home. Must have teenage sons. Air from the vents fluttered the pages of the manifest and the orange scent vaguely reminded Kane that he'd left his laundry in the dryer at home.

On his monitor, at twenty thousand feet, the world appeared smooth and bucolic. The flight was uneventful; the Griffin crossed the Mississippi, and Kane eased the drone down through the atmosphere. He steered toward a development northwest of Oxford. The flight plan had Kane banking south over the woods, then following a main road up to Warren's development, cruising lower as he closed in on the delivery address. But as he pulled onto Autumn Applause Driveway, still eight hundred yards from his destination, the Griffin banked a sharp left. His monitors blinked and blurred, and two went black.

"Motherfucker!" Kane screamed.

Schroeder turned his head. "In Oxford?"

"North. Sardis Lake." Current satellite maps indicated a clear street, but Kane's gauges were going nuts, and the damage to the right wing had the Griffin spasming.

"Can you land it?"

Kane trembled the flight stick, trying not to send the Griffin into a tailspin. He was two hundred yards from the driveway. He raised the nose. Another sound reverberated in his headset, and the Griffin banked hard to the right.

"Fucking shit," Kane said. "I'm not gonna make it."

The Griffin dropped hard, power to the rear throttle gone. Kane could see the Warrens' mailbox on the monitors. He jerked the flight stick, trying to ease the acceleration, but the street was

speeding toward him; individual homes were no longer on the screen. Kane yanked back hard on the flight stick, aiming for the driveway. All six screens went black. A tremendous shudder rippled through his hand.

"Motherfucker!" Kane yelled.

Schroeder scooted back. "Goddamn."

Kane checked the dashboard. Though the Griffin was down, the refrigerator was still attached. Heating gauges indicated NO FIRE. Tracking signaled that Kane had made it to the Warrens' front yard. He pulled up the satellite image. From the rear camera, he saw tire marks ripped across the driveway, digging a trench of mud and grass straight through the lawn. The Griffin had come to a rest at the edge of the flower bed in front of their living room window.

"On the plus side," Schroeder said, "you didn't hit the house."

Kane made the call: "Shepherd, this is Three Four. I have a Griffin down; repeat, I have a Griffin down."

"Three Four, this is Shepherd. We have your location. Do you have eyes-on?"

The eagle eye was buried in Ruth Ann Warren's lilacs and tulips. He panned the rearview camera left, then right, and caught a neighbor climbing out of his Lexus and pointing, like something out of a bad sci-fi movie.

"Affirmative, Shepherd. No looters, only friendlies."

"We're in route, Three Four. Is the package secure?"

Four of the six straps on the KitchenAid Super Capacity Three-Door Stainless Steel LG EX700 were broken but miraculously, the fridge was secure.

"That's not the last time we're going to shoot you down."

Kane froze. He'd never heard militia on a secure, encrypted channel.

"Do you hear me?" the voice continued. "William Kane of St. Louis, Missouri? I said, that's not the last time we're going to shoot you down."

Kane killed the mic. He continued watching on the rearview until a black SUV with the Connectivity logo on the doors rolled to the end of the Warrens' driveway. Then Kane switched off the monitor, and coded in the situation to Control: the Snipers had struck again. And it was, apparently, personal—he was almost certain the voice he just heard was Alice.

"So you did not recognize the speaker's voice?"

Kane shook his head. "No, sir."

Five men in dark suits sat across from Kane in a conference room that he had never set foot in before. It was on the third floor of the St. Louis complex's headquarters. He could see the hangar out across the yard, beyond the pebbled sidewalks, picnic benches, and corporate art of oversized parallelograms and oblong ellipses that seemed to be in various stages of somersaults.

One man, Mr. Piafsky, was doing all the talking. According to his profile page on the Connectivity website, he was a John Grisham fan, and since Grisham only shaved on Sundays, he too only shaved on Sundays. Kane didn't know if Piafsky bothered going to church, but since today was Thursday, his chin was speckled with graying hair. The other four men were methodically flipping through the report on Kane's "incident" as if they hadn't been in the room for the last twenty-five minutes.

"You understand the seriousness of this issue," Piafsky said. "And I appreciate you coming in early and walking us through yesterday's incident. These safety concerns have been ongoing for our company, and we're trying to keep our customers' worries to a minimum."

"Of course."

"We're working with the states to prosecute these people, but of course, we have to catch them first. Anyway, I would appreciate it if you continue to honor your employee confidentiality agreement and do not discuss this ongoing investigation with anyone."

"Yes, sir."

Piafsky closed the file in front of him, and with his head still down, theatrically raised one meaty finger.

"One last question, Sergeant Kane. When's the last time you spoke to your ex-wife?"

Kane blinked, both at the use of his rank and mention of his ex. "Alice?"

"You have another ex-wife?"

All five vice presidents laughed, and Kane resisted the urge to tell them to go fuck themselves. One of the appeals of his Connectivity job was that, most of the time, it was just him and Schroeder in a box delivering merchandise that regular people wanted, and all supervision was through daily reports that were automatically spit out. Work your shift, deliver products, go home. In the Nest, he could pretend he wasn't still being driven by the suits, by the men who made the decisions.

Kane shifted in his seat. Alice was small and blonde, which described most military wives he knew, except her expression was always etched with skepticism and distrust. She used to go on long runs, and when she returned, kicking her shoes off on the front porch, she'd stand barefoot in their living room, hands on her hips as if she'd expected her run to have taken her far away from home.

"I haven't spoken to Alice in almost two years."

"Does she still live in St. Louis?"

Kane shrugged. "I really don't know."

"Okay. That'll be all."

After returning from his fourth tour freshly divorced, Kane decided that flying for United or Delta was too boring for him; what was fun about flying from Los Angeles to New York and back again? Other than stewardesses, it seemed like a shit job. He thought Connectivity, too, was a shit job when he first started. But one of the many perks of working for Connectivity was that all his needs were delivered to his doorstep. When he came home, whatever he'd ordered two days earlier was there: pillows, comforters, laundry detergent, light bulbs, water filters, new Xbox controllers, both Michael Bay Criterion Collection films, paper towels, toilet paper, Blues hoodies in gray or blue. Even groceries. All delivered in neat, unbroken boxes from Connectivity. Even better was that when his shift was over, he could simply step away from it, hop in his truck, drive home, and not speak to anyone or deal with anything based in reality. Kane preferred puzzling out the confined, forced options of elaborate Xbox worlds. In those worlds there were always men with comic book muscles wrapped in unshaven stoicism set to destroy an alien horde. He liked people just fine, but the controlled world of video games was emotionally superior. The military's need to destroy by inflicting pain with surgical precision was pointless, and back in the civilian world, these memories made him recoil, his chin tucked and shoulders curled. Why speak about the unspeakable?

Other than one chance encounter, he hadn't heard from Alice since she left him. Kane had long assumed she was wholly indifferent to his existence. But this, apparently, was not true. It was both thrilling and terrifying to know he still had her attention.

According to the badge she presented, the FBI agent on Kane's doorstep was Special Agent Molly Lewis. She looked disturbingly similar to Alice. A petite woman, barely five feet tall in a dark suit and comfortable shoes, her hair was pulled back in a loose ponytail, and she stood ramrod straight and smiled pleasantly, as if she was his next door neighbor and welcoming him to the neighborhood. But she walked around his porch with a deliberate and contained power; like Alice, her manner was deceptive, and it put Kane on edge. She asked if they could talk, they sat down on his front porch, and she refused a cup of coffee.

"Caffeine makes me jittery," she said.

Kane nodded and wondered how he would get through his life without caffeine.

Agent Lewis seemed to be in no rush. She asked Kane about his military service in Iraq and Afghanistan, and then, in the effortless navigation similar to a first date, they discussed their favorite action movies. She particularly liked *Ronin*.

"I could keep this up all day," she finally said, pulling a notebook from her briefcase. Agent Lewis clicked a pen. "But I'm afraid I do have some official questions for you."

"Sure, go right ahead."

"When's the last time you saw your wife?"

"What did she do?"

"She's part of an ongoing investigation."

Kane sighed and shook his head. "Last time I saw her was at the grocery store. It was about a month after I started my new job, so, call it February 2013."

"How did Alice seem? Did she say anything about what she was up to, where she was staying?"

The last time Kane saw Alice, she had been stocking up on canned goods—tuna, black beans, peaches in syrup—at a southside Schnucks. She was in workout clothes, all black, her hair back in a ponytail, the muscles in her legs taut and strong as she stretched up on her toes to reach for items on the top shelf. She wore sandals.

The first thing Alice always did after finishing a workout was strip off her shoes and socks, which were soaked in sweat, and slide into a pair of sandals. They used to joke about how bad her feet smelled. Even from the far end of the aisle, Kane could see her dainty feet and imagine the horrible stench pouring out of her soles.

"Need help, ma'am?" he said.

She fell back on her heels. She smiled broadly. "Kane."

He reached up and plucked a bag of kale chips from the top shelf. "Not Pringles?"

"Different aisle. I'm trying to be more mindful of my body. CrossFit. Have you ever tried it?"

He shook his head. Alice's body had changed; her shoulders and arms rippled with new muscle, and her tights were shapely around her thighs. She radiated power.

"Still at Connectivity?" she asked.

"Yeah. Second shift now."

"Are you sleeping?"

"Not really."

"Tell me you aren't still playing video games all night long."

"I like video games."

"You need to make friends, Kane. Like normal people."

He looked over her shoulder at the butcher counter and the slabs of meat on display: oven roasted turkey, roast beef, honey baked ham.

"Listen, Kane." She put her hand on his forearm, and wrapped her fingers into the groove of his elbow. "I'm really glad I ran into you. I've been meaning to call, but I don't know, I just wasn't sure if I was ready to talk. But I want you to know something. It wasn't your fault. Any of it. You know that, right?"

Alice's face, flushed and open and clean from her workout, made his chest ache.

"After I left you, I met somebody." Her fingernails dug into his skin. "Older than you. He's dead now. He was dying when I met him, but I didn't know that. Something to do with his immune system and enzymes and receptor cells. His company stopped paying his insurance. Said he wasn't covered. I was there while he suffered. All I did was observe. Just watched. Like you do. But you know what got me through it? Forgiveness. I learned to forgive. I forgave him, I forgave myself, and I forgave the insurance company. So, I forgive you, Kane. I forgive you."

"Alice, what are you talking about?"

"When people die," she smiled vacuously, "they just die. It doesn't always make sense."

He shook his arm loose. "The fuck is wrong with you?"

"Nothing. Nothing is wrong with me. That's what I'm trying to tell you. Maybe you aren't ready to hear me." She put both her hands on her shopping cart. "Take care of yourself, okay?"

"Sure," he said. He stayed rooted to the ground until he no longer heard the wheels of her shopping cart squeak.

Kane blinked, and found Agent Lewis staring at him. Something in her face, so like Alice's, made him decide right then to keep this memory to himself.

"She'd been working out." He could almost feel her fingernails digging into his skin, a threatening *thank you.* "We didn't talk long."

"She didn't say where she was working? Recent changes?"

"I didn't ask, she didn't offer. My ex-wife changes careers the way normal people change clothes."

"I see. Do you have any current contact information for Alice?"

Kane pulled his phone from his back pocket, thumbed to "Alice—Do NOT Answer!" and showed the screen to Agent Lewis. Of course, he would have answered. If she had ever called.

"Has she tried to call you since you last saw her? Have any of your friends seen or heard from Alice?"

"No. Our divorce was actually easy. She didn't want the house or any of our things."

Agent Lewis handed Kane her card. "Would you get in touch with me if you do hear from Alice?"

"Sure, soon as you tell me what this is about."

Agent Lewis almost masked her suspicion. It was just a flicker, a flash of calculation that zipped through her eyes like a jet, and then morphed back into the "aw shucks" girl she had been pretending to be.

"Of course," she said. "What I can tell you is this: Alice is a person of interest in an ongoing investigation into domestic terrorism."

Kane frowned and gazed out over his lawn. He knew her answer was bureaucratic bullshit: Alice was in a lot of trouble. When she was into something, she was into it whole hog. For a moment, he sat silently with the image of Alice waging some sort of guerilla warfare, and he resisted the urge to laugh at the absurdity of his ex-wife's existence. Then Agent Lewis stood, and she offered her hand to shake. When she was at the bottom of the porch, Kane asked her one more question.

"Agent Lewis, what was the last raid you were on?"

She turned. "I beg your pardon?"

He raised his palms. "Just want to hear a story," he said.

"A parking lot bomb failed in Clayton," she said. "About six months ago. Real clumsy work, so he was easy to trace. He had a home out in Wildwood, and we went out there with full tactical. I was secondary through the door."

Kane gazed across the street. He knew before he even asked. "You lit him up."

"He fired on us. His two bomb-building buddies did not."

"Nothing more exhilarating than a raid, is there?"

Agent Lewis's eyes stilled. "No, Sergeant Kane. There sure isn't."

They'd met at a beach party in South Carolina when Kane was on a weekend pass from his training exercises prior to shipping out. At the time, Alice was a pharmacist, a year out of school and freshly certified, pulling down six figures for pushing a few pills around on a dish. That weekend, they played beer pong, raced dirt bikes, and dove naked into the Atlantic. It was the hubris of youth and the whopping benefits the military gave married couples that made Kane propose after knowing her for just eight weeks, and they tied the knot at the Charleston courthouse immediately after he returned from his first tour.

The boys had called Kane a gasshound and Alice was known to never sleep alone, but they'd immediately developed a fierce monogamy. After they met, he had seen Alice punch—not slap, punch—men that tried to touch her. He always proudly wore his wedding ring, and unlike his copilots, never had the need to take penicillin for a "kidney infection" from overseas trysts. If nothing else, Kane and Alice had fidelity. But his devotion blinded him to what, in hindsight, was a pathological unhappiness in Alice.

First, it was yoga. Then it was tae kwon do. Then it was motorcycles. Then it was organic farming, mulching with worms, clean water filtration systems. Everything was a new devotion for a few months and then it was gone, replaced with a new obsession. And the replacement process involved a furious anger with Kane for being so blind, so stupid, so complicit with the previous thing. The fights were loud and hateful, shouting that made him hoarse, leaving him with claw marks on his forearms and neck. Yet their divorce was a quiet, sad event. Even on the days when his forty-eight-minute drive to work was filled with nothing but furious anger at Alice, he always, eventually, came back to her last solemn words to him: *I'm so sorry you aren't good enough for me.* And he never could entirely convince himself that her words were untrue.

Since talking to Agent Lewis, he spent his entire drive to and from work thinking about the changes he had seen in Alice over the short life of their marriage. Being home on leave was always a fresh discovery that he wanted to immediately redeploy. He'd learn all about Alice's new obsession—crystals to wear around the neck and wrist that redirected the body's "good" energy or a pyramid scheme for "natural meal replacement" drinks in various colors of green or orange sludge—and when her encouragement for these new products was met with Kane's skepticism, the fighting began and didn't end until Kane was on a plane back to the Middle East. His deployments merely put off the inevitable. When they split, for a month of Tuesdays, their curb was a motley collection of Ikea and Best Buy furniture, and stacks of black garbage bags. Whatever the garbage men wouldn't collect, Kane loaded in his truck and drove to the city dump and chucked. Soon, he replaced all of their things with his things, all ordered from Connectivity.

Once, near the end, during an afternoon détente that Kane would always look back on with complete puzzlement, they sat on the back patio in the late afternoon. They had a case of Coors Light and a bottle of Old Crow—the same combination they used to drink in South Carolina—and Kane had grilled bratwursts on the grill. Earlier, Alice had received a Facebook message about one of their South Carolina friends, a guy named Travis, who had flipped his pickup truck heading home from the bars. Killed on impact.

"Do you miss South Carolina?" Alice asked. "That time before we were married."

There seemed to be a hidden accusation there about him, about that first walk up into a new woman's apartment. But the fact was, he didn't miss it. He didn't think about that time much at all.

"Feels like a long time ago."

"Only a couple of years."

"Lot changed in a couple of years."

"Don't get sad. Don't get all PTSD. There were almost a dozen of us, and we were really close, and we had so much fun, and we laughed all the time. We mattered to each other. We knew all about our lives, we had no secrets. I mean, you knew Maggie was fucking Kenny and AJ, right?"

Kane finished his beer. "Oh yeah. She hit on me more than once."

"She hit on me."

"No shit?"

"Swear. Don't know if she hit on all the girls, but yeah, she came onto me once. In the parking lot of a Sonic."

This made Kane giggle uncontrollably.

"Do you think they ever talk about us?" Alice asked. "What do you think they say?"

"I dunno. Something like, 'Kane went off to kill some A-Rabs and came home and he and Alice went off to start a family in the middle of Te-has.' I can hear them saying that."

"I don't have much of a role in that story."

"Mother of my children."

"Like I said."

"Look, South Carolina is over. I don't want to think about the past. At all. I know it sounds corny to you, but I did my duty. I just want to be left alone."

"Left alone to do what?"

Kane opened a fresh beer and stared out at the lawn he mowed earlier that morning.

"You don't have any friends. You don't talk to any of your Army buddies. You don't hang out with anyone from work, and you definitely don't want to see my friends. You take extra shifts at work but you don't like work and you don't spend the money, so what's the point? Don't you want something more?"

"I thought we weren't gonna argue."

"Is that all you want now? To come home at night and fuck around online?"

"And you have it figured out? With your painting classes and studying the Kabbalah and salsa classes and jewelry business and whatever else you dump after eight weeks?"

"At least I'm trying to be happy. Are you?"

Kane reached for the whiskey, poured a large shot, drank it, then chased it with his beer. When he looked up again, Alice was staring at him, her eyes already wide and pooling. Happy. What a ridiculous, arrogant idea.

"I thought," Kane said, "we weren't gonna argue. Not tonight."

She rolled her beer bottle between her hands, the fingers flexing straight as arrows, and then she chugged the rest of it in three gulps and set the bottle on the table. She fished a second one from the cooler between them, twisted off the cap, and drank most of that too. Then she stood and looked out at the yard.

"It's nice, isn't it?"

Their slab patio was surrounded by a garden bed where nothing grew. The lawn, luscious green and thick, the fresh smell of its cut still in the air, was a long rectangle surrounded by a tall wooden fence in need of a few repairs. In the back corner was a cluster of birch trees. There was no garage, no carport, just a long sidewalk leading to the alley, a gate with a lock on it to prevent kids or junkies or thieves in this still gentrifying neighborhood from creeping through their yard. It was uncomplicated and simple and Kane was proud of it.

"You should hang a hammock out there," Alice said. "In the shade of those trees."

"I should." Kane nodded. "We should."

Her gaze was focused on some point in the distance. She made a noncommittal noise. Arms folded across her chest, her eyes hard and unblinking, she still possessed a ferocity that Kane remembered from the first time he saw her, when she stood on Folly Beach and stared out at the Atlantic as if she was daring the waves to a fistfight. Beneath the sadness, there was still something brave and unbound about her.

Six weeks later, the divorce papers arrived for him at work, and he didn't see Alice again until that day in the grocery store.

In the driveway, Kane thumbed through his phone, found her number—last dialed almost two full years ago—and called. The line was disconnected. He flipped through the rest of his contacts, looking for friends of hers, her parents, someone, and discovered what he expected: he had deleted those people from his life.

Kane exited his truck and walked to the porch. He reached for the knob and saw scratches around the lock and handle, though the door was sealed. His heart rate jacked. He stilled, waiting to hear movement in his house. He waited, waited, then walked softly to his truck, unlocked it, and reached for his Beretta under the front seat. He removed the safety, chambered a round, and crept around to the back of his house. At the corner, he stopped and scanned his backyard, and seeing nothing in the neglected lawn, turned the corner and took the concrete steps to the kitchen door. He peered through the window, saw no one, and quietly unlocked and opened the door.

Inside, he aimed at both doorways, unmoving, waiting for his eyes to adjust to the dark, and listened to the stillness in the house. He crept forward. Still nothing. He stood in the hallway and pivoted his firearm around the room. Nothing. All the lights were off.

The floorboards upstairs creaked.

Kane's eyes darted up, but he held his position. He waited, then once again swept the front rooms. All clear. He swung wide of the steps, then inched forward, aiming the barrel up into the darkness. There was no way up those stairs quietly. He knew it. 911 time. He stepped back into the room, Beretta still raised, and fished for his phone with his left hand.

"Baby," a voice said. "Is that you?"

Kane froze. "Alice?"

"You coming up?"

He stepped to the bottom of the stairs, gun pointed up and directly at his ex-wife.

"Fuck are you doing here?"

"Waiting for you. Put that thing down and come up here."

"Alice. What the fuck are you doing here?"

"I'm in a little trouble and need your help. Can we talk, please?" She flipped a light switch, and there she was, bathed in light.

Kane lowered his gun. It didn't occur to him that Alice was wearing combat boots until later, after he woke up from the vicious blow that just then struck him on the back of his head.

When he woke, the lump at the base of his skull already throbbed. Must have been the size of a softball. He wanted to reach up and check but found that he was hogtied and on his belly in his own backyard. And in front of his eyes were his wife's black combat boots.

"Alice," he whispered.

She crouched down.

"We tied you up with your PlayStation controllers. Isn't that an image?"

He tugged on the cords, which were cool and rubbery against his wrists. "Let me go."

With her forearms on her knees, her fingers brushed the overgrown grass in his backyard. "We're building a bonfire."

Kane raised his chin. Men in dark outfits were carrying things out of his house and setting them in a large pile on the patio. His televisions. His couches. His dining room table and chairs. His blender, microwave, lamps, Jawbone, PlayStation, Xbox, box sets of his HBO shows. A steady line of men like an army of ants added to this shadowy pile growing at the foot of his house.

"We might torch the house, too. Haven't decided yet."

"Alice, listen to me—"

"No, I'm not going to do that." She reached into her pocket and pulled out a six ball, and wrapped a dustrag around it, then twisted it tight. Alice jammed the ball into his mouth. She yanked the rag behind his head, Kane bucking and twisting futilely, and she secured it with a sharp tuck to the back of his skull. Panting, dust on his tongue, shoulder grinding into the grass, he had a brief and startling revelation: these gags and knots aren't amateur work.

"We don't buy things, Kane. We're not materialists. Materialists actually want to possess good materials. As the Earth gets warmer, as animal go extinct, as people get sicker, we cannot let consumerism become an opiate. We are fighting back against the hostile takeover of our—"

She stopped. There was a long silence, and Kane twisted his gaze away from the house and up at Alice's face. She blinked rapidly, then raised two fingers to her mouth and drummed her lip. He'd seen this look before. She had forgotten her script.

"Hostile takeover, hostile takeover." She drummed faster. "Oh! Against the hostile takeover of our psychological, physical, and cultural environments by commercial forces. We are committed to—"

He roared into his gag. She sat down cross-legged, leaning her spine against his chest, and watched the pile of merchandise build on the patio. She turned his Beretta in her hands.

"Combat training was so illuminating, Kane. Like nothing else I've ever felt. Do you remember the first time you held a gun? No longer being passive and accepting things, but knowing that you were in control. It feels good. It's that thing I've been missing that you've always had over me. Control. Do you know that less than half of all your Connectivity cardboard gets recycled? It's more like thirty-four percent. We are literally standing on piles of our own waste. How do we control that?" She tilted her chin down and wiped the sweat from around his eyebrows. "This is just the beginning. We will shoot down your Griffins. We will burn their McMansions. It's all over, Kane."

One of the silhouettes crouched at the base of the pile, then stepped back. The fire started as a trickle, vanished, and then the pile cracked loud and flames leapt high into the air. She ran her fingers over his face, something like a caress, but light and detached, as if she was trying to draw his face from memory. Then, gently, she wiped his saliva from around his lips and curled her hand around his cheek.

"This is the freedom we've been looking for," she said. "You and me. I'm trying to save you. Don't you see this is for your benefit? This is your chance to be free from all your possessions."

His hands were almost loose. He was going to rip that gun from her hands, beat her skull in with it, then kill every one of those anarchist motherfuckers with his bare hands.

"Do you remember," she asked, "when you came home on leave from your first tour, and we had Thanksgiving in April? Remember how I made applesauce at Thanksgiving? Chunky, with some cinnamon?"

Kane nodded into the lawn. He clawed at the cords, at his skin, felt fresh scratches in his wrists.

"Cinnamon," she said. "What a word. Like a snake learning to speak. Sin-a-men. Sin of men. Sin to man."

And then he looked at the fire. Really looked at it. All the sound drained from the world except for crackling from the bonfire. He could no longer discern the individual items; it was just a black, cancerous mass surrounded by flames, a kaleidoscope of reds, whites, yellows, and deep purples, crackling and gurgling as if it was speaking in tongues. His mind went blank, even as the cords around his wrists loosened and the Beretta sat loose in Alice's hands. His eyes grew wide as if an answer to a question he had been pondering for a very long time had just begun to form in his mind. The flames grew higher, throwing back their reflections in the windows. The cords were loose. If Kane wanted to use them, his hands were now free.

THE PHOTOGRAPH

Annie received the phone call to return to New York on the same day her boyfriend Jason moved out of her house. It had been twelve years since Annie and her two best friends were selected at random by a photojournalist in the Mall of America for a spread in the *New York Times Magazine* about the everyday lives of teenagers. Her face lit up—she could actually feel the flush run through her cheeks—when she heard the photographer's name and the reason for the call: a retrospective photo shoot to revisit the image of three thirteen-year-old girls from Edina, Minnesota. In the original photograph, Annie and her friends were applying too much blush and lipstick, their hair straightener cords dangling from the light fixtures, getting ready for their school's Sadie Hawkins dance, a time in her life that Annie increasingly thought of with cheery sadness.

She refused to not be there when her boyfriend moved out: it was her house, the down payment had been all hers, the mortgage payments had never been shared, and she sensed the possibility that he would take something of hers, accidentally or not. This threat, however unfounded, felt like a horrible violation. But her thoughts were on New York, wearing Dior and reading *Vogue* and flashing a radiant smile at photographers and their assistants. Her suitcase was on the top shelf of the hall closet, and Annie wondered how many outfits she should pack for a three day visit.

The e-mail with a proposed itinerary was still open, the *New York Times* logo in the signature gleaming like a gold coin, when she sensed Jason hovering in the doorway. She set her laptop down on the coffee table and stood up, folding her arms across her chest. The friend that was helping him move out was not a familiar face, and he had smiled with embarrassment at her presence. She wondered if he was like Jason, the type of man to blame his girlfriend for the fact that he had been out of work for six months. She wondered, too, if he would decide to cope with this insecurity by cheating on his girlfriend with some slut across the river at Macalester.

"I'm all done," Jason said.

"If I find anything of yours, I'll set it aside and give you a call." She looked out the window at his friend, leaning against the pickup truck, smoking, the sweat glistening off his forearms. "Are you staying with him? Or her?"

His jaw clenched and his eyes focused at some point over her head.

"On his couch," he said. "I told you, I'm not with her."

"It doesn't matter. You know there's more to it than that."

"I know," he said sadly, and for a moment, she pitied him, and how it must feel to have been laid off twice while Annie kept getting promoted. Then he said, "I just can't believe you're chucking me when I'm still looking for a job."

"Are you serious?"

"Whatever." And he turned and pushed open the storm door, which swung back rapidly, and right before it hit, the hydraulic held it in place, just for a moment, until the door's weight eased and it closed with a satisfying click. The truck backed out of the driveway, the items in the bed shifting perilously, and then they were heading up the street and they were gone. She picked up her phone and dialed her brother.

"How did it go?" he asked.

"Great. Can you come over now?"

In ten minutes, Joel and his wife Bridget were there. Annie pretended to listen as he explained to her what he was doing as he changed the locks. Instead, her enthusiasm for New York vanished at the mere presence of Bridget. Her sister-in-law had been married to Joel for two years, and she and Annie had never been close. Bridget was Nordic and solid and, while certainly not unpleasing, she was a remarkable switch from the effusive and buoyant type her brother used to date. Bridget smiled tightly at her and asked if she was okay, calling her *dear* in a condescending tone that made Annie irrationally furious, and remained across the living room, politely disinterested, as if she somehow disapproved of even being in Annie's home. When Joel was done, he handed Annie the new key, and she wrapped her fingers around it into a tight fist until its grooves stabbed her palm.

"I'll be right behind you guys," she said. "I just need to pack a bag."

"You're staying at Mom's?" Her brother's expression coiled into a grimace, and she pictured what he was like when he was younger, bouncing bars in order to pay his way through school.

"He wouldn't hurt me. I just don't want to stay here tonight. That's all."

His eyes softened, and he was her brother again: more teddy bear than grizzly.

Within five minutes, she packed, got in her car, and started following her brother on the short drive to their parents' house. She assumed that her mother had told them everything about her relationship with Jason. What they didn't know, what Annie still hadn't decided whether or not to confide to anyone, was that she had followed Jason one night, trailing his car like something from a bad detective novel, and saw him leaving a bar with the girl. From across the street, Annie focused on her: tall and curvy with dark wavy hair and a slim nose, moving with the athletic confidence of a funambulist. Despite everything wrong with their relationship— her budding career and his lack of one, their inability to communicate their fears, their deadening sex life as Jason gained weight from inactivity, the growing disapproval of her parents, her disbelief that anyone else wanted to be with an unemployed twenty-five-year-old like Jason—what hurt Annie more than anything else was this inarguable fact: this new girl was prettier than her.

During dinner at her parents, everyone left her alone, treating her silence as a stage of grief and reflection. All through dinner, Annie focused on those weeks in junior high after the original *Times* photo came out. With Hannah and Kaitlin, she had walked down the hallways of their school like royalty and met the gaze of not just their classmates but their teachers and parents, too. It was intoxicating to be recognized and known simply for being herself. Even during high school and college, at any time she was brought low by a soccer match or poor grades or hooking up with the wrong guy or filling out job applications, the memory of that time could lift her mood like a warm summer wind, and Annie would momentarily close her eyes and glide on that feeling of admiration.

She helped her mother clear the table and brought out dessert—brownies and coffee for herself and her dad—and eased back into silence. She didn't quite see her parents as attractive, but she knew her brothers were handsome, desirable with their broad shoulders and easy smiles. The memories of their girlfriends drifted through her thoughts: large eyes and long hair, straight white teeth, bodies with just enough curves in the right places to make them seem vaguely like adults. It struck her then that Joel had married a girl who wasn't all that pretty, not in the sense that his previous girlfriends had been. The beginning of a question formed in her mind, then she brushed it aside like crumbs and sipped her coffee, ignoring her mother's insistence that she eat.

After, Annie returned to her old bedroom and turned on the desk lamp. She had cleared out the dresser and closet when she bought her house, and these spaces now felt like coffins emptied by grave robbers. Above her desk was a corkboard still covered in high school memorabilia: photos of her soccer team and senior prom, her scholarship letter to Wisconsin, Prince concert tickets, torn notebook scraps with inside jokes scrawled in her handwriting. In the middle, among all the clutter, was the original photograph that ran in the *Times*. She pulled it down, careful to not damage it further. The three of them were so young, barely into puberty, their shoulders and elbows bony, their brows and mouths protruding as they tried to look adult and ignore the photographer. They were sweetly unaware of how young they were. She sat down on her bed, holding the photo with two hands, studied her face. It wasn't until she was in her pajamas and staring at the ceiling that her mother came in and sat on the edge of the bed, and Annie told her about returning to New York.

As the plane descended into LaGuardia, Annie leaned against the window, gazing down through the fog at the runways and planes lit by the airport, just like when she first visited during Hannah and Kaitlin's junior year of college, twenty-one and freshly armed with the developing plan to move here together as soon as they graduated. Her hand tightened on the magazine in her lap, the six dollars she spent on it duly noted in the spending log secured in the inner fold of her wallet. This must be what it's like, she thought, for the defeated—the politician about to give a concession speech, a salesman who just botched the close, lovers returning from a failed rekindling to the wreckage of their lives. She held the photograph in her hand, its corners rounded, fingerprints visible when tilted at the right angle, smudges all over, a crease between her and her two friends from a moment during their senior year when she was angry with them but couldn't quite tear it to shreds.

Annie hopped in a cab curbside and caught the driver checking her out when she dipped into the back seat. This brought a thin smile to her lips, a small reassurance that she was still in the same class of pretty as her friends. She removed her compact from her purse and checked if her eyeliner had gathered in the tiny creases around her eyes, then closed it with a resounding click. She watched the seven minute news loop playing on the small screen on the back of the front seat, but as soon as they climbed the Queensboro Bridge and she could see the East River, she focused her gaze out at the city, pleased to feel a bit like a tourist again. It was startling to rush through the city, around cyclists and pedestrians, and look up to see the building rose far above her view. When the cab pulled up to the address on East Eighty-Fourth Street, Annie felt as if she had been jarred from a pleasant, unexplainable dream.

She buzzed her friends' apartment, and almost immediately, Kaitlin came flying down the steps. On sight of her old friend, Annie felt a twinge of jealousy: Kaitlin was beautiful. It was so natural, too, with her shapely face and shining smile, as if adulthood had filled her with light. In her T-shirt, Kaitlin's sinewy arms were the kind Annie never saw at the gym back home: lean, smooth, unfreckled, no fat. When Kaitlin reached her and wrapped her in a massive hug—Christ, she even smelled good—only then did it hit Annie that she had been hoping, all this time, that she was somehow better than her friends.

"You look great!" Kaitlin said. She pulled back, holding Annie in place. "I'm so excited! I've told everyone that you're back for a photo shoot and they're so jealous. Remember how they all hated us the first time?"

"Bitches," Annie laughed. "What do they know?"

"C'mon, let's go upstairs. Gimme your bag."

Annie followed her up three flights of stairs, noting that Kaitlin's hips were slim and she had that upper thigh gap that she had never been able to achieve, no matter how much dieting, Pilates, and yoga she tried. She counted how many locks were on their door—three—when they entered. Even just inside the doorway, Annie could sense how small the apartment was, how constricted.

"She's here!" Kaitlin screamed. She wrapped both arms around Annie and steered her into the bathroom. Hannah stood in front of the mirror, leaning towards the glass with her chin raised, running eyeliner over her lids. For just a moment, Annie was certain that a flash of contempt ran through Hannah's eyes before she broke into a smile, turning fully to face her, and giving her a strong hug that chilled Annie to her core.

It didn't take long for Annie to remember why she loved New York. To revel in the endless beeping of taxi horns, the crowds of people moving like oceanic waves through the streets, the variety of people—so heterogeneous, a kaleidoscope of clothes, expressions, heights—buildings rising and rising into the sky, the rank smell of the hipsters and bohemians mixed with the expensive perfumes and colognes of the rich tantalizing her from block to block, lights of restaurants and bars that never seemed to be anything but full. In part, it was the walking that so captivated her, the constant sense of movement, the steady impact in her heels that rippled up her legs that reminded her, with each step, that she was young and alive and going somewhere in this world.

They hailed a cab at Second Avenue, zipped on to the FDR, and headed south into the Village. Their first stop was at Jimmy's No. 43, which is a bar they stumbled into together on one of their first nights in New York after meeting—and then ditching—a couple of NYU law students. Annie's eyes widened at the drink prices, but Kaitlin placed a hand on her wrist and said, "This night is on us." They stayed for two drinks before heading to KGB, then Boiler Room, then, drunk and arms linked, they took a long nostalgic walk around Tompkins Park. The entire night, Annie wondered how she could possibly live anywhere else but here. Finally, at two in the morning, they caught a taxi home, the smell of alcohol pouring off their skin like perfume, their arms and shoulders sticky, pressing against each other as they talked too loudly in the back seat of the cab. Inside, they yanked their shoes off and made gin and tonics. Kaitlin stretched out on the couch, her eyes heavy with sleep. Annie and Hannah sat in the dilapidated easy chairs against the window overlooking the street.

"Dad helped me buy a place in Nokomis," Annie said. "It's really cute. On the weekends, maybe once a month, he comes down and helps me do work. We restained the floors last month. I don't know if we're going to do anything this summer. I mean, I love it, but I'd like to just live in my house, you know?"

Below, the heavy gears of a delivery truck reverberated in her ears.

"It's nice having my own place." Annie stared out at all the rows of lit windows across the street. "But it's hard not to feel that I've settled somehow. I didn't think I would miss being here so much. I'm really lucky to have my job back home, and I really don't regret taking it. I don't know. I guess I'm just wondering."

"I couldn't imagine going back. It's so Midwestern," said Hannah. "And look at this one." They looked back over at Kaitlin, asleep now, her mouth agape, her hands tucked neatly into her chest as if in prayer. "Remember how long it took her to sleep through the night when we first moved here?"

"I never really adjusted to this place. I know I could now. I'm different. More mature." Annie turned back to Hannah. "I think I might want to give New York another shot."

A silence fell. Hannah took a long drink from her glass, and the ice cubes rattled when she set it back down.

"I bet it's easier to get married in Minneapolis," Hannah said. "You wouldn't believe how many thirty-five-year-old women in this city have never been married. They say it just sneaks up on you. One day you're all Carrie Bradshaw and the next day, you realize you're never gonna have those two kids until you find a guy, and there's just no one out there."

"I don't care about that," Annie lied. "To tell you the truth, I feel like I needed to figure myself out first, decide if I wanted to stay there or come back here."

Hannah contemplated her with an expression Annie couldn't understand. She looked back out the window. She could feel the trains shaking beneath the city.

"Of course, we've got some time," she said.

"I don't know if I'll ever get married," Hannah said, staring into space. "It's just so much trouble. You see these women walking through Manhattan with their twins in a stroller, and you just know they had to get shots in the ass for years in order to conceive. And all these women are forty! So old! I mean, what happened to their careers? They're just at home all the time? I don't know. I never really thought about it until I got here, and now, the idea is just so bizarre."

"I could always sell my house."

"Weren't you seeing someone? What was his name?"

"Jason. He got jealous because I got a raise and a promotion and made more money than he did. Sounds silly, but he really had a problem with it." Annie frowned at her hands. "I feel like I'm never going to have sex again."

"You'll never have a problem finding that here. Just smile and toss your hair: that's all it takes for some of the assholes you meet at bars. I was seeing a married guy for a while. That's not a bad way to go."

"What?" Annie said. "Wait, who?"

"Just some guy. I didn't work with him or anything. It was only a couple of weeks and then I decided the fun was over and broke it off."

"How could you do that?"

Hannah shrugged. "It's really not that big of a deal." She finished her drink and set the glass down with a satisfying clunk on the coffee table. "Kaitlin, you still with us?"

Kaitlin's eyes opened and then closed, and she rolled away from them and faced the cushions. "Annie," she said. "Take my bed for the night. I'll sleep here. Just throw a blanket on me."

"Sleep sounds good," Hannah said. She draped a throw blanket over Kaitlin, then stood and stretched her bare arms towards the ceiling. "I'm off to bed. See you in the morning."

Annie took her drink to the kitchen and dumped it down the sink, and then chugged two glasses of water and refilled her glass before she crossed the tiny apartment and closed the bedroom door. She shouldn't have sounded so indignant at Hannah's affair. So she slept with a married guy—so what? But, frankly, it did bother her, and if that made her parochial and old-fashioned and Midwestern, so be it. She didn't want to feel shocked and offended but the fact of the matter was she was shocked, she was offended. People just shouldn't do things like that. She flipped off the lights, casting the room in gray and black shadows. In the dark, Annie stripped off her dress, leaving it crumpled on the floor, pulled on her Badgers T-shirt, and then slinked into bed, falling immediately into a heavy, dreamless sleep.

The shoot was in the Four Seasons, and the writer met the girls in the lobby. She had a long forehead and a haircut and glasses that screamed expensive. Annie couldn't remember the name of the reporter who had interviewed them the first time, but she knew it was a woman, and she vaguely recalled liking her, wanting to be her, even though she had no interest before or since in journalism.

On the twenty-third floor, they were led down a hallway that seemed to zig and zag endlessly, and then they entered a room filled with people. It was an executive suite, complete with a bar and kitchen and two opposing bedrooms. Everyone wore vaguely haggard looks, as if they had been drinking all morning. They were all women, and Annie realized she had been dreading the idea of changing outfits in a hotel suite surrounded by inquisitive writers and the precise and cold gaze of photographers. The room was stuffy, and all around them, massive photo lights stood like scarecrows; cables and cords to computers and equipment lined the floor like snakes. Annie's feet ached, even though she was in flats and had been told in advance someone else would select their wardrobe. That hadn't happened the first time. The first time, the girls were told to wear whatever they wanted, to "act like I'm not even here," and the three of them had spent all weekend racing through all four floors of the Mall, their mothers indulging their every whim, insisting that as long as the price tags remained on they could buy whatever they wanted.

The wardrobe coordinator frowned when she saw them. "I thought they were taller."

Annie lemoned her lips, a hot flash traveling down her neck and burning on her chest, and she knew she was making the expression that got her nicknamed "Mouse" in the first grade.

The coordinator narrowed her eyes. "Not a problem. I can work with them."

Annie twisted her gaze into the kitchen: coffee and pastries and fruit lined the marble counter. Last night's alcohol flipped in her stomach. Kaitlin touched her elbow and whispered in her ear, "You're gorgeous." Annie loved her for saying it, hated herself for needing to hear it. She smiled tightly and crossed the room for a cup of coffee.

She stood watching the coordinator choose their outfits. The coordinator sized them up, hands on her hips, arms jutting out like an accusation, pursing her thin lips tightly, then reached into one of the four long and full racks of clothes and grabbed an item seemingly at random. She only needed three attempts to find something for Kaitlin, selecting a lavender dress and a slim leather belt. She smiled at the coordinator the way she would smile at her parents: genuine and open, the oldest in a family of six that Annie had always been slightly jealous of. Everything for Kaitlin came together. Annie knew this wasn't effortless. Rather, it was a dogged optimism that Kaitlin possessed; if she gave it her best, whatever it might be, things would work out all right for her, and this state of mind is what seemed to be so graceful and reflexive, this was the thing that left Annie in awe of her friend, and almost made her forgive Kaitlin for not having called in almost two years.

She set down the coffee—which was remarkably good, and made her think about a coffee shop she dearly loved back in Minneapolis called Cherokee Street, and how maybe it would have been wise to turn down the free airline ticket back to New York for this short weekend—and fingered the fabrics in front of her, noting the quality of the stitching, the care that was clearly taken to putting all these clothes together.

"I have something for you."

Annie turned. The coordinator was looking up at Annie. In her hands was a pair of black slacks and a sleeveless plum-colored silk blouse.

"I'd like to wear a dress," Annie said.

"It doesn't matter. We're going to shoot you girls from the waist up."

"Kaitlin is wearing a dress."

Annie scanned the room. Kaitlin was in the bedroom, changing, but Hannah was there, her back turned, browsing the racks of clothing. It seemed she hadn't heard Annie's protest. Instead, Hannah tilted her right ear downward and flipped her hair back and over her left shoulder. Metal hangers clattered as the clothes were pushed aside, flipped nonchalantly, like a magazine in a waiting room. But Annie was certain Hannah had heard her, had heard the meekness in her statement, and that there was somehow a refusal in this gesture of feigned deafness.

She looked back down at the clothes in the coordinator's hands. She fingered the silk, pleased the shirt had a deep, plunging neckline. Maybe that would be enough.

After the shoot, the girls said their goodbyes to the entire crew—thank you, thank you, so nice to meet you!—and followed the reporter down to the lobby. It was both crowded and intimate all at once, as if someone had placed all the couches and chairs in just such an order to create the kinds of nooks and crannies children hid in when playing games.

The reporter clicked on a digital recorder and set it down on the low coffee table in front of them. Annie and Kaitlin sat on one couch to the reporter's right; Hannah sat on the same couch as the reporter, to her left. The reporter crossed her legs and flipped open a notepad, a pen appearing in her hand from out of nowhere. Annie noted that the reporter was left handed.

"We sent a reporter to Minneapolis thirteen years ago," she said, "to discover the everyday lives of young girls who were newly minted teenagers. Looking back, what are your thoughts on being thirteen? Kaitlin, I'd like to start with you."

Kaitlin nodded, her hands in her lap. "It was so much easier then. No Facebook, no Snapchat, you know? But it was still so fraught with both excitement and uncertainty. Being a teenage girl is always hard, and I'm lucky that I made great friends that I still have today." She took Annie's hand, squeezing warmly, and gave the reporter a genuine smile.

"When we were younger," Kaitlin continued, "we had our whole lives ahead of us. In many ways, we still do! Like, when the three of us graduated from Wisconsin, we all moved to New York together. It's been an adventure. It's still an adventure. As for the future, who knows where we will end up."

The reporter turned left. "Hannah. What about you?"

She raised her chin with what Annie thought was a haughty gesture.

"When I moved to New York," Hannah said, "I felt so incredibly young. I'm an associate producer for a TV documentary series, and often our subjects are children, so it gives me a unique perspective on the lives of teenage girls. Hopefully, I'll have children at some point, but I don't know. Since I moved to New York, I've sort of stopped planning. I think that a lot of girls are too young to self-edit, and it's so easy to put too much of yourself online. But of course, maybe I'm cautious because I got put out there in a big way when I was younger."

The reporter turned back around. Annie tried to smile, but something about Hannah's response angered her, made her feel like Hannah had treated the question as if it was beneath her. She couldn't fully understand why she felt this way, only that it was a tremendous effort not to clench her hands together and ignore the rising heat in her throat.

Instead, Annie said, "Thirteen is a tough age for every girl. It was for me. And it's tough for girls that age everywhere. Growing up in Minnesota, we were all taught the importance of friends and family, which for the three of us, is really the same thing. The three of us met in third grade, and I feel lucky that I met really great friends in Hannah and Kaitlin when I was young. They're still my great friends today. I don't know what I would do without them."

"All of you mentioned family," the reporter said to Annie. "Is there something special about being from the Midwest that makes your sense of closeness stronger?"

Actually, Annie thought, Hannah didn't mention family at all. She hadn't mentioned Kaitlin or Annie either. And this question seemed like the kind of question an East Coaster would ask a couple of Minnesota hicks, as if they lived in some exotic and mystical world of farmland and suppertime with all their aunts and uncles.

Annie said, "Hannah and I grew up on the same street, and Kaitlin was just one street over. I think there might be something special about our families, but not necessarily because we're from Minnesota. It's just how we were raised."

On the flight home, staring at the steady blink of the red strobe light on the wing of the plane, she couldn't remember any other questions directed at her. It seemed the majority of the reporter's focus was directed at Kaitlin and Hannah, as if there was a connection between the three of them that inherently excluded Annie.

After six weeks—during which Annie had returned to Minneapolis, setup a daily e-mail about recent sale prices for homes in her neighborhood, and started sending her résumé out to New York companies, with Kaitlin and Hannah's address listed on the résumé—an e-mail from the photographer arrived. The text of the e-mail was polite and impersonal, and Annie skimmed it quickly before downloading and opening the PDF of the spread that would run in the *Times*.

She held her breath as she took in the original and new photo.

Her initial response was like being poisoned: a nauseous turn of her stomach, her mouth comically open, a ringing in her ears. This couldn't be the real photo they were running.

She flipped back to the original. Objectively there were similarities: the same three girls in the same order in front of a mirror. The rest, however, was so different. For whatever reason, the photograph they used was one that Annie couldn't imagine was worthwhile—they had taken dozens of shots, hundreds, and what they used framed the mirror, showing the viewer the nondescript walls of the bathroom. At least a fourth of the photograph contained these beige walls. The angle of the shot showed empty space to the left, a mirror reflecting, essentially, nothing. Though the girls were lined up in the same order as last time—Kaitlin, Hannah, then Annie—this photograph was so misaligned that Kaitlin was now in the center of the image; Annie's arm was actually angled out of the mirror, out of the photograph, as if a portion of her simply did not exist.

But that wasn't what was horrible. What was horrible, couldn't be changed or fixed from a better angle or a better photo, was this:

Annie was the ugly one. Annie was the one who wasn't pretty any-more. Annie was the one made to wear pants, whose blonde hair looked shaggy and unkempt; the one whose nose seemed too big, eyes too large, who looked like, yes, a mouse. Her friends—flawless brown hair shaping their confident and defiant expressions, with their sleek arms and short dresses and faces that fit their bodies—were beautiful. Heartbreakingly so. Annie wasn't. And the proof was on her monitor in brilliant, shining pixels.

She stood up and scanned the floor, afraid one of her colleagues would see her on the verge of tears. She strode to the nearest con-ference room and closed the door. The click of the latch signaled a release, and she slumped into the nearest chair. Everyone would see that photo. Everyone would see how ridiculous she looked with her flat hair and frumpy clothes and how plain and ordinary and dull she was compared to her friends. A thought zipped through her mind: *Jason was right to leave me.* She pressed her fingers into her forehead. *Stop it, stop it, stop it. You broke up with him. You threw him out.* She closed her eyes.

"This is about you," she whispered.

After several minutes, she stood, walked back to her desk, e-mailed her boss that she was sick and was heading home, hit send, logged off, and went straight home. She turned off her phone, changed into sweats, and took a bottle of wine from the fridge. She sat on the couch, fired up Netflix, and willed away any thoughts of the photograph.

The Sunday the article came out she turned off her phone, went to her parents' house, and spent the day on the couch watching football with her father. She loved his presence, his periodic cursing at the various plays, things she understood well enough, if disinterestedly, thanks to her brothers and father. When she was younger, she liked to watch old movies with her dad, letting him choose whatever he wanted, just so long as she could rest her head against his chest, feeling his body rise and fall as he breathed. Nothing else had ever made her feel so safe.

Around halftime of the second game of the doubleheader, Joel and Bridget arrived. Annie kicked at the blankets tangling her feet and sat upright. She swiveled on the couch and watched her sister-in-law like an art student studying a master painting hanging before her, its colors and lines and textures so clear while her sketchbook was filled with failure after failure. Bridget glanced at the television, then back at Annie's father with disinterested alertness. Her lips smiled; her eyes did not. It was as if Annie wasn't in the room.

At dinner, Annie was seated across from Bridget, and she stole glances at her all throughout dinner. Annie's one word answers to all questions convinced everyone to stop speaking to her; they knew how chaotic and painful the last few months had been, and she was given tremendous latitude to be moody and inscrutable, which she gladly took advantage of to take in her sister-in-law's wide shoulders, her pale flat face, her flaxen hair pulled perpetually into a ponytail, her high neckline sweaters that flattened her breasts, her long mannish hands and the way they enveloped her fork and knife. Why her?

After, Annie stood outside on the deck, a blanket wrapped around her shoulders. It was a scene from one of her father's war movies: one soldier, bone tired, pain so constant it was normal. Above, a light snow fell, coating the deck and the yard in a thin sheen of white. She twitched. Standing there with the warm lights of her house and family behind her, she couldn't fully understand why she was so miserably unhappy. Men leave. Friends leave.

Family ignores your flaws and tell you pretty lies. What was so tragic about being unremarkable?

Everything. Everything was wrong with realizing there was something that you wanted beyond your reach. To be loved by strangers. To turn heads. To be admired, to make others jealous. This was petty, she knew, small and unsavory of her. But two people who knew her, who had once loved her, Jason and Hannah, found her unworthy of not just her love but to even throw a glance at her. The last year—the cheating, the breakup, the photograph—all confirmed that Annie fundamentally lacked something that the world demanded of a woman. And there was nothing she could do about it. These doubts about herself, which had become more and more frequent, came like a vertiginous spiral of dark thoughts, and then her shoulders curled forward so instinctively that her body couldn't resist. The choking in her chest began, but as soon as she heard the sliding door keen open, she sucked in a deep cold breath and pulled herself upright.

The footsteps were heavy, and she knew who it was without pulling her gaze away from the woods at the edge of her parents' property.

Bridget said, "Are you all right?"

"People have to stop asking me that."

"Anything I can do to help?"

"Is that a serious question?"

They watched the snow.

Softer, Bridget said, "Everyone is worried about you. No one knows quite what to say."

Finally, Annie said, "Why does Joel love you?"

Bridget took a step forward and turned her questioning eyes on Annie's mouth, as if she couldn't quite believe it was capable of making sound.

"I just want to know," Annie continued. "You just appeared one day. All his other girlfriends were"—she licked her lips—"they were different."

She braced herself for harsh words, a withering gaze, maybe even a slap. She suddenly became aware of how much bigger Bridget was than her, how tiny she was by comparison. But Bridget's gaze softened, and instead of hitting her, her eyes lingered so long on Annie's face that the panic rose again in her chest. She blinked rapidly, hoping to hold back the tears, and her breaths came out raspy.

"Why," she asked again. "Why?"

"I don't know," Bridget said, "what you mean."

Her hands remained at her side, down by her hips, unclenched. Annie sniffed. When she was able to look Bridget in the face, ready to apologize and beg for forgiveness, she found that this would not be given. Her sister-in-law's gaze was stoic, neither bovine nor stupid, but a willful refusal of the question. She knew something that she would not reveal.

At two in the morning, Annie was still wide awake. She turned onto her side and stared at the wall, failing to get comfortable again in her old twin bed. Her eyes adjusted to the gray light, and she turned over, listening to the silence of her house and the strong winds blowing outside. She gazed at the empty space on her old pinboard. It looked strange up there, the last remaining vestment of her old bedroom, with all these paper memories of her teenage years, sun faded and brittle. She studied the empty space between all her awards and letters and ribbons and photos, then slid out of bed and opened her purse. She took out the photo and ran her thumb over their faces, then tacked it back up among all of her old things, where it belonged, and wondered what her thirteen-year-old self would think if she could see Annie now.

WHO ARE YOU WEARING?

The head of the first of Justin's costumes sat at the edge of the manager's desk. It was hard for him to focus on the manager interviewing him rather than the large, disembodied head of a three-eyed Martian with jagged teeth, its pelt of green skin, and the large antenna protruding from its back. Then Justin remembered, with the sort of bizarre hopscotch of thought that seemed to be as familiar and mysterious to him as breathing, that it was eight weeks until Halloween, and perhaps he had to wear a new costume every day.

"I'm just glad," the manager said, "to have someone with experience for this position."

"Do you need experience to wave at cars?"

The manager, Brad Butler, chuckled and tossed Justin's résumé on his cluttered desk. "The last thing I need is to hire someone who is going to quit on me. Some people have no idea how claustrophobic those things can get. So, yes, experience does matter here. Even if it was a long time ago."

Justin's first job was at a Six Flags in Eureka, a distant southern suburb of St. Louis, where he had his first experience as a mute but friendly cartoon character. For one brutal summer, Justin had dressed as various Hanna-Barbara characters with oversized heads, delighting small kids and inviting terrorizing behavior from teenagers. He got a break every ninety minutes, and as soon as Justin was out of public view, he yanked off the headgear, collapsed into the nearest metal chair, and hung his head, watching sweat drip from his face in large drops that splattered on the concrete. Why he hadn't quit after day one, he didn't know. And now that he had been laid off not once but twice from his post-college jobs, here he was, back to the humiliation of wearing costumes. At least there was some comfort that his face was hidden from those he was supposed to serve.

"Days and weekends are okay?" Brad asked.

"Yeah. I have another job waiting tables so I just need a little notice to make my schedules sync."

"That's a lot of work."

"Saving money. I'm applying to law school." He imagined then wearing a Halloween costume to the exam center for the LSAT. Ronald McDonald, maybe. Or Jabba the Hutt, but tell everyone he was Antonin Scalia. "What's my first costume?"

"A bumblebee?" his girlfriend Amy repeated that night. "Why a bumblebee?"

"There was a kids' movie with bees. So, they're kinda in this year." They were sitting in the living room of their two floor apartment in Richmond Heights; she was on the couch, her laptop and paperwork spread out on the cushions to her left, the Edward Jones logo bright and triumphant on all the documents. He was looking up at her from the floor, the smell of fried food clinging to his work shirt and pants, and he leaned away from her, the carpeting digging into his palms. "What should I ask to wear?"

The next five minutes were peppered with their ideas ranging from Adolf Hitler to Katy Perry to Michelle Obama, all of which made them laugh, and he remembered that moments like this were good, and too often rare. Two years ago, when they graduated, Amy too had been hired straight out of college. Unlike Justin, Amy hadn't been laid off twice but been promoted, twice. With the sports bar and now the costume shop, he was working almost every night, which kept them frequently apart, with the exception of Wednesdays, which they designated Date Nights and which neither of them seemed to enjoy.

Amy always seemed to know what she wanted. She possessed the generic beauty of Missouri girls: straight hair, large eyes, thin hips and legs. She was the kind of person who would treat a baby as an upscale accessory. She was extraordinarily secure with herself and her ambitions, and at times, despite moving to St. Louis together, Justin was afraid of her.

"Where do you want to go tonight?" he asked.

Amy looked down at her ThinkPad and the presentation she was working on. "I don't care. Wherever."

"We could stay in."

"We can go out. Maybe see if Nathan and Lindsay want to join us?"

He shrugged. He liked her friends only enough to not be bored in their presence, and yet, he was conscious of how often their date night had become a couples night. He stood.

"Sure," he said to the window behind her. "Would you close that? I wear a rubberized sauna all day. I'll turn on the air."

She picked up her phone. "I'll text Lindsay," she said. With her other hand, she pointed at him with her wine glass. "Get me more of this, would you?"

Justin was dressed as Tigger, waving at the passing crowd, his prosthetic tail curled up behind him like a treble clef and acting as a counterweight to his oversized head. He concentrated on his breathing and, through Tigger's mouth, watching the cars zip up to and then break hard in front of a series of intersections.

"Hey, Tigger!" a passenger yelled. "Where's Winnie? Is his head stuck up your pot of honey?"

The kids in the back seat roared with laughter. Tigger kept waving.

He could deal with the fucking morons in their cars. But he could not deal with the heat that rippled up from the sidewalk through the rubber soles of his outfit and into the bones of his feet. What he really wanted was grass. Green, cushy grass, a slim tree with a canopy of branches he could glide under. Tigger was restricted to pacing back and forth in front of the store's parking lot on a cracked, uneven sidewalk that never had any pedestrians. It wouldn't even be fair to say he was sweating. Sweat came in droplets. This was a steady stream, a broken faucet, dripping down his entire body. When he got his mid-shift break, he was actually surprised there weren't wet footprints on the ground.

The Halloween Superstore was owned by a media conglomerate so generic that Justin couldn't remember its name. All he could recall is that this particular store front always changed: it was a separate building on the decrepit strip across from the Galleria Mall, wedged between a Jared and a Burger King, both of which appeared to have no customers.

He was not sure why he brought home the zebra mask. It was after eight, his shift over, and he stood in the storage room, stripped down to just his lacrosse shorts, and he stared at the long row of rubberized animal masks: sheep, donkey, grasshopper, dog, cat, ferret, elephant, hippo. Their features were exaggerated in a creepy cartoon fashion, and it felt as if a big game hunter had freshly killed and skinned the beasts, leaving their carcasses rotting on the other side of the room. Justin picked up the zebra mask, pressed the material between his fingers, and imagined how freaking hot wearing the dumb mask would be. He glanced at his phone, walked to the back, slipped on a shirt and his shoes, grabbed his backpack, punched out, stepped into the rear parking lot, and only then did he realize he was still carrying the mask. He glanced at the door, figured, *fuck it, I'll bring it back tomorrow*, and hopped in his car, tossing the zebra mask on the passenger seat.

He parked in an unshaded spot at his apartment complex, and grabbed his backpack and the zebra mask. The unseasonable night was muggy and suffocating. Amy was in the kitchen fixing dinner while watching a show on her iPad.

"What is that?" Amy asked.

"Oh, this?" He slipped the mask over his head, spread his arms wide, and turned his palms up. He shook his hips, slow, and stepped into the room. Amy watched, her hands unmoving over the bowls and spice on the kitchen counter.

Justin laughed, yanked off the mask. "I didn't mean to bring it home. I just forgot. I'm going upstairs to change."

Amy nodded, watching his hands.

Later, Justin tried initiating sex. He stood behind Amy, kissing her neck, running his hands down her hips, then finding her belt. She acquiesced, but didn't making the moaning sounds, the running commentary she once used to make. She spun around. Kissing, they undressed, and he pushed her back onto the bed. Naked, staring at her, Justin leaned forward, and then Amy bent her knee and pressed her right foot into his stomach.

"What?" he asked.

"Do something for me."

"Sure," he grinned, thinking she wanted him to go down on her.

"Put on the mask."

He laughed. "What?"

"Put on the zebra mask."

He shook his head, and started to bend toward her pussy. She pressed her right foot harder, standing him upright.

"C'mon," she said. "Try it. I'm serious. Put it on."

He squinted down at her as if she was out of focus. She wiggled her toes against his ribcage in a combination of playful tickling and sexual impatience. He turned his chin toward the dresser where the zebra mask lay. Finally, he crossed the room, picked up the mask, and with his back still to Amy, slipped it over his head.

"Get over here," she said.

And he did, keeping the mask on, his expression of dull horror hidden from her. He was shocked at how wet she was when he slid his cock between her legs. She bucked and talked the way she used to when they first met, and gripping her ankles tight against his face, she came hard, and shortly after, he did too, his breath acidic in the mask, sweat rolling down his hidden face.

"That was so good," she said, rolling onto her side. "Oh, wow."

Justin peeled off the mask and tossed it on the carpet. "Yeah," he said, thinking this was both true and false.

The lights were off and through the blinds, shadows laddered across their bedroom, a slate gray world that was neither light nor dark. Naked atop the sheets, untouching, Amy on her side and facing away from him, he stared up at the ceiling wondering what the hell just happened.

To Justin, his manager was a man of indeterminate age. He could picture Brad as a high school kid, the one who was vaguely popular without being a jerk, who was good looking and knew it without being too cocky. His hairline was receding, and he slicked too much gel into his thinning hair. He had large forearms but a thin chest, and his stomach protruded slightly over his belt. He wore a wedding ring and one of those Lance Armstrong bracelets, and Justin was always aware of how infrequently Brad had to go outside. They rarely spoke to each at work and even then, Justin thought of him as a manager not as a person.

So it was a surprise when they closed the store on a Monday night just two weeks before Halloween and Brad asked Justin if he wanted a beer. Justin still wore the bottoms of that day's costume—Woody Woodpecker—and had his backpack in his hands, the zipper tightly shut over his LSAT books and the Ronald Reagan mask he had swiped earlier in the shift. So, playing cool, Justin simply nodded. Brad handed him a twenty and told him to walk to the Shell and grab a twelve-pack of whatever, then meet him out back. Justin returned with a case of Coors Light to find Brad sitting on a milk crate with a cigarette between his fingers. He pointed Justin to sit on the cooler next to him.

"Don't tell me," Justin said, "there's beer in here, too."

"Nope. But I found it in the office and it doesn't have leaks, so I think I'm going to keep it once we move out of here." He cracked open a beer, handed it to Justin, then opened his own.

"Where do you go from here?"

"Let's see, I'll open up a Christmas store. Another temporary one. I'm not sure where."

"You don't know where you're going next?"

"Haven't for three years." Brad chugged his beer, crumbled it in his fist, then set it softly on the concrete and opened another. "The company sends me on the road for Halloween, Christmas, and Valentine's Day. Then I head home for six months."

"Where's that?"

"Des Moines. It's actually a pretty good gig. I miss the school year, but then I'm home with my kids all summer. I don't get to see my wife much, but no job's perfect."

"I'm not touching that one."

Brad laughed, which made him belch. "Not what I meant. I just meant, you know, the travel is okay. I have this studio apartment that the company pays for, company phone, car, gas, and I don't have to sit in a cubicle the whole goddamn year. They also pay me more when I go on the road. For a fuckhead like me, it's a pretty good living."

"I thought taking a break from school would be a good idea. It wasn't. I can't wait to go to law school." Justin pressed his head back against the brick. "Did you want to do this?"

Brad laughed. "Are you kidding?"

"No, I mean, I don't know, just, how did you make up your mind?"

"It was made for me. I got married, she got pregnant, accidentally, and I couldn't fuck around anymore with figuring out what I wanted to do. Diapers cost money. I got my degree in environmental sciences—why, I don't know. I didn't expect to end up in Iowa of all places, but that's where my wife's family is from, so that's where we ended up, and weirdly, this company that nationally sets up temporary stores is based there, and boom, there you go." Brad finished his second beer.

"Lotta my friends went to Chicago. Or Dallas. My girlfriend's family is here."

"Y'all live together, right?"

Justin nodded.

"Yeah, man," Brad said. "That makes it hard."

Justin wondered what *it* was, what *it* meant. The fear he felt, the fear that prevented him from asking Amy why they had to fuck wearing costumes, the fear that prevented him from taking any kind of risk, the fear that rooted him to law school, gnawed at his stomach like a parasite. He couldn't ask Brad what *it* meant. He couldn't risk being seen like that. Instead, for the next hour, they talked baseball, and Justin didn't give another thought to Amy or his stolen mask or his going nowhere career. He just thought about Cardinals baseball and home runs and strange managerial moves and what the fuck was with that pitch?, getting a nice buzz from the beer, until Brad said, quitting time, and they gave each other a bro hug. And then Justin was driving home, hoping five beers and working a double at the restaurant tomorrow was enough reason to not wear a rubber mask while Amy writhed in ecstasy under his sad, thrusting hips.

It was strange what people yelled at him from moving cars. The most common was "Hey, FUCK YOU!" to which Justin responded by continuing to wave like a trained monkey as the offending car zipped by. It was hard to see where they came from, but occasionally, some object like a rock pinged off his head. This never hurt—there was too much padding around the oversized costume head—but the sound echoed in his elliptical costume head and his balance was momentarily shook. To actually knock him over, it would take something massive—a kid whacking him with a two-by-four or a brick slamming into his knees—and given the hostility spewed at him, this wasn't inconceivable. Every now and then, a car would swerve in his direction, sometimes even bouncing up onto the curb, before straightening and zipping away.

When he was hit by something that left a visible mark on his costume—usually, a Burger King milkshake—Justin had to leave his post, walk around to the back of the store, enter through the store room, strip off his costume, and immediately place it in a large dry cleaning cart that was picked up once a day. The company, it seemed, anticipated these attacks. And being in the back of the store frequently made it easy for Justin to slip a new costume into his backpack and borrow it for one evening before changing into a clean costume and heading back outside to get pelted with batteries and have incoherent profanity hurled at him.

At home that night, Justin untied his Snow White bonnet, and pulled the red skirt back down over his shrinking dick. Amy's eyes were closed, her hand thrown back against her forehead like a fainting starlet from the thirties, her ribs slick with sweat, legs quivering. Justin used to be careful about keeping the costumes clean, but he no longer cared if his sweat or come was on the inside of the outfit. Not since Amy started requesting that he bring home women's outfits. This week, he had been a slutty corn on the cob, Miss Scissorhands, and Dorothy. He even had props; on the bed was a basket with fake straw and chocolate eggs. Amy rolled onto her stomach, snatched a candy, and popped it in her mouth.

"I love the props," she said.

"Yeah, me too," he lied. "Too bad we only get them for one more week."

Her eyes went down and she studied her palm while she continued chewing. Then she said, "What do they do with the extra inventory?"

"Box it up and ship it back. Whatever we don't sell will still be good next year. Princess Leia doesn't go out of style."

"Right." She pulled out a strand of the fake grass and wrapped it around her finger. He started to strip off the costume. "Could you take a few?"

"Inventory is electronic."

"Buy them?"

"You earn more money than me, go ahead."

She shrugged. Naked, Justin slid to the floor, resting his head back against the bed. She was over his right shoulder, and he was facing the bathroom.

"Are you going to take a second job?" she asked.

"I thought I'd focus on studying once this gig is over. LSAT is in December, and with more flexibility, I can get some of the better shifts at the restaurant."

They were quiet for a long time. Then Amy asked, "Did you ever cheat on me?"

"No," Justin lied, thinking about their first year together, when they were juniors at Mizzou. "Why? Did you?"

"No. I was just wondering." Justin happened to know she did cheat on him their senior year, twice, but found, both now and then, that he didn't particularly care all that much, a feeling of indifference about their fidelity that puzzled and then frightened him. He wondered how many days of his life he spent afraid, afraid of failure, afraid of choices, afraid of choosing failure. He ran his hands over his knees.

"Is this what the costumes are about? Some way of cheating while not cheating?"

"No. I don't know. I mean, it was weird, you put that mask on the other day, and I was instantly turned on. I was really surprised. You know Halloween is my favorite holiday. Always has been. I just didn't think of it as sexual."

Justin ran his hands over his knees.

"Four years together," she said.

"Yeah."

"Still love me?"

He turned. She was resting her cheek atop her folded arms, staring off toward the bathroom. The curves of her body still glistened with sweat, and her crossed ankles, rocking back and forth metronomically, stopped in mid-air. She wouldn't look at him.

"Of course, I still love you."

He leaned back, and sprawled out on the carpet. Lying right against the bed, all he could see of Amy were her pretty feet.

The company Halloween party that Amy dragged them to was in Clayton, tucked back among leafy lawns, hidden behind gated streets that made finding the house a little difficult. He was dressed as Superman and she was dressed as Wonder Woman, and before they left for the party, she had bent over their kitchen table and he fucked her from behind, wondering only after they were in the car if the reason they had been in that position was because she couldn't see his face.

All the lights were on in the great windows along the front of the opulent house. Inside, women wore a wide variation of Sexy Generic Occupation and the men wore dumb hats so they could explain their dumb outfit to each other (Justified! Gangster! Teddy Roosevelt!). Justin entered a kitchen of granite countertops and rustic farmhouse furniture, poured a drink, and then hurried to the back porch, where the cool October air and the tastefully strung lights skimming the sky above the back patio were a welcome relief.

More than forty people mingled on the brick patio and into the backyard. He glided into a conversation about movies. He flexed his biceps, showed off his red boots, discussed which Superman movies he had seen (all of them), and which one he liked best (*Man of Steel*). He introduced himself as Amy's boyfriend and gladly received advice from the lawyers about law school. He shook hands and made jokes and grew so relaxed and comfortable that it took over an hour before he realized he hadn't seen Amy the entire time. With a nod and a polite "excuse me," Justin finished his drink, set the glass on the porch railing, and wended his way inside. He was feeling good, a little surprised by how much he liked everyone at the party, wanting to slip his arm around Amy's waist, finish each other's sentences, flirt with each other, get drunk and be the happy couple he imagined they always would be.

He searched the costumed faces: Amy wasn't in the kitchen. He bumped into someone in a suit with a knife in his back, slipped around a Tinkerbell, and tapped a Double Dare contestant on the shoulder, whose costume consequently slimed Justin's hand with green goo. Out of the kitchen, he stood at the archway of a long great room that ran the length of the house, guests sloshing by him with drinks and laughter and big smiles. Across the neat cluster of expensive furniture, tastefully angled and staged, sequestered from all the other guests, stood Amy and a man dressed like a vampire, huddled together in the distant opposite corner.

The man was stunningly handsome, and from the way he set his feet and stood tall with his shoulders back and hip cocked, he knew it. Even his ears seemed perfect. Amy stood almost beneath him, so close they were magnetized. They weren't kissing, but they might have been, and their mouths were close enough that they could do so again at any moment. They both laughed, their teeth blindingly white, and then their hands, the ones shielded from the rest of the room, raised ever so slightly. Their fingers wrapped together, clutched and held, and then they both let go and their hands dropped back against their thighs.

Justin turned away. He stood rooted to the floor, his gaze locked on the patterns in the veneer of the wood floor. His hands mechanically fisted. Then he strode to the front door and left, pushing through a just arriving group dressed as the Fantastic Four, and went to his car. He drove home, stripped down to his boxers, and flopped down on the couch. He dropped his phone on the floor, yanked an afghan over his body, and turned away from the room, staring at the cushions of his couch as if, like an angry Superman, heat could come from his eyes.

When he woke up, he was looking directly into those same couch cushions. Weak light filtered through the cracks of the blinds. He rolled over and set his feet on the ground, listening for any movement or noise in the apartment. He picked his phone up from the floor: no texts, no calls. Clutching his phone like a weapon, he walked upstairs and found the bedroom undisturbed and mockingly neat—bed made, closet doors closed, even the clutter on top of the dresser seemed organized. There was nothing in the bathroom: no purse, no wet washcloth, no toothpaste in the sink. She never even came home.

Justin and Brad sat in their respective spots—cooler, milk crate—behind the store. Halloween was over now, and Brad got Justin an extra ten hours this week to help with the sale (ALL COSTUMES 75% OFF!!!) and box up what remained to ship to the distribution center in Tennessee. The building's rear lights threw down a powerful, harsh glare. Across the lot were their two cars, and inside the trunk of Justin's car were two duffel bags of clothes, his laptop, a small box of books, and his external drive of movies and TV shows. When he had packed it earlier this morning, it had seemed sad, owning so little, nothing of real value in the apartment that he wanted for himself. Maybe there was a lesson in this. He wasn't sure.

He finished his second beer, cracked a third, and rested his head against the brick wall. Brad was going on about the Chiefs. Justin flipped through his texts: three people offered a couch for him to crash on, one landlord had written back about an efficiency in Richmond Heights, and Amy wrote, "Let's talk when you've found a place to stay ok?"

"I have tickets next weekend," Brad said. "But I'm not sure I can stomach watching them lose 20-17, you know? I can just suffer watching it on television."

"Maybe you should give up football."

"Why would I do that?"

"Because it sounds like it makes you fucking miserable."

Brad laughed. "It does! But I still really like it. It's good for blowing off steam, right? I mean, who doesn't like sitting on the couch for three hours doing nothing?"

Justin slipped his phone back in his pocket.

"Hey. You all right?"

Justin pulled the tab off his beer and held it between his thumb and forefinger. "Yeah, actually, I am."

"Two more of these and then I oughta get going."

Long before he started working with Brad, months, maybe years, Justin had been unhappy and adrift and afraid. Both the job and his relationship with Amy were now over. It was like being released from a small cage after a long incarceration. He sipped his beer and observed the trunk of his car as if he expected it to perform an extraordinary magic trick.

The next day, Justin and Amy met in the Central West End at a coffee shop tucked away on a street just north of Forest Park. He had never been here before and wondered how she found it. He was seated with a cup of coffee he didn't really want at an outdoor table under the shade of elms. She arrived with her face tight as if she had been crying, but when she sat down, he already knew that their minds had been made up a long time ago. After a perfunctory greeting and forced small talk about their days apart, Justin said, "I want to break up. I'm sorry, but this isn't what I want."

"I don't think," Amy said, "you know what you want anymore."

"You're right. But I do know what I don't want. And I don't want this."

Amy gave him a look he hadn't seen from her in a long time. Then she gazed down at the table between them, her smile rueful, as if she was lost in a long-forgotten memory. She palmed his apartment keys, and said, "I really have to go." She stood, leaned over, lips against his ear, softly said goodbye, and kissed his cheek. This kiss finally broke him, and his eyes pooled watching her walk away, watching her turn the corner, watching her vanish. He sniffed, pushed down his tears, and lowered his forehead to the table. He pictured his relationship with Amy, all four years, from when they met to these last strange weeks. She seemed to know something about herself that Justin hadn't appreciated or understood. He sat up and went inside for a refill. Back outside, he pulled his arm jacket tight. On the sidewalk spotted with black circles of gum were cigarette butts and a few scattered leaves fallen from the bare branched trees. Soon, it was dark and the cold air felt better, soothing, a balm; hours later, when he finally stood up to leave, he was surprised by how good he felt.

Months later, hustling across Lindell on his way to his law class at St. Louis University, he saw her again for the first time, leaving the Moolah Theatre. She looked happy and appeared purposeful with her stride. They cross paths from time to time; St. Louis is a small big city where everyone seems interconnected. Just last week, he saw Amy in his neighborhood. He no longer recognized the friends she was with. It didn't really matter. Each time he saw her, he remembered a period of their life together that was bleak and fearful. Then the memory was over, and he thought of her and their relationship fondly, and Justin knew that she was happy.

Years later, he crossed the street and gazed up at his high rise, then entered the lobby to take the elevator up. When he came home in the evenings from his law firm, he entered his condo with his tie loosened, a junior associate with fatigued muscles in his back and legs, and he sensed he has stepped into a place of great security and warmth. The light in the living room was bright, the view of the city panoramic. Far below on Washington Street, men and women of all ages streamed out into the night. This vibrant stretch of St. Louis had blossomed over the last decade, the kind of place Justin always wanted to live. In the window, his reflection was ghostly and clear. He could see his eyes, his jaw, and the way his mouth curled into a smile when he thought of the direction of his life. Justin looked out on the city for a moment longer, then turned back into his new, bright home.

You, Only Better

The photo shoot was held on the sixth floor of a newly renovated condominium in Adams Morgan, close to Meridian Park, which was sometimes called Malcolm X Park and sometimes Needle Park, depending on who you were speaking with and what era of DC they remembered. Tucked away in the southeast corner of the neighborhood, the building had once been a storage facility for local companies. After decades of decay, a developer had snatched it up and chopped the eight floors into high-end living space, a renovation that preserved and emphasized the brick walls while sliding in the modern amenities of marble countertops and low-flush toilets that were demanded by people who could afford to live there. The backbone of the building remained brick, but the front facing walls were now glass and steel with a large lobby that no one would spend any time sitting in.

Amanda stood at the curb, clutching her camera bag to her hip, staring at the steel edifice. A stench of vomit and energy drinks drifted off the sidewalk. Her boyfriend Colin hopped out of the car, his aviator sunglasses unable to hide the exasperation in his face, but when he saw her looking at him, he forced a smile. It was a smile that got free desserts at restaurants, upgraded seats on airlines, and the so rarely heard phrase "let me see what I can do for you."

"What do you have?" he asked, keying the trunk open.

"Camera, laptop, purse."

She looked at her phone—they had twelve minutes—and slid it into the back pocket of her jeans. Their part-time business, Cocktails and Collars, was a two-hour photo shoot lubricated with a cocktail or two that produces photos her clients could use for their social media or professional résumés. She was the photographer, Colin the makeup artist and bartender. This afternoon, they had three clients: the first at 11:00, second at 1:30, and third at 4:00, just enough time in between each for a brief break and, if necessary, running a little over to get a few additional shots. Two hours for each client at a rate of $500. She would have preferred earlier sessions, but she had quickly learned her target demographic spent Saturday mornings sleeping off the previous night. She tilted her chin up toward the bright sunless sky, the day like something out of a sci-fi movie, and pictured herself standing in one of those high windows and looking down on herself on the street, pointing the camera, twisting the lens, adjusting the aperture, and then pausing to inhale a deep breath before taking the shot.

They showed ID to the security guard, gave the names of their three clients, and took the elevator up to the sixth floor. She tapped in their temporary key code, and after the LCD light changed from red to green, Amanda stepped into the condo's broad, spacious entryway, the walls on both sides decorated with black and white panoramic photos of the city. In a few steps, they were in a spacious, open living room. The galley kitchen was to their right, and down at the opposite end was first a bathroom, then the master bedroom. In front of them were floor to ceiling windows facing north and, in the distance, Rock Creek Park.

"Nice," Colin said. "Lighting is perfect. Karen hooked us up."

Amanda nodded in agreement. Their friend Karen was a realtor who specialized in this part of DC, and giddy over Amanda's business, offered this space for their photo shoot. Amanda knew

Karen was showing the condo tomorrow and guessed that she'd have offers on it first thing Monday morning. She approved of the staging—generic furniture and their muted palattes; clients would stand out nicely against such a background. She set her bag down on the salvaged-wood dining table with the fake tulip centerpiece, and surveyed the room, looking for ideal places for clients to sit, stand, lean, perch. Exposed brick ran around the perimeter, and interior walls were painted the kind of cool gray found in Ethan Allen catalogues. She lifted her camera to her eye. The phenomenal lighting softened the room with a filter quality that she often tried to produce in her photos. There was an incongruity of place and person, an askew quality, like trying to see with only one contact lens, everything hazy and slightly distorted.

She raised and lowered the camera. She had long imagined that is what holding a gun was like, a power both hypnotic and captivating. Point, frame, click, capture. With the camera in her hands, both sword and shield, she walked the room, stopping at random and pivoting in a slow circle, absorbing the layout, the light and shadow, synthesizing the contours of the massive open room.

Just like a great first date, these photo shoots are a limited commodity.

Amanda wrote dozens of lines like that on her website to attract clients. Writing corny, winking sentences for a month of Sundays made them ubiquitous in her mind. She threw away most of them, and yet now these catchphrases constantly carbonated her thoughts.

With three sharp knocks, their first client, Daniel, announced his arrival. Colin opened the condo's front door, and the men shook hands. Daniel wore an unstructured navy blazer and brought with him, as instructed, additional clothing: a gray blazer, collared shirts with unfrayed cuffs, T-shirts with designer labels. Dark blond, well groomed, clean shaven. Not particularly tall, shorter than Colin, he wore his blazer with the comfort of a man who slipped one on every morning. Crooked nose and wide eyes, but not bad looking. A little nerdy. Nonthreatening. Colin took Daniel's drink order, mixed their first round, and the three of them clinked glasses. He made her drink—a sugary bourbon cocktail— weak. Daniel drank gin, which Amanda found disgusting.

We'll mix you up a good old-fashioned cocktail and grease the wheels a little before you hop in front of that camera.

"Good martini," Daniel said, returning to them. "So?"

"Let's get started," Amanda said. "Why don't you walk around a little bit, and then we'll apply a little makeup for you."

He paused a beat before saying, "Are you saying I don't look good?"

Amanda laughed, throwing her chin up, overselling the joke. She could tell he was funny in a sardonic way, never cracking more than an amused, thin-lipped smile, always getting in the last word.

She pulled out her phone, accessed the Wi-Fi, opened the playlist she had created for client number one. The music piped in from the recessed speakers in the corners of the living room. The first songs were always a bit upbeat, but never too loud—celebratory lyrics, happy music—and as Daniel walked the length of the apartment, Amanda's camera rapidly caught him from behind, the way he attempted to loosen his walk, twirling his wrists. He competently ignored the camera. She had used her employer's software to run a background check on her client and his social networks, and along with making sure she was programming a playlist that would make him relaxed and happy, it also let her know that her client was not a sociopath.

Colin stood next to her and whispered, "Do you find him attractive?"

"He's just a job."

"Like a whore?"

She whipped her head around. "The hell is wrong with you?"

But Colin remained in profile, smiling out at the client, whose arms were spread wide as he strolled back to them.

When Daniel returned, Colin pulled out a chair, and opened up his makeup kit. He directed Daniel to a chair, slipped tissue around his collar to keep his clothes clean, and stared into the client's face, studying its contours before beginning his work. She looked up from her camera. There was a calm to Colin when he applied makeup for a client, almost serenity. He had never spoken of missing the theater, of doing the kind of work he so loved in college, which he had given up quietly, with little to no fanfare, to take a corporate job and launch his career.

It'll be you, but hotter—because you want your Tinder date to recognize you when you finally meet IRL, y'all.

Months ago, Amanda and Colin had sat at a crooked table near the front door of the Codmother, an underground dive bar on U Street that reeked of urine. They had stopped because, through the window, they had seen open tables, and they were just buzzed enough to not wonder why this would be the case. With her finger, she stirred her whiskey and soda served in a plastic cup, the drink more cheap gin than tonic.

"Everyone has a Tinder account, right?" she said. "But the photos are often super sketchy. Shit from a summer barbecue five years ago, or a bathroom selfie, or something like that. No one is going to swipe right on that."

"Eventually someone always swipes right."

She shrugged. "Okay, probably. But, what if you get people to take better photos of you? And not just your friend or roommate, but a stylized shot of you. The best version of you."

"Wouldn't you be a little suspicious of that?"

"I'd rather someone cared, put some effort into it, you know? Plus, those photos can be used for something else. Anything else. We're all self-promoting and branded now, right? So, you have a set of photos not just for Tinder, but for LinkedIn, for Instagram, for whatever. Plus, I sell it as a fun photo shoot. Mix a cocktail, change outfits, play music, take a ton of photos, whatever. Like, lifestyle shit."

"People would pay for that?"

"Hell yes, they would. You know the people we work with."

Colin nodded, and stroked his chin. He had been doing this more since he grew a beard.

"What would you charge for this?" he asked.

"How much do you think I could get?"

"If you're selling a lifestyle experience? A lot."

Amanda asked, "Would you do the makeup?"

He belched quietly into his drink. "Makeup?"

"To charge what I want to charge, the clients should really stand out. Everyone wears makeup. Or should. You know that better than anyone. And, plus, how many people have had a professional do their makeup?"

"I'm not a professional."

"Fuck that. You're the best! You'd be so good at it! It's the kind of glamour treatment that something like this needs. Something intimate and amazing. You'd love to do this. Don't you miss it?"

The last question, not meant to be an accusation, clearly jabbed at him in a way she hadn't anticipated. His eyes dropped, searching for a memory, and a faint smile stretched across his face. Amanda knew he was no longer here, but back in the past, minutes before curtain, applying makeup to the face of each actor and actress, accentuating their expressions to highlight the very best of both character and actor, an effect that would move the audience but be invisible under the hot blaze of the stage lights. Amanda reached out, took his hand, and gently squeezed until he looked up, smiling, and nodded.

Ain't no shame in your Tinder game.

The second client was also a male—Clark, an old man's name, a Midwestern name. Longish brown hair. Could use a haircut. Seemed like a kid out of the nineties. The kind of man who always wore a T-shirt and jeans. According to the screening emails he sent to Amanda and Colin through their site, he was a structural engineer who had graduated college and spent the next four years playing bass guitar with his band, traveling the country in a white Econoline van, playing new gigs every night, and periodically returning to Indianapolis to record a new album, which they distributed online and at their shows. On a trip to Virginia Beach he got stoned and watched the ocean, thought about what five years of college had taught him and how his lifeline had an end date, and promptly quit the band, sold his meager possessions, and took an engineering job with a defense contractor. He worked long hours and owned a record player and claimed to love women. Amanda found his lack of awareness about his own sexual appetites and narcissism to be commonplace. If only he knew how to be honest, how to be direct, people—women, in particular—would respect him. She wondered why he was here, why he needed her help, before remembering that, to him, that wasn't the point.

Amanda asked, "What outfits did you bring?"

Clark dropped his ratty duffel bag on the couch and opened it. He pulled out clothes, laying them across the back of the cushions, showcasing four matching button-downs and chinos. He even brought belts and shoes in both brown and black.

"Do you have any neckties?" Colin asked.

"Sure. Do we want that?"

"It's important to have options," Amanda said. "We just want to make sure we present you in a range of different ways so you can choose which ones you want to use."

He changed quickly in the bathroom, and each time he returned, Amanda and Colin cheered him, hooted and hollered (*Fun, fun, fun, fun,* she repeated to herself), and then she fired off a series of shots with Clark leaning against a brick wall, gazing in his serious, affected way toward the light from the windows. The playlist moved to peppy, upbeat tracks, and the men bantered in the easy, light way that men do. This was going well, she told herself. This is good.

What's wrong with a little makeup? Shouldn't you feel as fine as you look?

If asked, Amanda would say Cocktails and Collars was their business, but she knew that wasn't true. She knew she was being ungenerous. Colin's makeup work made the clients pop in the photos and, perhaps more important, made them feel at ease and valued. Because Amanda and Colin were together, they presented proof of what each client was after: a partner. Yet, with each photo shoot, with each weekend of work, Amanda resented his presence at work she considered hers.

And this was hers: she built the business on her own. On a Saturday morning, two weeks after discussing the idea with Colin, during which he never brought it up again, she flopped down on the couch before her roommates were up, pulled the French doors of their living room closed, and opened up a blank document. She already owned a great camera, a gift from her father for getting her new job in the capital, and a phone filled with contacts. By noon, after three cups of coffee and no breakfast, Amanda had a registered domain, five webpages with pull quotes of her corny catchphrases, SEO rich text, placeholder images, and a budget for hourly space rental, all with a profit margin—with all factors included—of 27 percent. For a side project, it was a good start.

On the weekends, she was hungry, hungry in a way she wasn't for her weekday job at a management consulting firm. The click and whirl of a camera like the snapping of jaws, the satisfaction of being in control of the subject—nothing else made her so imposing. Everyone came to her asking to capture his or her "real" self, and Amanda nodded and smiled and took their payment, knowing that all photographers lie: she only captured the surface of things. What lies beneath remained there in the stillness of the shot, especially in this city, where context and nuance are means to deniability, where lying is as natural as breathing. She framed her clients, made them glow, gave them the personality they always wished they possessed.

Expect a "wat r u up 2?" text from your ex. Probably more than one!

After Clark left—buzzed on four drinks and insisting that they were awesome, just awesome—Amanda and Colin moved unspeaking through the apartment. She drank a large glass of water, and then sat down in the club chair, the fatigue of being on her feet rippling through her hamstrings and hips. On the coffee table were two oversized books, one of Washington, DC, and the other of Degas paintings. She resisted the urge to flip through the latter. It would make her ache for a Saturday alone, wandering the museum unaccompanied, absorbing each painting, eras of bygone cities and countryside and all the contortions of the human body in its beauty and depravity. Phone off, no camera. The slow lazy walk of the flâneur without work e-mails, without conversation, without Colin. Without any shit that routinely made her feel worse about her life. Made her anxious and dissatisfied and unsettled in a way that felt so regular and common. Made her cruel.

She looked down at her camera and the photos of Clark. He was a mildly attractive man, his hair longer than she liked and certainly out of vogue, but she had to admit it framed his face nicely, even if she was sure he never thought of it that way. The black and whites of him against the brick wall were best; the contrast made him striking, and the chiaroscuro hid a few of the blemishes of his face: the growing gin blossom, the budding wrinkles of a long-time smoker. She also liked the one of him at the living room table, half in profile.

At the time, Clark had been sitting across from Colin. They had discovered a mutual love of the Chicago Bears and started a deep if short discussion of the team's defense and the decades long search for a quarterback, a problem she knew about from years of autumn Sundays when Colin obsessed and groused about Bears losses with devoted pigheadedness. Staring at this photo, she remembered the way Colin had been just outside the frame—a glass of rye whiskey in a squat circular glass, his fingers lightly off the drink, which was deep in his palms, as he twisted the glass unconsciously while he spoke.

At the time she captured this snapshot, Colin had been relaxed but purposeful at the table. He knew he was working. He knew that the conversation about the Bears, while perhaps genuine, had an ulterior motive: put the client at ease. Colin's duplicity was on full display. This duality, while not unique to DC, did seem ubiquitous in this city; Amanda had learned the hard way to be careful of using surnames or identifying characteristics when discussing people in public. The fluidity of it was striking as too was her ability to remember him, see him so clearly, even though he wasn't in the frame.

She looked up from her camera. His back to her, standing over the sink, water gushing, he cleaned the highball glasses by hand. He wore a long sleeve plaid shirt rolled to the elbows, his taut forearms on display as he scrubbed each glass clean. Then she remembered what he said earlier, about being a whore. She shook the thought from her head, and popped the USB card from the camera.

Gender ain't a thing. We make everyone as amazing and hot as you know you are.

The third and final client was a woman. Whitney. She wore glasses, dark frames that shaped her eyes nicely, her hair thick and shoulder length around her symmetrical, beautiful face. "Jesus," Amanda whispered to herself. Whitney walked into the room and stood with her hands on her hips, then spun back to them, a toothy smile spreading, her eyebrows raised.

"This is cool!" she said. "What a great space. You don't always shoot here, do you?"

"A friend of mine hooked this up," Amanda said. "We switch locations all the time. Makes it exciting for both us and the client to use different venues."

"I still can't believe I'm doing this. It feels so weird."

"That's because we haven't served cocktails yet," Amanda said.

"Nothing wrong with that," Colin said. "Take a look around."

They both watched Whitney stroll through the apartment. She dropped a gym bag next to the couch, then walked to the windows, where she placed both hands on her hips and stared out at the park with a look of delight. She asked to use the bathroom, and after Amanda pointed down the hallway and she disappeared, Colin whispered, "She's hot."

"Why would you say that?"

"Because she is. What? What's wrong with saying that?"

"Because she's a client. And because it sounds like you're comparing her to me."

"You're overthinking it."

"Am I?"

"Beauty is an objective quality."

"What the fuck are you talking about?"

"Jesus, forget I said anything, okay? I'm sorry. Leave it alone."

She opened her mouth to say more—*No, I want to talk about this*—but found, actually, she didn't have anything more to say to him.

What did she think of Colin when she first saw him? When he caught her looking at him at a Soulard bar back in St. Louis, she held his gaze, and he crossed the room as if she were physically pulling him closer. When he was next to her, she stared at his neck, her eyebrows raised, her smile a dare. For the next two hours, she had his undivided attention, and he was charming in his insouciance that toed the line of arrogance, but he was in on the joke, self-aware in a way most men his age were not.

Now, moved away from her, standing by the window, hands in his pockets, chin tucked, looking down on the streets below, Colin struck her as bored. The meticulous disheveled look he cultivated appeared sloppy and middle-aged, and his eyes struggled to focus, sloth-slow blinking, as if he was fighting an urge to nap. He arched his chest, hands on his lower back, his expression one of bored aggravation. The long Washington hours were wearing on him, and his weekly outfit of dark suits and white shirts, she had to admit, fit him; out of uniform, he appeared a bit lost, a bit misplaced, a toy returned to the shelves in the wrong aisle.

Whitney's shoes clopped on the wooden floors. "Even the bathroom is amazing."

"We think of everything," Amanda said. She opened up the Client #3 playlist. "Drink?"

After the shoot was over, they sat across from Whitney, who sat with her knees together and ankles apart, staring into her vodka glass, holding it with two hands. It was her second, and the ice had completely dissolved. Amanda was then aware that even though the drinks were weak, she and Clark had been drinking all afternoon, loosening her thoughts, making her legs wobble and fogging her thoughts.

"This was fun," Whitney said. "I'll recommend you two. Do you two find it weird? I mean, as a couple, setting singles up?"

"Not really," Amanda said. "It's like being a wedding photographer, only in the first stage rather than the final."

"That's clever. It's such an appealing visual, you two together, doing this business together."

Amanda smiled vacantly at Colin. Together.

"I went out with a guy," Whitney continued, "who told me that he was so happy that I wasn't a model. He said he was done with models, that all he had dated were models. He said I was a 'plain Jane beauty.' Unbelievable."

"Maybe this will help," Amanda said. It was a dumb thing to say. She hadn't yet mastered the sales language of closing. But Whitney literally shrugged it off, and stared at some point over Amanda's shoulder, her body very still. Amanda eagerly waited for this dating horror story she knew was coming.

"Do you remember," she said to Amanda, "what it was like before you met him?"

"Sure, absolutely."

"Do you remember being afraid?"

Amanda had heard these stories. Told them too. She looked down and saw Colin had loosened his grip on her hand, but somehow he knew completely removing it was the wrong thing to do. Did he think it was wrong for work, or for her?

"I mean, some are funny," Whitney said. "You know, they send texts that are just like, 'Wanna fuck?' And, the worst thing is, that probably works, right, if you send that out a hundred times a night, you really only need one person to say yes. Or, they are just so awkward when you meet for coffee, self-deprecating themselves over and over again, you wonder how they even made it out of high school."

"I remember one guy," Amanda said, "who went on and on about his college girlfriend. I mean, for almost an hour. Nonstop. A soliloquy!"

"Did anyone try following you home?"

Amanda's smile vanished. She nodded.

"He seemed so nice," Whitney said. "He wasn't a big guy. I don't really like tall men. We went to that place in Dupont, the one with the tree growing in the middle of it."

"Firefly," Colin said.

"Yeah, that's it. We sat off to the right, this little raised area. I can't remember who suggested it. We had a drink, and then we had an appetizer, and another drink. I always had one of my friends text at fifteen minutes and one hour. You know, in case you have to get out of there, like, 'Oh it's my mom and my dad has cancer' or something. It was fine. I thought I'd see him again, you know. So he signals for the check and he says, all charming, 'Want me to get this?' And I laugh, and say sure, and he gets quiet. I mean, I said, sure. Sure. What's the big deal? But you know how it is when you can almost see this, I don't know, like a shadow or something drop over a person's face?"

Amanda dug her thumbnail into her palm.

"I asked him," Whitney continued, "about what his week was like, you know, gently hinting about getting together again, and earlier he had mentioned something about a weekend trip with his buddies. His response is real terse. The temperature had completely changed. When the waitress returned, the charm is back, right there, his face lights up. And when she turned and walked away, he said, 'Women always want me to pick up the check.'

"So I try to laugh it off and say, 'I'm sorry, I misunderstood, here, let me split it,' and he says, 'Nope, too late now.' I apologize, reach for my purse to look for cash, and I'm feeling really flustered you know, completely embarrassed, I mean, that's not what I meant. But, you know, just say something, right? Splitting a check, no big deal. And, I'm acting like it's my fault! He won't talk. He won't even look at me. He signs and then just sits there and says, 'I'm going to finish my drink.' And, so, I think, okay, nice to meet you, and I stand up and he won't look at me and I just walk out. Firefly is a short walk to the Metro. Not super far, two blocks. That's all. And I'm halfway there, and he grabbed me."

Whitney looked at neither one of them, instead staring at the space between them, and her eyes hardened in the late afternoon light.

"I didn't hear the footsteps," she continued. "I don't know why not. I just wasn't thinking about it. But yeah, all the sudden, there is this hand on my right elbow, and he pulls, hard. I was so stunned I didn't say anything. My mouth was open. And he leans right into me and says, 'What's your fucking problem?' His spit sprayed all over my face. He said, 'You think you're so great, don't you?'

"I stumbled when he pulled me, and I was off balance, and so he sorta yanked me upright, and that's when I screamed. I just screamed, as loud as I could, 'Get your fucking hands off me!' People turned around. I mean, isn't that crazy—there were people around. It wasn't, like, a dark alley or something. Right in the middle of a sidewalk. And he throws his hands up like I offended him and he backs away and says, 'Fine, be that way, be that way.' I couldn't breathe. These two women stepped in front of me and said, 'Are you okay?' and I must have been in shock or something because I just couldn't figure out what happened and who they were, and then next thing I know I'm having a panic attack. So they walked me over to this café that was right behind me, and they sat down with me until I could catch a breath and then I started crying."

"I'm sorry," Amanda said. "I am so, so sorry."

"He left a bruise. On the inside of my elbow. Three little marks, his fingers. I wore long sleeves for two weeks. In July."

She picked her glass back up and frowned down at it. She didn't drink.

"Every woman has a story like that. Mine's not even that bad."

They sat in silence. Whitney put her drink down again, and when she stood, they stood too. Amanda watched Colin's discomfort, crossed then uncrossed his arms, then he took a step back, shoulders slouched, and ultimately jammed his hands in his back pockets. His expression was in shadows, grayed out in the early evening dark, and even though he was right next to her, the light made his face appear far away from her, receding like an unwanted dream. She blinked at him and yet the distance remained.

"I don't think I really want the photos," Whitney said. "I'll still pay you, of course, but I don't think this is for me."

"You don't have to decide that now," Amanda said.

"I already did." She set her empty glass on the coffee table and stood. "Thank you both. This was fun. Just, I don't know. I'm going to try something else."

They watched Whitney gather her purse and bag of clothes, cross the room, and close the door behind her. Colin shrugged, said he'd get started on cleaning up, and gave Amanda a goofy grin. They had dinner plans, remember? She had forgotten.

Amanda didn't know it at the time, but that afternoon's photo shoot was the reason she left Washington. The reason, four weeks later, she would meet Colin after work, break up with him, and delete his name from her phone. This realization came slowly, not quite an epiphany, more like an initial spark, perhaps not the one that lights the fire, but one of those first frustrating snaps of a lighter, when butane and metal first meet, the first of several false starts, the click of tinny metal, a flash of yellow, the first frustrating

flicks of thumb before the brush is lit, the kindling catches, the wood alights, cracks, splits, and the flames climb high and give the comfort of heat.

She turned her back on Colin and went to the window looking down on the street. Below, Whitney stood outside on the sidewalk. No one was around her. She reached into her purse, and then stood tall and gazed across the street. Amanda couldn't see her face. Whitney did not move, wasn't using her phone, just stared, as if hypnotized, at the unmoving activity in front of her. Amanda raised her camera, and at the point it reached her chin, she lowered it, and held it by her waist in both hands. The photographer hungry, the subject harassed. An ecosystem. *There she is. I alone am here to see it.* Amanda watched the client, tried to imagine what she was thinking, and stood by the window, looking down, watching, as the day grew dark.

THE GOOD SHEPHERD

Every eight weeks, a Fayetteville Farms truck delivered dogs to the Sullivan farm. A six-man crew unloaded crates of canines, each worker filing into the four industrial-size barns and herding the dogs into neat rows and stacks of steel cages. Pruitt Sullivan's job was to safeguard the tens of thousands of dogs, keeping them warm and fed and hydrated, fattening them up until Fayetteville Farms returned to collect them for slaughter. It was a routine Pruitt knew well, one that defined the rhythm of his grandfather's, and then his father's, chicken farm here in rural Arkansas for as long as Pruitt could remember.

The Fayetteville Farms men came in a series of semitrucks with long trailers, and from his porch, Pruitt could hear the frenetic barking. He knew he was not to interfere while the Fayetteville Farms men unloaded the dogs, but it always struck him as something he should interfere with. The men got out and didn't mill around; they went straight to the back of the trailer, entered an electronic keycode to unlock the doors, opened them up, and led dogs out, the large ones on leashes and the smaller ones in crates. The dogs trotted with merry curiosity as if they were stars of a small town parade. These were dogs of all sizes and breeds, but the majority were mutts with obvious pit bull in them.

But what really unnerved Pruitt was that the Fayetteville Farms men wore baggy green suits with thick, rotund helmets, their skin protected from the air. Like they were delivering something toxic.

The dogs were led to what had been his grandfather's chicken houses—now converted into appropriate storage for the dogs—a series of thick low buildings with studded round silver ventilation fans every fifty yards in order to properly ventilate the barns during the hot Arkansas summers. On both sides of each barn was a massive bay door that could slide open like a loading dock, and this was where the Fayetteville Farms men entered with the dogs.

Today, the green men were followed by a Kia sedan, and from this car stepped a man of medium height, medium build, and nondescript clothes. He stood erect, hands held directly to his side. He spun and scanned the entire farm before walking briskly toward Pruitt, taking the steps to the front porch two a time. He offered his hand to shake; he wore neither a watch nor a wedding ring.

Mr. Sullivan? I'm Dr. Thomas Cook with the Fayetteville Farms Company. I'm a vice president of research and development. I was wondering if you had a moment to talk.

Of course. They shook hands and moved down the porch away from the front door. What can I do for you, Mr. Cook?

Please. Call me Thomas. How's your operation going?

Fine. Nothing to add. I send in my weekly reports via the server. Everything I observe and record is there.

I know. I've read your reports, Pruitt. Very detailed. Very thorough. Is there anything you want to add? Something that you felt uncomfortable about putting in a written report?

No. Why?

Cook shrugged. Sometimes with our farmers, I find it helpful to speak in person. More of a connection, an understanding.

Pruitt frowned. His reports, using a proprietary software provided by Fayetteville Farms, detailed the weight, body fat percentage, and heart rate of each dog, along with twenty-six additional metrics of their health. His report also included information about the water filtration system, air temperature and quality, stool consistency, and other details that were measured daily and broken down in his weekly reports with an executive summary, spreadsheets, pie charts, and bar graphs. Pruitt didn't miss a thing. Including the fact that since Cook had stepped on his porch, the dogs, who normally barked off and on all day long, had gone silent.

You should get more exercise, Cook said, studying Pruitt's face. You should run. Every morning. It's just like basic. Get up, head outside, and run.

Pruitt wondered how this man knew he had served. I don't remember enjoying that.

Running is glorious. Cook turned. He smiled out at the yard like a preacher beaming at his congregation. With our work, it's easy to forget the simple things that make our lives so beautiful. Like the dawn. Feeling our bodies warm as we move through the world. I love to run, Pruitt. I love it so much. The way your legs burn with the effort and the steady sound of your breathing in your throat and ears. You used to run, I can tell. You should get back to it.

I'll think about it. Pruitt cleared his throat. He sensed that Cook knew something about him, about family obligation that could be steered and cemented through doubt and fear and shame, and that this pale man was peeling back a darkness that he wanted to remain hidden and unearthed.

You do that, Pruitt. Cook reached into the left pocket of his pressed, clean chinos and withdrew a business card. If you have any problems or concerns, you give me a call. I'm happy to help. But the most important thing, Pruitt, is that you buy a pair of running shoes and get outside every morning. I promise this will be a big help.

Pruitt said sure, took the card, and looked over Cook's shoulders. The Fayetteville Farms green men were coming back from the dog houses, free of leashes, carrying the empty cages, their delivery work finished. They climbed into their trucks and when they turned the ignition and shifted into gear, Thomas Cook said goodbye and walked towards his Kia. Pruitt watched them leave, then stood on the porch staring into the distant Ozark hills for several minutes. Then he went inside, opened a beer, drank it greedily, sat down at his computer, and spent fifteen minutes comparing running shoes before ordering a pair that would arrive on his doorstep in just two business days.

The morning after Cook's visit, the dogs started to die.

Pruitt found one of the dogs nearest the door dead, keeled over on its right side, unmoving. The dead dog was in a ground level cage near the door. All the dogs were housed and stacked tall in cramped wired cages, six high in six rows, running the entire length of the house. A CAT forklift truck was parked against the far wall. Vulcanized bags for urine and fecal matter, coated with a chemical designed to prevent sores, were attached to each dog, and directed into a trough behind each cage where the waste poured down to a massive treatment vat at the end of the building. He moved down the rows and found that eight other dogs were dead, collapsed on their sides, their mouths and eyes rigidly open. Pruitt pulled his shirt collar up above his mouth and nose and then beelined for his dilapidated garden shed. He returned to the dog house wearing a white surgical mask and yellow latex gloves that stretched up his forearms. The dogs bayed and barked and howled as he searched for the dead bodies, detached their catheters, and dumped their shit and piss from the clogged tubing onto the stainless steel pan beneath their cages, which already held a mixture of blood and puss that had come from their mouths and paws. He slid the bodies out from the cages, careful not to spill their waste on the dogs below. Their rotten bodies were like deflated balloons, their tails sloughing off the bodies when he tried to scoop them out of the cage.

The dogs always barked wildly at the sight of Pruitt, not, he believed with joy or fear but with the simple awareness that his presence meant food, and they were always hungry. The food that Fayetteville Farms provided Pruitt to feed to the dogs was a formula, created in research labs using the best of modern science to synthesize the appropriate combination of proteins, carbohydrates, amino acids, vitamins, and minerals to maximize muscle growth and density in the dogs. It was also laced with a material that coated the dog's stomachs to encourage them to eat more. All around him, stacked above his head, these dogs were overweight; their bodies were both muscular and blob like, whales with snouts and tales. Far worse than their barks was the rhythmic clatter of their stupid tails banging against the cages, a trilling drumbeat of bone on metal that amplified their state of confinement.

Pruitt dumped the bodies in a wheelbarrow. He looked up at the fans, pictured the pathway of the air pushed through the ventilation system, and wondered if the room was somehow too hot or cold. Per the company's instructions, he kept the room at sixty-one degrees. He didn't know how they reached this calculation. He didn't know what precise formula was in their food, what clear chemical treatment he added to their water, or why the regulations for cages width, length, and height were so specific. He wasn't even allowed to stack the cages five or seven high. It had to be six. Which was roughly the same number of dogs he could dump in a wheelbarrow before it was full and he had to cart the dead out into the yard.

He picked a spot downwind from his house, dug a large and deep grave, spread a tarp along the bottom, and then dumped the bodies.

Despite his daily, insistent phone calls, Fayetteville Farms didn't come any earlier. They continued to arrive every Tuesday morning They continued to unload dogs and lead them into the cages.

Don't y'all wanna take a look at this? Pruitt asked the man with the clipboard.

Pruitt lead the foreman to the pit. Flies hovered above the bodies, and the stench was horrific. When he looked down, all Pruitt could make out were the teeth, twisted and grinning, like happy snarls.

Did you put this tarp down? the foreman asked.

Seemed like the smart thing to do.

Sure was. Okay. We'll collect the bodies, and bring you a fresh tarp.

What's the problem?

Don't know until we get them to the lab.

Want me to change anything?

The foreman looked down at his clipboard, squinting at it as if the words were written in a foreign language. He then spoke slowly, as if he was uncertain of the pronunciation of his words.

No, don't make any changes. Average dog weight and mass are in-range. Chemical elements in the food and water are all clear. Could be the temperature, I suppose.

Pruitt pointed down into the grave. Temperature explains that? Them dogs are bloated and purple. Look like goddamn grape jelly.

The foreman looked directly at Pruitt. We don't yet know what's going on. I want you to keep everything the same. Same foods, same cleaning process, same temperatures.

So I get paid the same amount?

The foreman clucked his tongue. You're paid based on the weight of the dogs we pick up for slaughter. Not for the dogs that are dead.

This ain't my fault!

Frankly, Mr. Sullivan, we don't know that yet, now do we?

Pruitt looked down at the grave and made a quick calculation of how much money this was going to cost him.

My margins are already slim, he muttered.

The foreman laid a hand on Pruitt's shoulder. It's gonna be fine, Pruitt. You'll see. Gonna be fine.

Not to Pruitt it wasn't. He was up all night, sitting on his porch, the beers under his feet, shotgun leaning against the house, drinking and watching the dog houses. There was no howling, just the occasional scratch of claws against the cage, a dog shifting in place in their presumed sleep. He half expected those dogs to come barreling out of the house, a pack of Cujos, to tear his skin and muscle from his bones with their sharp, devilish teeth. Sometimes, he wished they would.

Three years ago, a chicken flu swept across America and even today, no one can identify what caused this specific strain of H5N1, why it only attacked chickens rather than starlings or chickadees or cardinals, why it only attacked the birds that the average American ate ninety-four pounds of every single year. What was clear was that chickens were unsafe and Congress was not about to export a product that could be unsafe, despite no one getting sick from American chickens in Europe or Asia.

Instead, the chicken companies just decided to change products. That three thousand unwanted dogs were executed daily struck someone as a market inefficiency that could be made profitable.

The political machinations of this shift never much interested Pruitt. That's not what he remembered about those turbulent six months when legislation was whipped and rammed through, when rebranding of food from the same people that rechristened chicken as poultry occurred, when Americans dissociated their beloved pets from the food on their plate.

What Pruitt remembered about this time was his father's suicide. His father, the fourth generation of Sullivan men, a family that had moved from Providence to Arkansas for a large swath of land and the opportunity to live somewhere other than city slums, at first treated the paperwork from Fayetteville Farms with earnest focus. After all, Sullivan men had a standing relationship with the company, going back decades, long before their financial contracts effectively made the Sullivan's tenant farmers. The living room table was soon covered with paper, first slim white envelopes, then large manila envelopes, then stacks of paper filled with legal jargon and threatening letters from law firms. The pure amount of paper that corporations, banks, and law firms could generate to someone as insignificant as Pruitt's father was spectacularly cruel.

It always struck Pruitt as peculiar that he cannot remember the sound. What woke him was this sound he couldn't recall, a single shot from his father's .38, a shot fired by his father into his temple, standing out in the backyard in a spot that, to Pruitt's knowledge, held no significance. It was a Saturday morning, the light creeping around the blinds of his window, and though he couldn't locate the sound, he continued to look around his bedroom in search of a source, as if his body knew something his brain did not. It was as if his father walked outside that morning, started to walk toward the chicken coops, and then thought, why bother? His father did not leave a note. Pruitt figured that his father, who never liked to trouble anyone for the simplest of

things, hadn't wanted to burden him with one more piece of indecipherable paper.

Cook returned exactly one week after the first dogs died, right after
Pruitt had finished a run. He had waited until the day's heat was at
its peak, the humidity pressing into his body like a hot iron, wring-
ing him out. He found that he couldn't run as far as he wished but
that each day he ran a little bit farther, a little bit faster, and that
skipping a day of running made him feel squirrely and on edge.

You've been running, Cook said, staring at Pruitt's shoes.

Every day.

It's quite addicting, isn't it? And invigorating. Nothing makes
you feel more alive. Pruitt, I could talk about running all day long,
but I received a message that you have some concerns about the dogs.

Pruitt scanned the yard, checking his 25, 50, and 100 yard
markers as if he was still in Iraq. There was no one. There was a Kia
sedan in the driveway and no other cars. The world was still, and
the dogs had ceased barking.

If I've interrupted your dinner, Cook said, I can come back
another time.

Pruitt thought about the pretzels he had been munching on
while he drank beer and listened to the Cardinals game on the radio.

Now's good. Would you like to come in?

It's nice out. Let's sit on the porch.

Beer?

Yes, thank you.

Pruitt pulled what remained of the case from his fridge and
came out to the porch. He took a seat and handed Cook a beer,
which he opened but did not drink. Pruitt opened his beer and
took a deep gulp.

So, Pruitt. What's wrong with the dogs?

Isn't that what your green men are for? I don't know. I'm following protocol. Temperature is set correctly, AC is working. Their food is the formula y'all give me, and they're getting the right amounts. Water is filtered, unpolluted, and clean, just like y'all demanded.

Cook turned and looked at the chicken houses. Pruitt still thought of them this way—chicken houses—though they hadn't had chickens inside them in almost two years. The only noise was the steady hum of the fans that cooled the buildings.

That's spooky, Pruitt said. Usually them dogs are barking and howling.

Dogs are different from us. They understand things instinctively that we do not. Cook turned back to Pruitt and stared at him. Were you in the service?

Three tours.

And now you're home.

I did my part. Now I got a chicken farm without chickens.

The food industry has changed.

My granddaddy started our family farm. Couple of chickens in a pen, and next thing you know, boom, he's got this great big business. My daddy is who sold to y'all.

Do you ever talk about the war with anyone?

Not much to say. Pruitt crushed his beer can and opened another. People always ask shit like, Did you kill anybody? Or really general stuff. What's it like over there. They don't really wanna know the answer. They just like being near soldiers, pretending they're heroes, too.

Tell me.

Pruitt stilled. You know, there's actually a lot of downtime when you're just sitting there waiting for the next assignment, when nothing happens, and all you do is play *Call of Duty* and shit. And you're not really thinking about going out there, but you're also not not thinking about going out there. Just keep playing that game, moving your hands over them buttons, and if it goes bad, you just start a new mission. We played for hours.

Tell me more, Cook whispered.

He could feel it, then, the way that his mind zeroed in on the monitor, the way he could ignore the heat and the tent flaps and sand that seemed to embed in his skin. Just keep playing those games until the sergeant said it was time to move out. Not peaceful, exactly, but cocooned off from a world that required his full attention.

Pruitt wasn't sure how long he talked, but when Cook said, Well, Pruitt, thanks for talking to me. I'll be seeing you, it was like a trance had been broken. On the floorboards were eight empty cans of beer; Cook's remained untouched on the railing. Pruitt staggered upright and watched the Kia pull out of the driveway, and once the car was out of sight, the dogs began to bark and howl.

Soon, Dr. Thomas Cook appeared on Pruitt's porch every Wednesday night. He would knock on the door and politely decline to come in, preferring to remain outdoors. He asked Pruitt to turn on the Cardinals game, though he otherwise never showed any interest in baseball. Pruitt would open a beer and hand it to Cook, and he would always graciously say thank you, then never take a sip. He always stood, his ramrod posture like a sentry. And Pruitt would talk.

He talked about his deployment. He talked about the desert, the inexplicable heat, the weight of all that gear he had to carry on his back. He talked about the first time his squad was attacked, and how chaotic it was to have bullets zipping around his body, to not know who was firing at him, or from where, or when there was an explosion since there wasn't fire and bright oranges and reds but just dust, so much dust, clouds of it rolling over him, coating the back of his throat. Pruitt had never been wounded in combat, a fact that always seemed to surprise people back in the States. His friends had died, some immediately from an explosion—one moment there and the next gone in that cloud of dust—others slowly in triage from shrapnel or bullets that couldn't be dislodged from their pale, skinny bodies. I don't feel lucky, he said to Cook, or blessed or anything. The whole thing made no sense.

Not that it made any sense when he received his honorable discharge and returned to Waldron, Arkansas, to discover that his family no longer owned their chicken farm but were effectively tenant farmers. His grandfather, oxygen tube in his nose, dying from the lung cancer brought upon him by a lifetime of Marlboro Reds, explained that Fayetteville Farms offered more money, a lot more, if they signed a contract to provide their chickens exclusively to the company.

So we're tenant farmers? Pruitt asked, running his hand across his still military short hair.

We're partners, his grandfather wheezed. Not the same thing.

Contract don't read that way.

Your father and I agree. This is the best thing to do. We can't afford the land we're on and we can't afford to compete in the market as individuals. This is a guaranteed income.

You sure?

Goddammit, you weren't here, were you?

Pruitt shrugged and spit tobacco juice off the porch. His grandfather shook his head, the tubing around his nose remaining firmly in place. He had a blanket over his legs despite the fact that it was early summer.

We will be fine, his grandfather said. Your father knows what he's doing.

Three months later, his grandfather was dead and Pruitt and his father were the sole proprietors of a chicken farm, where every eight weeks, a Fayetteville Farms truck would come to pick up chickens for slaughter, the terms and conditions of the chicken houses built to their specifications based on the best science. Fayetteville Farms, of course, did not pay for the necessary upgrades: that was on Pruitt and his father. They took out bank loans and for a few years, the money was good, the work was straightforward. Everything about their financial arrangement was just fine. Until one day, like high winds and storms that suddenly form into a tornado, it wasn't.

What happens to those dogs? Pruitt asked.

Cook smiled thinly. They're slaughtered.

I know that, I mean, you know, how.

I see, Cook focused on a point over Pruitt's shoulder. It's quite elegant. We control all facets of meat production now. We collect dogs from shelters all throughout the region, check their health, then bring them to you. We genetically test their breed, or breeds, as it usually is with mutts, and scientifically determine the best food for their size in order to optimize growth. That's why your houses are so different, why particular breeds are taken to particular houses. We want to make sure they are eating the proper mixture of carbohydrates, proteins, and amino acids. We transport these dogs to you, you feed and care for them for eight weeks, and then we bring them back to the plant, where they are funneled into chutes.

Chutes? Like a slide?

It's beautiful to see, the efficiency. Cook's eyes were glassy. The dogs are hung upside down on hooks and decapitated, then skinned. They travel down a line for disassembly. A line of people in hairnets and white aprons and white masks and white hats cuts them apart by hand. Then we take the meat and batter it, cook it, and freeze it, sealing the product in airtight bags. Then we ship them to the appropriate markets.

Don't seem right. Cook stood very close, towering over him, and a tremor of fear bubbled through his chest. I just want to live in peace.

And you will, Cook said. You always will.

He was lightheaded, feeling weightless and unsteady. He set his beer can down on the arm of the chair.

Something ain't right, Pruitt said.

That is so true, Pruitt. That is very, very true.

The dogs were quiet. No scratches, no sounds. Pruitt rolled his head back. He closed his eyes, and when he opened them again, it was dawn. Cook's car was gone. Around his feet was a larger collection of beer cans than Pruitt remembered drinking; there was even an empty bottle of Old Crow floating in the cooler water. Did they drink whiskey? Pruitt's vision fogged, and he stumbled into the kitchen and made toast and drank orange juice and tried to shake the visions from his head, the visions of dogs attacking him, his legs churning, feeling teeth grip his flesh and pull the muscles from his bones.

On the morning of his father's suicide, Pruitt had slid out of bed and tugged on the jeans and T-shirt he found on the floor directly next to his bed, the discarded pile of a drinker. He thumped barefoot into the hall and down the stairs, his mouth dry and cottony. He drank two glasses of water from the kitchen sink and then went to the coffee machine, the pot of coffee freshly made but only half filled, and assumed his father had been up for a while. His father had always been an early riser. Pruitt poured himself a cup and set it down on the counter. He stared at it for a moment, chewing over the idea of pouring a splash of bourbon into it, aware that his was the behavior of a drunk. Yet the idea gripped him like a fist, and he didn't quite know what to make of this desire, this need.

He picked up his coffee. No bourbon. He stepped out on the back porch and took a long gulp of the hot coffee, savoring the way it almost burned his throat. He held the chipped Razorbacks mug with two hands and leaned against the railing. It's pretty here, he thought, a thought as clear and sonorous in his mind as the desire for bourbon had been just a moment ago. Funny how the brain works. He shook his head and lifted the mug to his lips. When his eyes were over the mug's lip, he saw something in the yard that didn't look right. Now his brain seemed to slow down. This was a shape. This was the shape of a man. This was the shape of a man that resembled his father. This is my father. What's he doing in the grass? Why isn't he moving?

This was the moment that Pruitt always came back to, this moment of discovery. It wouldn't have mattered if he had known his father shot himself; the bullet that went into the right side of his father's skull had killed him instantly. And the grief he felt, the type of terrifying, bone wrenching he would feel for months—even now, sometimes, when he walks away from the dogs and back to his father's home— would always be unavoidable. There was nothing to do. Yet, Pruitt could not shake the belief that his hesitation to see the world for what it was in all its misery and pain was a character flaw so deep and intractable into who he was that he could not help but puzzle over it, turn it in his hands, feel the hardness of this enigma, and study this flaw with inexhaustible patience and Sisyphean futility.

As the summer dragged into autumn, Pruitt watched his bank account dwindle. Fayetteville Farms never discussed the toxicology reports on the dead dogs or Pruitt's decreasing monthly earnings. The men in the green toxic waste suits continued to collect the dead dogs, continued to deliver new ones, continued to get their data reports from the computers that help control the dog houses. All of it was programmed by Pruitt: the automated feeders, the ventilation systems, the water lines, the thermostats, and he had been following the guidelines with precision. And still dogs were dying.

Pruitt hadn't been sleeping. He might as well be in the desert again. Now when he brought the dead dogs out, he knew the living were barking and growling not at the corpses but at Pruitt. It was his fault. All of this was his fault.

It was late October and Pruitt sat at the dining room table, the entire surface covered in paper—bank statements, legal threats, credit card statements, torn envelopes, foreclosure warnings—and in front of him was a plate with a half-eaten Pop-Tart. He didn't know what to do: his mailbox was filled daily and his phone rang all day, always unanswered, from numbers he didn't recognize. His voice mail was filled; he didn't even bother with his e-mail. All across the area, chicken farmers had gone bankrupt. His father had seen that coming for years. But the dog farm was supposed to be the way out of his problems. How did he not see this coming?

When the dogs stopped howling, Pruitt knew that Cook was here. He sat upright and listened carefully for the sounds of the Kia crackling along the gravel, of footsteps, of a doorbell. There was no noise. He had a sudden, powerful wish to have his gun. When Cook knocked, Pruitt took a deep breath, closed his eyes, and then said as loud and calm as he could, Come in.

Cook entered, the screen door batting once against the frame, and he looked down the hallway into the darkness before turning and facing Pruitt. He smiled at Pruitt, then smiled at the papers covering the table. He stepped closer, stood tall and true at the opposite end of the long table, and wrapped his fingers on the nearest chair.

It's not over yet, Pruitt.

I'm broke, Thomas. Can't make the payments.

There is always a solution, Pruitt. Always. You just have to think through your problems, consider the possibilities. Look at Fayetteville Farms? Chicken, beef, pork. What to do, where to go. Why not dogs? Why not a different type of meat? Who would have thought of that? Only a company unwilling to break, unwilling to say 'It's over.' Do you see my point, Pruitt?

The dogs are dying, Thomas. It ain't my fault.

Cook released the chair and walked along the side close to the windows. He ran a finger along the table as if checking for dust, and when he was close, he stopped and made a fist.

Did you really do everything you could, Pruitt?

Sweat ran down Pruitt's face; he was hot and cold at once, his skin sticky. Yet, he could not move, as if his limbs were no longer a part of his own body. Fear gnawed at him. He thought about the papers he would have to sign to declare bankruptcy. All of it would be gone: his grandfather's land, his father's business, his entire life. It had been just six months, barely a half year, since the first group of sick dogs had arrived.

I'm lost, Pruitt said.

Cook smiled cruelly at Pruitt. He raised his fist, uncurled his fingers, and placed his hand on Pruitt's shoulder. His touch was shockingly cold and a tremor of shame ran through his chest. I'm sorry, Pruitt blubbered, I'm sorry I'm sorry I'm sorry.

I know you are, Pruitt. But what I want to hear is what you're going to do about it. Break down to build up. Do you see? Do you understand?

Pruitt raised his head and looked the length of the dining room table, across the hallway, beyond the dark family room, and out the window into the woods. With a calm whose source he could not find, he said, Yes, I understand.

Good. Cook released his shoulder and without another word turned away, crossed the room, walked out the front door, and drove away. Pruitt sat with his hands in his lap, listening for a long time to the silent night before rising and walking through his house to turn off every light. He showered, shaved, and then slipped naked between his sheets and stared unmoving at the ceiling until he fell asleep.

In his nightmare, there were shadowy figures outside his blinds. The silhouettes moved toward his air conditioner and lifted a sack and tilted it toward the window. The air conditioner kicked on and the machine blew a thin white powder into the room. Poison. Pruitt knew it was poison. Yet his legs were paralyzed. He kicked and kicked and they refused to move. The cloud drifted toward him, swimming like it had arms, like it was gently paddling over to his face. When he opened his mouth to scream, no noise came out. He tried again. Nothing. He stretched his jaw as far as he could and screamed from the pit of his stomach, a burn rippling through his throat, and an ear-piercing silence filled his ears.

Pruitt sat up. He was awake. Sunlight laddered through the blinds. He was soaked in his own sweat. He bolted to the window, fingered open the blinds, and saw the driveway was empty. He pressed his forehead against the pane; the cool October air had made the glass soothingly cold. Pruitt tapped his head against the pane. Then he did it again, harder. He heard the glass crack.

Pruitt pulled on his jeans and work boots and went into the living room. He took his shotgun from the closet, loaded the weapon, and pocketed extra shells. He ripped open the front door and aimed the barrel out into the yard. He checked his 25, his 50, his 100, and the tree line. No one. The stench of his own sour breath filled his nostrils. He stepped outside, and when he was certain there was no one waiting for him, he raced to the nearest dog house.

He entered and immediately the barking began. He logged into the computer and tapped in his code. The lights turned on. Pruitt keyed in his command. The monitor stated, Are you sure? Pruitt confirmed it, and all the low level cages sprang open. Pruitt scrambled between the rows, and reaching behind each dog, unlatched the catheters from their hind ends. The stench was horrible. The dogs staggered out of their cages and snarled. Pruitt went from cage to cage, unlatching each dog. He climbed up the ladder and detached each and every dog. His hands were covered in shit, piss, and blood, and he wiped it off on his jeans and jacket until it no longer did any good.

Still carrying the shotgun, he strode to the CAT and turned the key. He turned the forklift toward the cages and brought them down as many at a time as he could. The dogs stumbled out of the cages; some fell out, some limped, some collapsed on the concrete floor, panting with their tongues out. Some of the dogs in the cages were already dead. A few dazed dogs stumbled out through the open barn door and stood sniffing the Arkansas air.

Run! Pruitt screamed. He fired two shots into the ceiling. The dogs howled and scattered into a semicircle, staring at Pruitt. It didn't matter. They would know. They had to know. Pruitt raced to the second house, looking back over his shoulder at the pack of dogs standing uncertain in the field.

He kept thinking he heard sirens—police cars, fire trucks, he didn't know what—but no one came. Nothing stopped him from dislodging all the dogs, from emptying all the cages, and then there were thousands of dogs, thick and muscular like small bulls, not running for their freedom but standing in confused groups surrounding their cages. Pruitt, covered in the waste of dying and deceased dogs, stood and watched as their muzzles turned up toward the sunless sky, their nostrils tremoring with the distant smells of the Ozarks. Not a single one barked. The silence of the dogs was unnerving, and Pruitt knew that he stood with his mouth open, that he wore an incredulous expression of amazement and fury and horror. Why did they stand there? Why didn't they run?

REUNION

after Cheever

The last time I saw the man who almost became my father-in-law was in St. Louis at Terminal C of the Charles Lambert International Airport. I had taken the MO-Ex shuttle from Columbia to St. Louis, a ninety-minute ride on a bus with a broken heater. During the ride, a few light taps on the window became a steady freezing rain that soon included snow. It was optimistic of me to think that I was going to make my flight to Washington, but that's where my life was then. I always imagined I would have a career where I would spend time in airports, a traveler, an important person focused not on where I had been but on where I was going. At worst, my frequent flyer status might get the airline to put me up in one of the hotels on the other side of the highway, and I could maybe get a complimentary meal and have quiet drinks at the bar by myself.

Waves of rain and wind hurried me off the shuttle and into the terminal, the floors slick with gray puddles of melted precipitation, black footprints covering the wet mats on the other side of the sliding doors. Travelers in business-casual wear packed the terminal, tapping their cell phones with one hand and with the other, dragging their wheeled carry-on baggage behind them, congesting the walkways. I hoisted my duffel bag up over my head and let the strap fall against my shoulder, freeing my hands, which I blew on as if they were cold. The bag, a free gift from a company picnic ten years ago, was the right size for weekend trips like this one, an economics conference in DC. The strap of my duffel bag cut into my shoulder, and I stood before the monitors, figuring that "Delayed" probably meant "Canceled," but when I asked the attendant at the United counter, she insisted that since the flight hadn't been officially canceled, if I switched flights now, there was a rebooking fee of one hundred seventy-five dollars. So, I cleared security and wandered the terminal, watching angry passengers berate disinterested and powerless gate attendants. On the televisions throughout the terminal, the CNN weatherman swept his hand across the digital map showcasing the winter storm sweeping across the country, demonstrating how the entire Midwest would soon be under thirteen inches of wet winter snow.

I wanted a drink, and wiped my hand across my mouth as if I was thirsty, a silly and empty gesture. I often act like I'm on camera and being observed; I don't know why I do it, but I can't seem to stop either. Gray plastic buckets sentried the terminal, collecting rain water from the leaky roof, the carpeting beneath them permanently stained from years of neglect. In all the newsstands, tchotchke stores, and restaurants, people were furiously waiting, passing their time with magazines they didn't want to read and food they didn't want to eat. Between gates C14 and C16 was a long shallow restaurant called Mulligans Sports Pub, its dark walls hung with generic country club décor of dark wood paneling and framed black and white photos of Jazz Age golfers. The kitchen was on the right, and the bar ran the length of the back wall with one exception: on its left, there was a single floor-to-ceiling window that overlooked the runway, and in front of it, one table only big enough for two seats. I couldn't tell if anyone was there; it was a nook easy to miss. I crept closer, feeling hopeful.

Terry McKenzie occupied the second chair, facing away from all the noise, his head up and focused on the sports highlights flashing on the television overhead. I froze. It had been almost three years since I had last seen him, and to be honest, I wasn't yet entirely sure it was him. I adjusted my duffel, and took a step closer to stare at his profile. It was him. The airport noise vanished, replaced by my heartbeat echoing in my ears and a feeling like a closing fist in my chest. I couldn't not see him. I walked over, and stood next to the adjacent chair.

"Hey, Terry," I said.

He turned. He had large eyes, bigger and softer than normal, often unblinking but somehow sympathetic, like a teddy bear. In front of him was a tall plastic cup of iced tea, the straw hammered down between the ice. He seemed to need a moment for his eyes to focus. When I last saw him, he had a beard, and now he only had a thin goatee, his bare cheeks riveted with age lines charting his decades in way that made him distinguished.

"Well, this is a surprise," he said.

"I saw you sitting here, and I thought I'd come over and say hello."

He stood. Terry couldn't flatten his arms or fully bend his elbows: he had a congenital radioulnar synostosis, a fusion of the proximal ends of the humerus and ulna bones, fixing his forearms in a degree of pronation. With his barrel chest and bent arms, he always appeared ready for a fight. When we shook hands, his iron grip gave my soft professor hand a strong pump. "Why don't you sit down? I know there isn't any space anywhere."

"Thanks. You heading to Foxborough?"

"Belichick keeps winning, I keep going."

"I keep rooting for the Dolphins to make the playoffs, but it doesn't seem to work."

He was a sports cameraman, and on his way to Boston in order to drive down to Gillette Stadium and setup for the Patriots play-off game on Sunday evening. When we first met, I peppered him with questions about all the different events he covered, which was just about everything: NBA, MLB, NHL, NFL, Olympics, World Cup. He once told me St. Louis Blues hockey was his favorite: indoors during the winter, two eighteen-minute breaks between the periods, and at the end of the game, he could hop in his pickup truck and drive home rather than to a hotel. But the NFL paid the best, and for nearly a decade the best team was the Patriots, which meant Terry was outdoors in the northeast for football games during December and January.

I asked about his wife.

"Ellen is fine. She's working for Enterprise now. Gets to work at home for a few days each week, and only drives into town twice a week."

They lived in Edwardsville, Illinois, on the other side of the Mississippi, and "town" meant St. Louis. The waitress came over. I ordered a beer, and to my surprise, Terry asked for the same. After the two pints were put down in front of us, Terry took a large gulp from his without looking me in the face.

We talked, as we always used to, about sports: baseball, which is my favorite, and football, which is his business. Despite his years of work in the industry, Terry wasn't a huge sports fan like I was; he watched the games for the production, the camera shots and angles, the broadcasters, the replay, the cuts, all things he loved to talk about while watching. He had radiated glee when he took me on a tour of the Billikens' new arena, the unblemished fiber optics cables and piping wired into the exposed ceiling, the blinking high-speed connections and outlets, a large docking area for the production trucks, camera wells with easy access and great sightlines. All of it, he said, was built as if the university's engineers and architects had actually consulted with the producers and cameramen who worked the games.

Finally, I asked Terry about his daughter, my ex.

"She's fine." He nodded to himself as he spoke. "She and Peter are doing well."

"They're moving to Dallas, right?"

"Baylor University Medical Center. It's supposed to be very good."

"That's great." For about a year after we broke up, she and I kept in touch, and then she met Peter and I got updates on her life solely through Facebook. I knew they got married last year; I knew she was officially an orthopedist. Beyond that, I didn't care much what she did. I say this without malice. It remains a strange feeling to me that someone I loved and lived with for nearly three years stirred almost no feelings or memories. It's almost like she never existed, which is, perhaps, why our relationship ended.

Terry asked, "What about yourself?"

"I'm tenured now," I said. "I published a few articles and then my book came out last year."

He tilted his glass in my direction. "Congratulations. What's the book about?"

"Monetary mechanisms and bank runs in the twentieth century."

"I'm not gonna read that one."

I laughed. "No one but a fellow economist would."

We stared out the window for a while. Fat flakes of snow rained down on the concrete, and plow trucks rolled across the tarmac, scraping and pushing the snow off the runways. We both watched the snow. The air reeked of cheeseburgers and fries, and the bar was three people deep, all laughing faces growing red from alcohol. When our waitress stopped by, I figured she wouldn't get back to us anytime soon, and ordered accordingly.

"I'm sorry," she said, "We aren't permitted to serve doubles."

"Then just bring me two."

I don't know why I switched to whiskey. I glanced at Terry, but he didn't comment on my order. In college, I had tended bar at the airport in Pittsburgh so I knew that tables next to the windows were popular; people could sit, waiting for their flight, and watch the airplanes taxi, see the grounds crew wave their directions to the pilots or unload luggage onto motorized carts. Back then, sodas were two dollars, with free refills, and if paid for in cash, I would simply never ring them in and pocket the money, earning myself somewhere between thirty and fifty extra dollars every shift.

Terry crossed his arms and leaned back and continued to watch the runways. When our waitress returned, she refilled Terry's iced tea and I poured my two whiskeys into one glass.

"My father," he said, "was in the war. Europe."

"My grandfather flew in the Pacific. B-17s."

"My dad was stationed in England. He bombed France, bombed Germany, wherever the Nazis were, wherever the orders sent him, he bombed. When he got back from the war he had a factory job. Never left Wisconsin again. Even our family vacations were in the state."

Once I had been to Terry's father's house in northern Wisconsin—I can't remember why my ex and I drove up there, but we did—a concrete slab of maybe eight hundred square feet that once held nine children. They were German Catholics. The house had only three bedrooms, and downstairs in the concrete basement, past the winter freezer and the jars of preserves, there were hard bunks where the oldest kids had slept so they could get some privacy because sleeping down there was better than being upstairs and close to their parents. These bunk beds were hand built of unadorned white oak, and made me think of internment camps.

"I got the World Cup in 2006," Terry continued. "I wanted to fly my father over, give him the chance to see Berlin again. My mother had recently died, and I thought the travel would do him good. I was a little surprised he agreed to it, but it made me happy, and maybe he knew it would. I gave him the window seat on the connecting flight from London to Berlin. He sat up straight when he looked down on Berlin. He turned to me and said, I bombed that city. Twice. He held up two fingers. Twice, he said again. I asked him how he felt about that. You know what he said? He said, nothing. Back then, he said, I hated them. I wanted to bomb them to hell. Now look at it. It's beautiful. And I don't feel anything. Not one thing. He didn't seem the least bit sad about it."

Terry looked out at the tarmac. "I've always felt a little funny in airplanes ever since."

I never knew my father; he left my mother and me when I was five years old, fleeing Pittsburgh for San Diego, where he met and married a woman with whom he had three new children. He never invited me to visit, and I never asked to go. Instead, twice per year, on Christmas and my birthday, he sent a greeting card, often with a sentiment that didn't mirror his indifference, with a check enclosed and "college fund" scribbled in the memo space. The amounts on the check increased over the years, but the frequency remained the same, and as soon as I turned eighteen, the cards stopped arriving altogether.

I followed Terry's gaze. I loved living in fantasies where I could be heroic. Imagine: bombs dropping on the airport, the runways cratered, electrical wires tumbling from the ceiling and dangling like nooses, concrete pillars falling and crushing travelers, suitcases spilled open and pouring out clothes like internal organs, and me, rushing through the chaos trying to stay alive. It wasn't an entirely unpleasant image.

"I'm gonna call Ellen," he said, pulling out his phone. "No point in staying here for the rest of the day."

"You want me to step away?"

"That's a good idea."

I nodded, stood, and walked out of the restaurant, slinking my way around suitcases and travelers. The rebuke stung. I had only asked out of politeness; I hadn't actually expected Terry to shoo me away. I had wanted to hear Ellen's voice and the familiar rapport between them, how they spoke to each other, needled each other, negotiated, mildly complained, the familiar dance I had seen them do for years. I wanted to know if he told her that I was there.

I walked out of the bar and hurried to the nearest restaurant, two gates down, and elbowed my way to the bar and ordered a twenty-four-ounce Schlafly. I left a large cash tip, drank half in one gulp, breathed deeply as I stepped away from the crowd, and then drank the rest. I left the glass on an occupied table, ignored the "Hey!" yelled at me, and walked back to Mulligans. Terry was still on the phone, so I went to the bar and ordered a shot and a beer, then lingered at the edge of the restaurant, making sure I didn't take my drinks outside the seating area. After he hung up, I stood in the concourse for another beat, pretending not to be waiting for him. My beer was half empty. Down the length of the hall, passengers slumped against the wall, sprawled out on the floor like schoolchildren. Everyone had a laptop or cell phone plugged into an outlet or pressed against their ear, or both, their expressions bovine and desperate. I watched the steady accumulation of icy water in the gray buckets on the floor, the drip hypnotic and numbing.

I pocketed the shot glass and sat down roughly. Terry eyed my beer but said nothing.

"I'm not afraid," I said, "of taking a job back east, a job in New York or something. I've been looking for a job out there, but I haven't had much luck and the university gig is pretty good. And I haven't been out in the working world in a long time, and it's pretty nice at the university. Teaching, and all that. I never thought I'd live in a college town. I don't know."

"That's a tough decision."

"It's not bad! I go to conferences. I get to travel. When I'm here, it's just work. I don't do much else. I get my research done. So."

"So."

"I'm not scared to leave. I'm not saying that. I'm just saying, you know, it's pretty good here. You travel all the time, right? You're never home."

"I'm home as much as I can be."

"Right. Right. I know that's true."

Because his work life took him on the road over two hundred days per year, when he was home, Terry's presence was one of tensed relaxation. Frequently when he was at home and my ex and I were visiting, Terry was on his back deck, pacing the length of his house as he talked on the phone to a friend whose story needed to be heard: someone who had become a new father, been laid off, had a mother die, a car accident, a new child, a costly renovation on a house, or any number of the normal human disasters and celebrations that happen to us every day. In need, they would call Terry, and he would go outside, winter or summer, and stalk up and down with a steady cadence of affirmation as he listened, and listened, and listened. Sometimes, after my ex and I moved away, the person on the end of those calls was me.

He leaned back in his chair. "Ellen is going to come pick me up. There's no way a flight's getting out of here. Maybe you should do the same. I'm pretty sure they aren't going anywhere."

"That's your advice."

He smiled, and I could feel him pulling away from this conversation. Our waitress appeared. I ordered another round but Terry just shook his head. He stood up, slipped on his coat, and put his hands in his pockets.

"This is a good spot," he said. "If you decide to wait it out, I'd hold on to this table. Take it from a guy who flies a lot. I'm gonna go. Airport police won't let cars linger for anybody in this weather, so I want to be there when Ellen pulls up."

"Sure. Sure. Yeah, that makes sense. Well."

"Good to see you again."

"You, too." I stood up and he offered his right hand to shake, but I spread my arms and hugged him. He patted me with his one free hand, the other remaining in his coat pocket. All the muscles in his back tensed, and with his ramrod posture he politely patted me on my back, a rapid rhythmic tap telling me to hurry up with my feelings and move along. But I held. I held and squeezed until he squeezed back and the drumming stopped, and maybe for a moment, he was willing to step back in time with me.

"I'm sorry," I said.

But if he heard me he didn't acknowledge it; he turned away without looking at me, carrying his suitcase back toward security, and then veered down one of the exit tunnels. He was gone. I imagined him standing on the curb, a hand over his eyes like a salute, looking east for his wife's car, then turning and looking east and seeing the storm clouds approaching, the miasma of cobalt gray and ice weather. Right then, the car would pull up and he would hop in and his wife would say *let's go* because it was a long drive home and they had to stay ahead of the weather.

The patter against the window turned my attention away from the restaurant and back to the runways. Out in the cold, plow trucks trudged across the concrete, the clear gray paths almost immediately recoated by snow and ice. I wrapped my hand around my fresh, cold glass of beer, blinking at the images in front of me. Something made me look back across the restaurant, beyond the men and women occupying each table, ignoring the travelers hurrying to nowhere in the concourse, and focus on the arrival and departure monitors. The flights in the terminal remained unchanged. STL to DCA, Delayed. STL to SAN, Delayed. Delayed, the monitor said, over and over again. None of us were going anywhere. There wouldn't be a hotel room for me if I kept waiting; I pulled out my cell, found a hotel across the highway, and dialed. I liked airports. I liked hotel bars. They weren't permanent, but they were always welcoming and looked the way you wanted things to look. What did it matter? The hotel had me on hold. When I got through, I booked a room, and when I was told check-in wasn't until 3:00 p.m., I told the clerk I didn't know what time it was. He laughed, but that wasn't what I meant. I hung up, still thirsty, looked at the monitors, and waited for the delay to become a cancellation.

Until We Have Faces

Ryan drummed the steering wheel of his car outside of Great Ohio Financial, a firm where, in five minutes, he had an interview for the nebulous job of "investment property assistant." The job was listed under the finance sector on Monster, but the description focused more on property management, vaguely describing the role as a "multitasking real estate position." Ryan wasn't going to be picky, not after months of searching and scoring just one interview for what turned out to be a pyramid scheme selling natural vitamin supplements. He tilted the rearview mirror and searched his face: the swelling was down, the bruising gone. From the passenger seat, he picked up a portfolio that his girlfriend Ali purchased for him yesterday at Office Depot; inside were two extra copies of his résumé. He took a deep breath, then exited the car.

The firm was located in a strip mall in western Cincinnati. Garbage cans along the sidewalk overflowed, spitting out soda lids and cigarette boxes, and the empty newspaper bins chained to the support beams were so sunfaded that the name of the paper was unreadable: could have been the *Enquirer* or the recently defunct *Post*. New "Obama 2008" stickers were plastered on their sides. Ryan touched the knot of his tie as he crossed the sidewalk for the door.

Inside, a soft computerized chime announced his entrance. Fake ferns stood in the corners, and the couch cushions lacked indentations from seated bodies. Track lighting was turned to highlight the framed posters on the wall: Cincinnati's riverfront at night, pencil sketches of Victorian houses, black and white photographs of mustached men opening restaurants.

"Welcome to Great Ohio," the receptionist said. "How may I help you?"

"I'm Ryan Riordan. I'm here to see Garrett Scherzer."

"That's me." He came down the main walkway, a coffee cup in his hand, stomach lurching ahead of him like a dog straining against a leash. The top three buttons of his white dress shirt were open, revealing a tanned, waxed chest. His shirt sleeves were rolled in neat and precise folds up his forearms and his handshake was quick, which helped Ryan hide his wince when Garrett squeezed. "Good to meet you, Ryan. Follow me back."

"Mr. Scherzer, excuse me." The secretary smiled cautiously. "We received the Isaac Henderson documents. You'll need to take a look at them immediately."

"Is this going to piss me off?"

She answered by handing him a sealed overnight FedEx envelope. Scherzer held it away from his body as if it could infect him. "Isaac Henderson. Not how I want to start my day." He spun on his heel. "Sorry, Ryan. C'mon back."

Only half the desks were occupied. Men leaned toward their dual computer screens, spreadsheets on display, and spoke into their headsets in a rapid and controlled tone while tapping their pens atop the stacks of file folders in front of them. The unoccupied desks were spotless, as if their previous occupant had needed to be sanitized and forgotten.

"Have a seat," Garrett said, pointing to the chairs in front of his desk. His glass office occupied the entire back wall, and without opening the FedEx envelope, he dropped it on his desk, which was already buried in piles of red binders, oversized green file folders, and yellow legal pads covered with numbers. Above a wall of steel filing cabinets, there was a panoramic shot of a mountain climber on a bright, brilliant mountainside, the only photograph in the room. Beneath the glass window that overlooked the entire office was a long, dilapidated couch. Scherzer sucked on his teeth and scanned Ryan's résumé then dropped it next to the FedEx envelope.

From the shelves behind him, he grabbed two large binders and handed them to Ryan. Their slick blue covers gleamed dully under the fluorescent lighting.

"I'll need you to study these," Scherzer said. "I'd like you to take the realtor licensing test in three weeks." He opened a filing cabinet, the metal screeching, and pulled out a series of forms. "Directions to the class site in Mason. It's a one hundred twenty-hour course, so it is essentially going to be your full time job to go. We pay for the course and the exam. If you fail, you're terminated, and we bill you for the reimbursement."

"I'm sorry?"

"You're here for a job, right? Well, I'm offering a job." Scherzer said, folding his arms across his chest. "I googled you this morning and just read your résumé. If you want to do a formal interview and have me ask you about where you want to be in five years and all that other fucking bullshit, you're in the wrong place. I'm here most of the time, and I often sleep on the couch behind you. I need field reps. Your cover letter mentioned handyman work, right?"

"Sure. A little drywall, floor refinishing—"

"Which is what I need. Your job will specialize in foreclosures and sub-prime mortgages, and if you don't know what that means, don't worry, you will soon. I need field reps that can clean up a house with some basic maintenance, change locks, and make sure the utilities get paid. It's all about having a good system. Once you've shown me you can handle the system, you get your own properties. If you can't hack it, you'll be let go."

Ryan touched his thumbs together. "What about the outside of the house?"

"Also your responsibility. Listen, this business is about properties, not people. Don't let anyone tell you differently. You always need to see the value in a property, no matter how bad it is. Don't say things like, 'Lots of room, oversized garage' because that just screams shithole. Instead, you find the good in a property. Emphasize the hardwood floors or something. But you really only learn to see those things when you work on them with your own hands. That"—he pointed at the binders in Ryan's lap—"is pretty easy."

Ryan said, "When should I start?"

"I'll get your paperwork, fill it out, and you can start the real estate class next Monday. How's that sound?"

It sounded like a job. And a job, any job, was a reason to get out of bed every morning, not lay there and watch Ali get dressed while he shoved his head back under the pillow. If they were going to live together, as they had begun to discuss, he would need to pull his weight, and if this job got him there, so be it. He shook Garrett Scherzer's oily hand with vigor.

Ali was the manager of a Clifton wine bar called Seven, the *V* in the signage above the entrance in the shape of a wine glass. Seven had two large windows separated by the main entrance, each with an Obama "HOPE" poster in the bottom corner. At the bar, they rotated seven daily servings, always and only seven wines, their names and vintage written in colored chalk above the bar's back wall. They were served in glass carafes large enough for generous pours. There were six beers on tap, all from Cincinnati brewers, and also cheap beers like Michelob and PBR for two dollars, which was popular with hipsters. Seven was two massive rooms, bisected by a partial wall of wine crates climbing to the ceiling, sorted by region, all of which Ali could discuss in detail. The second room, beyond the bar and the seating area, was not only a display area for bottles of wine for sale but also for two regularly occupied ping-pong tables. Ryan had his own small part in the business: the entire seating area of the front room was composed of discarded tables and chairs that he found by scouring the dumpsters around UC at the end of each semester. The hodgepodge of chairs—chintzy wingbacks, office, folding, armless, all with fabrics from across the color spectrum—gave Seven its charm.

Ali came back around the bar, and opened a bottle of High Life for him, then pushed her wavy black hair behind her ear, and leaned his way.

"I got the job," he said. She wrapped her hand around his forearm and squeezed, and he recapped what transpired in Scherzer's office. When he was finished, he asked, "Does that seem strange to you?"

"Corporate, maybe," Ali said, "but not in restaurants. You could turn it down."

They both knew this wasn't true. Even the seasonal landscaping he had done in the past no longer needed extra help. Since he failed out of college six years earlier, he had already been laid off three times, and he couldn't entirely convince himself this was bad luck.

"I get benefits and a 401K after the first month."

"Retirement. What a fucking joke," she laughed. She stood sentry at the bar, her lean arms folded in front of her as she stared out at the floor. "You're gonna have to take all those movies back."

He thumbed the label of his beer bottle. Ryan had passed his time borrowing DVDs from his library branch, which at least got him up and out of his apartment. "I'm sorry it took so long."

She squeezed his hand. "We should be celebrating, not complaining." Something over his shoulder caught her attention, and she stood tall, flashed a friendly bartender smile, and came from around the counter back onto the floor.

Ryan spun around on the bar stool and watched. Ali's family was Chinese; they had immigrated to San Francisco when she was three. At first, his friends gave him shit about catching the yellow fever, but no one he knew viewed their relationship—white man, Asian woman—as anything unusual. Or, at least, they didn't say so. Weeks into their relationship, late at night, naked beneath the sheets and lit only by the streetlights filtering gray shadows around them, Ryan told her he didn't even notice her race. Ali shifted her weight, turning on her side to look at him in profile, and calm but angry, explained how that was total bullshit, and recounted just a handful of the hundreds of time she had been fetishized for her looks by teachers, boyfriends, coaches, supervisors, administrators, loan officers, flight attendants, car salesman, waiters. Let alone the cultural expectations of her family. You don't see my race, she said, you not only don't see me, but invalidate me. You're saying my view of myself and my experiences aren't real. You know that, right? That's not what I mean, Ryan said. Maybe not, but it's what you said. In the dark, he took her hand. You're right, he said, I didn't understand. I'll do better. She said it was all right, but she ignored the squeezing of her hand and rolled away.

Ryan leaned against the bar. Ali worked the room, bantering and laughing with the still early crowd, mostly post-work happy hour drinkers, regulars who always tipped well, always knew when to not be so chatty because she was in the weeds. She came back around the bar to pour her table's drink order, and Ryan checked the time on his phone.

"Hang here tonight," she said. "Play some ping-pong, and help me close the bar."

"A bunch of us were thinking of going to J-Hall."

"Your face is finally healing up, right?"

"I won't fight."

"Not if you stay here, you won't."

When they first met, Ryan believed she had found his pugilism charming, a sign of masculinity perhaps, a willingness to stand up for his word and honor. But, lately, he just seemed to get in fights for the hell of it, for something to do, because there was no one else or no singular thing to be angry at but all of it. If his anger found an outlet in the guy running his mouth about Obama, or the Steelers, or vinyl records, or something else, what was wrong with putting that guy on his back? Especially if Ryan occasionally got his ass kicked and ended up face down on a sidewalk. The fights were always fair and always honest, two things he rarely could say about the rest of the world.

He spun around and placed his phone flat on the bar. Ali looked down at him with a mixture of feelings: pity, anger, love. He finished his High Life, then said, okay. She smiled in relief, leaned over, and kissed him. After she left to deliver her table's drinks, Ryan counted out two more bills from his wallet, flattening the creased corners, the warming and powerful pleasure of being able to afford his beer. It did, he had to admit, feel good—really good— to have a job again. For at least one night, this would be enough.

The real estate classes were held north of Mason, far into the Cincinnati exurbs in one of several identical beige buildings, each twelve stories high and distinguishable only by the building number posted next to the sidewalk. Ryan's all-day class, held in an amphitheater style room, was filled, and disposable coffee cups were left on desks, chairs, the sinks in the bathroom. Anyone that didn't arrive fifteen minutes early had to sit in the aisles, and the breadth of information was tremendous. The students were a hodgepodge: kids clearly just graduated from high school with awkward stride and gangly limbs, as if they hadn't yet grown into their bodies; adults the same age as Ryan, wearing khakis and polo shirts and smug expressions, confident this was the way to wiggle out of their corporate jobs from underneath the thumbs of incompetent midlevel managers; seniors with hair neatly combed, believing this real estate boom was the way to save their retirement and become the millionaires that forty years of work hadn't gotten them close to. At night, sitting at his kitchen table with a cup of cold coffee, Ryan examined the figures and terminology—calculating commission rates, writing habendum clauses into contracts, defining *non-homogeneity*, avoiding negligent misrepresentation—he thought: *we all reek of desperation.*

During the third and final week of classes, they were let go early, and Ryan raced home ahead of rush hour traffic. He changed quickly and headed out to the nearest ATM. The afternoon sidewalks, empty and still, provided no people to dodge and zip around. Waves of heat rippled off the street, the occasional bass of cars thumping out of open windows. He passed small, ugly houses with FOR SALE signs in the yards, yellow lawns, and quick paint jobs splattered on the porches that were unable to make a creaky starter home attractive. Those without signs remained in regular disrepair: crooked fences, weedy gardens, crooked and broken window screens, askew gutters, and a looming sense of defeat.

At the intersection, where a corner store had metal tables set out on the sidewalk and the people dragged them out of the sunlight and into the shade through the day, a sundial for the neighborhood, Ryan turned the corner and found his bank's ATM. The plastic cover above the machine showcased the name of the bank, written in blue ink on a red background, and in the lower left corner there was a small hole; from it a crack rippled out like a spore. He inserted his card and typed his pin code; the silver keypad was directly in the sunlight and hot to the touch. The screen presented him with his options, and he hit WITHDRAWAL and then asked for two hundred dollars.

Insufficient funds, the screen said. The machine spit out his card.

"The fuck?" He pressed his card back in, tapped his pin code again, and then selected BALANCE. $57.24.

He sucked in his lips and slammed his fist into the screen. The screen didn't crack. He hit it again. And again. Didn't even shudder. He shook his head, the pleasing pulse of pain shooting up his arm.

Ryan put his hands on his hips and stepped back. He had deposited his check three days ago. How was he tapped out? He hit EXIT and yanked his card out of the machine. Ryan scanned the building—he couldn't remember if there was even a bank attached to the ATM. There wasn't: above him, rows of glass windows in a hideous fifties-office style stretched up six floors. Where was his bank? He remembered when he opened the account at the campus student union, the teller said, *Our goal is to make sure you never need to set foot inside a bank again.*

Back at home, he pulled out his cell and called Great Ohio, but no one answered. He called Garrett, and after two rings, he was kicked to voice mail. He didn't want to sound weak and pitiful, asking why his check hadn't hit his account yet. He flipped his phone shut, then stood with his hands on his hips and studied his spartan apartment: a couch from his college apartment facing a huge television, a coffee table, a PlayStation. White walls with two framed George Bellows reprints from the art museum, gifts from Ali when he moved in. This was a home of a person who not only couldn't afford to furnish it but also didn't know if he really wanted to, didn't know why he owned anything, and didn't know if this lack of yearning was a failure of imagination or character. Perhaps it was both. He went to the kitchen and fished an unopened Gatorade from the fridge, and drank it furiously. He and Ali had plans to go to dinner tonight, one of those Hyde Park places with starched tablecloths and candlelight and the kind of wine meant to be savored. A paycheck was supposed to make this feeling of smallness go away. Now he would not only have to live with it for another day but also admit to Ali, someone who always saw the best version of him, that he had somehow screwed up again.

He pressed a fist against the wall and considered punching holes in the drywall—plumes of white dust in the air and splashes of his blood on the walls. He closed his eyes and leaned his forehead against the wall, considering, then took the empty Gatorade bottle in his hand and slammed it on the floor. The bottle ricocheted into the air, hit the ceiling, and bounced several times before rolling to a stop, and then Ryan jumped on it, hammered his foot down on the plastic again and again and again, that satisfying crunch of something beneath him breaking.

At dinner that night, Ali nodded at his story. "And what did that accomplish?"

"I dunno. It made me feel better."

"For how long?"

He set his fork against his plate. Everything had happened just as he imagined: telling Ali in person, her understanding, her willingness to pay and not let the snafu ruin their night, the rich salty bite of halibut that he loved, wine that was delicious though he didn't taste any hints of apricot or mud or whatever the fuck the waiter had beamed about. Yet asking him to describe his feelings to her was the hardest thing to do; often, he couldn't think of words other than *happy* or *angry*, as if he was a small child. He pictured it: hands on his hips, the bottle crushed, the steady hum of the fridge, and his stomach growling with hunger.

"It passed," Ryan said.

"So there you go."

"But not really. My check is who knows where. My problem isn't exactly solved."

"I know. But punching things doesn't change that."

"Unless it's a person."

"An ATM isn't a person."

Ryan resisted the urge to lecture on corporate personhood and its R2-D2 sidekick, the automated teller machine.

"Garrett," Ali said, "will call back. It's not the end of the world."

"I know that. I'm just tired of feeling shit on."

"Welcome to the world."

"Why are you pissed at me? I took it out on a plastic bottle, and you're acting like I went postal on school children."

"Because this isn't how an adult behaves! Adults don't throw temper tantrums and break shit or punch things just because they don't get their way."

Ryan waved his hand at the room. "What is this? Look at me being civilized as fuck and eating with a fork and drinking wine and shit."

"All of which I'm paying for. So stop being an asshole."

He glowered at his food. They ate in silence for several minutes.

"What if," Ali said, "you see a therapist."

"With what health insurance?"

"You want to talk about something else."

"Yes."

"What are we doing when your lease is up?"

He set down his fork and rubbed his forehead and closed his eyes.

"If you don't want to live with me," she said, "that's fine."

"That's not it."

"Then what is it?"

Someone once told Ryan that in a relationship, you shouldn't make any big decision the first year. Don't buy a couch, don't buy a car, don't move in together. Don't get married. And so forth. He only had a vague recollection of being given this advice when he was at a party in college, not who said it, or the context; it was just one of those peculiar phrases seared into his memory. But they had been together more than a year now, and still, he was afraid. What he had seen and learned in the last few weeks told him that the housing bubble was far worse than people knew; already, talks of not just a recession, but a new Great Depression. Everything would collapse. People were still just in the pull of a building wave that hadn't yet reached its power and apex; it was still rising, ready to crash down on everything in front of it. And like a fool, he stood feeling the water pull away and into the wave, watching it grow above him, too terrified to move, too terrified to make a choice.

She had been sad when she met him. This was obvious to Ryan, though he didn't realize until they had been together for months that this sadness was what had attracted him to her, the way she was removed from her group of friends that night, sitting in a circle with four other women but leaning back as if she expected them to vanish. Ryan stood next to her at the bar when she went to get a drink, and when he offered to buy a round for all of her friends, she simply said, "waste of your money."

Their relationship started as convenient: seeing each other once a week was just fine for both of them. She was tough. His wit didn't work on her, and she didn't so much see through him as see into him, as if she knew his stories about high school football, boxing, landscaping for rich people and their long rolling lawns in Indian Hill, parking cars for Mount Adams restaurants and learning the intricate variations of manual transmissions, were all a blustery disguise. The intensity of his attraction to her, and how quickly he knew he loved her, made him wonder if he had ever truly loved anyone before.

Unlike him, Ali enjoyed working. Her conversation with the people that came into Seven was a breezy banter honed from years of working in a comic book store where the customers were uniformly a little awkward, a little shy, a little needy, a little introverted, a little too eager to find their own tribe. She knew the right amount of physical pressure to put on a person—a light hand on the back, shoulder, or forearm—or the emotional pressure of a winking permission to order a third glass of wine or a more expensive vintage. The key was that her pressure felt more like permission, the intimacy of a trusted friend, someone who looked you in the face and understood your worries before you even spoke.

Last summer, Ali closed her comic book store, Maverick's, which she had owned and operated with her brother Jerry for almost five years. He had been killed in a car accident the year before, shortly before Ryan and Ali met, and it was several months before she had even mentioned she had a brother. She said very little about Jerry, details trickling out in fleeting asides—Jerry had been an all-state cross country runner; Jerry could walk the length of a room on his hands; Jerry was terrified of dogs; Jerry loved country music—and Ryan formed an image of her older brother in his mind, a steady person comfortable with who he was and a beacon for his little sister.

The liquidation occurred over four weeks. Ali attempted to unload everything in the store—all the comic books, trading cards, toys, figurines, posters, buttons, hats, autographs—at as high a price as possible, first offering a 25 percent discount, 30 percent on bulk orders only to find that nothing sold. It was as if the words *liquidation* and *closing* and *everything must GO* were signals of mortal weakness: Why pay a premium when the store would bleed itself out? And, of course, it eventually did; Ali lowered her prices to 50 then 70 percent.

Ryan had mowed lawns from 8:00 a.m. to 3:00 p.m. for four months that summer. When he visited her after a shift, he had no place to shower. He would park in the back alley for delivery and garbage trucks, stripped off his work clothes and dumped them in a gym bag, and changed into clean gear to wear inside. The scent of fresh cut grass and gasoline clung to him. But during the liquidation, Ali wanted his help, or maybe just his presence, either of which he was happy to give. He slouched on a wooden stool and worked the register while she spoke to customers with intimacy and kindness. She looked people in the face, smiling with her eyes, her interest in people genuine. Ryan just didn't have that.

"I'll be fine," Ali said to a pair of collectors.

"Who bought this place?" one asked.

"No one, so far. The company that owns this space owns the whole strip, and they just lease out the individual stores. Who moves in doesn't really matter, as long as they pay the rent."

Ryan glanced over. The speaker was a middle-aged man: hairline receding, eyeglasses appropriate for a librarian. Ali was nodding at him.

"I gave this my best shot," she said. "I'm really sad I have to sell."

"What are you gonna do next?"

"I don't know. Something will work out. It always does."

Ryan knew she had the job at Seven lined up. Interesting she didn't tell these two about how she had also sold many comics from her personal collection to read up on the finer nuances of wine.

They hugged her before they left, and then Maverick's was again quiet. Ali and Ryan had already pulled down the sound system, and all they had was a clock radio on the back wall that, for no particular reason, neither one of them had turned on today. On the opposite wall comics were faced in alphabetical order, the holes of sold out titles like broken teeth, with handwritten signs about the discounts stuffed into empty spaces like gauze.

"Did you eat?" Ryan asked.

She shook her head. "Can you grab us something?"

"Sure. You okay here?"

"Yeah. It'll be mostly kids until after five, and then the adults come by. Those are the really chatty ones."

Ryan jutted his chin toward the door. "Who were they?"

"Charles and Alan? They live around the way. Nice guys. I think they make audio equipment or something. Anyway, they really like the manga stuff. Come by every other week or so."

"They seem nice." He stood and fished for his wallet. "Some anniversary, huh?"

"What?"

"Our anniversary. One year this week."

She crossed her arms. "Jesus. I forgot. Sorry."

"It's cool. And, technically, it's later this week, not today."

"From what? Our first date?"

"Yeah."

"Huh. I mean, I knew it was around this time. I hadn't really forgotten, not completely, but with everything . . ." Her voice trailed off.

"I know," Ryan said. "I get it."

"No, you don't," Ali said. "But that's all right. I could go for pizza. How's pizza sound?"

It sounded fine. Ryan ordered a large with mushrooms, sausage, and peppers, and after fifteen minutes, he walked across the street to pick up their order. It was a hot, miserable day, waves of heat visibly rising off the concrete, and by the time he returned with their food, Ryan was once again damp with sweat.

"Fucking gross out," he said.

Ali didn't reply. They set the pizza on top of the glass countertop. Underneath, Ali showcased her best sports memorabilia: autographed baseballs and footballs, signed photos. Only a few of them had sold, but Ali had placed SOLD signs next to several items in order to convince people they were valuable and high demand.

Ryan chewed on his second slice. They ate in silence, and the first bite told Ryan he was ravenously hungry.

"Do you plan on keeping any of this?" he asked.

"Maybe a few things. I sorta don't want to. It'll feel like a reminder. I've become less interested in collectables than I used to be."

In her apartment's second bedroom that she used as an office, on the desk in neat stacks paper clipped together, the paperwork trail of Ali's efforts to keep the store alive—years of tax returns, sales reports, income and expense reports—covered the countertop. He didn't remember seeing many of these collectible items anywhere in her apartment. She lived by herself in a two bedroom in Northside, a building that looked derelict on the outside, but beyond the new security systems—keypad, steel fencing, closed circuit cameras—it was a nicely renovated brownstone with tall windows and refinished wood floors. Her office felt like a pop art museum, decorated with framed comic book posters and autographed footballs. But the rest of her spacious apartment was not. Reprints of Cézanne landscapes decorated her hallway and living room, a sharp contrast from the muscled and exaggerated bodies of superheroes. Bookshelves free of figurines and bobbleheads were lined with her college textbooks and novels Ryan had never heard of, let alone read. Her home life was an understated and muted palatte that was clean and comfortable. Ali seemed to keep her work life boxed into that small corner literally in the back of her apartment. Why was that? Compartmentalizing? Hiding? Smart? Ryan wasn't sure. What he was sure of is that she did it, and did so successfully. It worked for her. She was solid and certain of who she was, defined by something more than just a job.

"Plus," Ali continued, "these fetch the highest price."

"Are you in trouble?"

"If I wasn't, I wouldn't be selling the store, would I?"

Ryan shrugged. Ali dipped her crust in garlic sauce.

"The store," she continued, "is for business. People know what they want now. But my costs for a physical place with the rent, electricity, heat, security, a part-time staff, all of it, just doesn't make sense anymore. Not with all these comics that never sell no matter how carefully I curate my sales titles. I have to carry all these titles that just never sell, or at least, not enough. Even this is a shame, this seventy percent off shit. I'm getting better prices on eBay selling to some guy in California."

"You could run it from home."

"Maybe. I'd still have to stock inventory somewhere. My apartment isn't big enough, neither is the limited basement space. And, honest? I want to quit. Collect the money that I can and be done with it."

"Why?"

"I did this with Jerry. He helped me write the business plan, helped me find the location. I needed him to help me get the business loan. They might have liked my number but they loved that my number came from a man, a man in front of them wearing a suit who was Chinese and happened to be an engineer. They trusted that. My loan and my rate got approved real quick."

She set her slice down.

"I'm just tired. Being a business owner never stops. Never. The store hours are really just the beginning of it. But every waking hour I'm thinking about this place, and I'm just exhausted. I've had enough. If I was really listening to myself, I would have packed it in a long time ago, but Jerry and I did this together and after he died, I felt like this was all I had left of him. I couldn't close. I couldn't. And that only made me more miserable. Took me way too long to figure that out."

"What changed?"

She looked at him. He loved her. She loved him. He knew that; they both felt love and said the words for months. But, now, in this look, there was something more, something deeper. It was vulnerability, the kind of vulnerability that, for years, was the sort of thing that men found and pounced on, whether it was with their fists or the firm words given with a smile: *I'm afraid we have to let you go.*

"When we first opened," she said, turning her gaze out the window and onto the empty parking lot in front of them, "Jerry and I came here the night we got the keys. Ordered pizza. Just like this. Same place, too. We were drinking tequila and Mountain Dew out of coffee mugs. We didn't have stools or chairs yet, hadn't thought about how we didn't have any place to sit, so we sat on the floor, and bullshitted about the store, what it was, what it could be. And it was mine. I owned something. I started something. Four years of being my own boss, being the boss. Yet, without my brother, I don't know, it's not the safety net, but the feeling that was for and about something bigger than myself. And, then, eventually, you get tired of grieving. The grieving becomes self-serving. I wake up one day and I'm not thinking about my brother. Or, I go the whole day without thinking about him. It's just sorta over. You move on. Which at first I tried to resist, but you know, that's being human. You move on. I guess I've just finished moving on.

"I wake up thinking about the day I won't wake up tired. I dream about it the way some people dream about food. I can taste it. Really. I finally know what it means when people say they are too tired to sleep. Opening the store, unloading a truck, tagging inventory, hiring people who are unreliable because I'm offering minimum wage at strange hours, website updates, bank deposits, supply chains for my piddling business. And at night, I keep thinking about my business. First thing in the morning, running in the park, it doesn't matter, I'm always thinking about it. It just never ends. It has to end. It's over."

Now, Ryan would know about the stores next to the pizza shop, the ones that were boarded up. He would know why the foreclosure rates in this neighborhood and all the surrounding neighborhoods throughout the city were rising. Over ten percent, a number he knew was terrifying and signaled doom, a number that continued to climb. He would know the paralyzing fear and depression of people losing their homes and businesses. But that was next year. In the moment, he was just a guy stinking of a day's work on rich people's lawns and in their gardens, arms folded across his chest, unsure what to say to someone he loved. All he knew was to listen, and perhaps in moments like this, listening was enough.

Ali ran her finger around the pizza box.

"I'm a failure," she said. "And that feels okay."

"You're not a failure. Sometimes, people know when to walk away."

"Sounds like something Jerry would say."

"Wish I'd met him."

"You would've liked him." Ali pushed herself upright, flexing her arms against the counter. She stood tall and gave Ryan a look he couldn't understand. Then she went to the back office and shut the door, leaving Ryan to sit at the register and wait for customers that weren't coming.

On a Wednesday afternoon, Ryan drove through Price Hill, his suit jacket on the back seat and his tie loosened. His forearm resting in the open window glistened with sweat, and he kept his wrist turned out into the breeze to keep the sun from reflecting off his watch and into his vision. He drove by a Baptist church, then a Catholic school, wound downhill toward the city, then passed Elder High School, where in one game his junior year, he had twelve tackles and an interception in a losing effort. On treeless streets, dilapidated storefronts promising payday loans were separated by rowhouses with boarded up windows, and pickup trucks rolled through stop signs, then revved their engines and made reckless left turns through traffic.

Scherzer had explained to Ryan that as a subsidiary of a larger bank, Great Ohio Financial was a dumping ground of responsibilities: mortgage brokerages, property management, section eight housing, and foreclosures. The firm employed twelve people under Scherzer, all of whom had a finger in each of these four fields. Ryan started with easy work: filing bank and legal documents, helping and shadowing the other agents, and as promised, maintenance work. It surprised him that the company didn't specialize in a particular neighborhood: Ryan was sent the full twenty miles across Cincinnati, from Westwood all the way across town to the eastern edges of Mt. Washington, the homes varying from clapboard cottages with boarded up windows to Tudors and Dutch Colonials and Georgian Revivals with weedless lawns in good school districts. If there was any sense of order to where people who couldn't pay their mortgages lived, he didn't see it.

Garrett told him to look presentable at all times; anyone, he insisted, could be or could become a client. Shave twice a day, get your haircut every three weeks. And be a fucking killer. Walk like a panther; picture the sale as a gazelle whose jugular you have to rip out. Carrying this ridiculous image with him all day, Ryan worked the property list in his briefcase, swinging through a range of Cincinnati neighborhoods that he now viewed with new, untrammeled vision. Nothing in the documentation truly explained what had happened to the family that once lived there. Sometimes, he was checking up on a two-story colonial in Oakley, a mixed class neighborhood north of Hyde Park; other times, he would find broken windows or stained carpets or cabinets ripped from the shelves. People were stripped away like lead paint. They were gone and the bank was hoping to unload the house. The real estate sign staked into the front lawns never mentioned foreclosure; there were several variations of the "upscale" signs that Great Ohio Financial used— aristocratic fonts, two-tone color schemes, clean lines, a local phone number, everything understated and nothing flashy. He would park in the driveway in front of the garage, whether it was a detached single or a three-car monstrosity. He would key in through the front door, or punch a security code, and walk through the space like a mournful ghost. Breathing in the hot Ohio summer air after he left a property often was an incredible relief, like walking out of a courthouse after hearing all the charges against you had been dropped.

Ryan's last stop of the day was in Price Hill, the foreclosed home of Isaac Henderson. He parked in front of the bank-owned house. The lawn was yellowed and spotted with dirt patches, but a new wrought-iron fence surrounded the property. In the driveway, a late model sedan with no hubcaps leaned to the right; there were empty holes in the back where the stereo speakers had once been. Ryan rolled his sleeves down and slipped on his jacket. He tried his key on the locked gate; unsurprisingly it didn't work. He stuffed the keys in his pocket and hopped the fence.

No one answered when he knocked on the front door. His key didn't fit this lock either; all the locks, he was certain, had been changed out. At least he could report that the house was still occupied. He walked around to the back, surprised to find the walkway clear. The insides of all the windows were covered with thick, dark curtains. At the back door, he knocked again. From the nearest window—over a kitchen sink, judging from its height and shape—a voice asked who was there. Ryan frowned at what seemed to be the only open window on the entire house.

"Ryan Riordan. I'm the realtor for the bank."

"You're trespassing," a voice said, clear and sonorous.

"I'm not trespassing, sir. The bank owns the property. It's my job to give it a full inspection."

"What bank?"

"I'm with Great Ohio, but we represent First Buckeye National. They're based in Columbus."

"A Columbus bank owns my home in Cincinnati? That's ridiculous. I think you're making that up."

Actually, Ryan agreed: it did sound ridiculous. He stepped to the window, narrowed his eyes. Beyond the filthy opaque screen, the shapes of a kitchen formed in the darkness: silver pots and pans on the stove, a looming refrigerator, all the countertops covered with carryout containers. Henderson seemed to be standing just out of his view.

"Did you rekey all the doors, Mr. Henderson?" Ryan asked.

"This is my house. I'm going to call the police."

"That's an excellent idea, sir. We can both show them our IDs and clarify who's the rightful owner of this property."

Ryan stood tall and waited for an answer. The paperwork indicated this was a "Henderson, Isaac," but from the experience of the last three months, it was possible not only that this was a false name, but that this wasn't even the same person.

After a long minute of silence, Ryan said, "Could we start over, Mr. Henderson? I'm not trying to fight you. I'm not the bad guy. The property is in foreclosure, and I have the authority to offer you two thousand dollars to vacate immediately."

"You're paying me to leave my home? On which you're trespassing?"

"Mr. Henderson, the property is in foreclosure. It's no longer yours. This is essentially free money I'm offering you."

"It's my home. You people know that."

What the man knew, Ryan calculated, is that Price Hill police had to investigate armed robberies, homicides, and domestic violence; throwing out homeowners, regardless of who legally owned the place, wasn't a priority. Henderson probably figured he could be here anywhere from one to six months without losing the home, and when the sheriff did come to evict him, he could simply slide out the back door and get a new NINJA loan—no income, no job, no questions asked—from another bank and squat in a different house for at least a year or two. At least, that's the way the last few years had worked; Ryan wasn't sure if 2008 would be that way. But he was pissed, and so was Scherzer, and when motivated, they could find a way to make evictions move faster. Ryan left his business card on the window sill; as far as he was concerned, he was done for the day.

The bar Ryan liked to drink at was called Yesterdays. It was on the southern edge of Mount Adams, the last bar on the street before a long, steep descent down and out of the neighborhood. The inside was a single long and narrow room with brick walls and one pool table and a jukebox of nineties music favored by college students. The bar ran the length of the left side. Out back was a small patio with metal tables and chairs, an *X* of Christmas lights crossing the air, citronella candles in tiki torches in the corners. It was on this back patio that he found his friend Andy with a plastic ashtray full of cigarette butts and three empty beer bottles in front of him.

"When are you gonna quit?" Ryan asked.

"When I get around to it. Nice tie."

Ryan shrugged. He had left the jacket in the car and rolled his shirtsleeves. Heading back to his apartment to change seemed like too much effort. He pointed at the empties and Andy nodded, so Ryan headed back inside. He raised two fingers at Matthew, who replied by nodding and then sliding over a pair of Shiner Bocks. Matthew was finishing his doctorate of psychology at UC and had worked in Yesterdays for as long as Ryan had been drinking there; he was a barrel-shaped man who moved with a catlike quickness and strength that Ryan admired.

Ryan and Andy had played football at Colerain: Ryan at free safety and Andy at fullback and linebacker, a couple of guys who liked to hit hard and talk about the gridiron with the kind of reverence that made head coaches weep. He had been stunned when Andy went to Kenyon and played football for the tiny liberal arts college, but maybe he knew something about the world Ryan didn't—Andy lettered for four years, went to law school at Case Western, and returned to Cincinnati to work for Procter & Gamble. Now Ryan studied his friend in his cargo shorts and flip flops, leaning back and smoking a Marlboro Red, his beer on his bare knee, thirty pounds heavier than he used to be. Ryan wondered if this was the type of life he too was seeking.

On Wednesdays, the bar never filled up. At a table across the patio, Ryan heard two men laughing and one of them said, "Ching, chong, chung." Ryan ignored it, and he and Andy discussed the Reds recent winning streak in detail, particularly the back end of the bullpen. They were on the West Coast, and the game wouldn't come on until late. Someone at the bar ordered a couple of communal pizzas to be delivered, and Ryan and Andy went inside for two slices each and then went back to the deck. They bullshitted about their football days, their wins over Princeton, making it to regionals, and a particular play where an interception went through both their hands—Andy first, then the tipped pass through Ryan's—for a touchdown. It was an easy, lazy night, their cold beers occasionally punctured by a shot of rye until they felt pleasantly drunk.

Once the Reds game was on, they went inside and sat at the bar, which was now filled with regulars. Though there were a handful of women, always arriving with a boyfriend rather than on their own, this was a bar mostly for men in their twenties, working men who had not yet married and had young families that kept them at home. Ryan found his attention wandering from the game to imagine what all these guys did for a living, whether they worked with their hands, behind a computer, and how often they—like him—found themselves out of work. The unemployed slouched and fidgeted in a way he recognized from his own periods without a job. Every month at Yesterdays, there were more men slouching and fidgeting.

The two men Ryan overheard outside were now standing directly next to him at the bar. After one of the Giants players, an outfielder from Korea, struck out, the man next to him chuckled, "Fags can't hit sliders."

"What's your problem?" Ryan said.

"Do what?"

"I heard you earlier. That racist ching chong shit. What's your fucking problem?"

"It's a joke, asshole," the man said, turning his wide shoulders toward Ryan. "Who fucking cares? Arab, Asian, whatever. Listen, buddy, I fought in Iraq and lemme tell you, they're all a bunch of fucking savages over there, okay? So shut the fuck up."

Ryan nodded. "Thank you for your service. I mean it. Seriously. My bad." He turned back to the bar, and after the veteran stared at the side of his face for a moment, he too turned toward the television. Then anger, even hatred, rose up in his chest, and knowing what would come next, he said loud and clear, "But you're still a fucking asshole."

The soldier turned but Ryan's left fist was already cocked back. He connected with the soldier's nose, and then rammed his knee into his groin. Ryan tackled him and drove him into the ground, slamming his hand into the man's throat. He raised up and hit him once, twice, before his buddy kicked Ryan in the ribs then pulled him up and threw him against the pool table. The second man landed one strong punch to Ryan's face, directly under his right eye, before Andy grabbed him by both arms and pulled him off Ryan. The first soldier was still on the floor, gasping for breath, and Ryan lunged at him. But before he could throw another punch, two sets of arms pulled him up and back, almost lifting him off his feet, and steered him away toward the front door. Matthew came out from behind the bar, pointed at the soldiers, and said, "Get him to the bathroom and clean him up." Then he looked at Andy. "Would you get Ryan the fuck out of here?"

Outside, Ryan laughed, ignoring the throbbing under his eye. "That was fun."

"What are you doing fighting GI Joe?"

"Did you hear what he said?"

"Yeah, he was an asshole." Andy shook his head. "Nice tackle, shithead."

"I feel awesome!"

An hour later that feeling was long gone. After Andy got him home and forced a glass of water and four ibuprofens down his mouth, Ryan was alone, stretched out the length of his couch with an ice pack against his ribs and an open but untouched beer on the floor. The room was lit by the muted television looping the late night *SportsCenter*. Who was that guy? Ryan couldn't stop thinking about it, and whether the soldier had gone home to a wife—was he wearing a wedding band?—or children, someone in the morning who would ask about his swollen, battered face. Ryan couldn't picture his face. Other than being blond, he couldn't remember anything about him. It was so strange, and so disturbing, to not have any idea who he was. One of the things he had long loved about boxing was how at the end of the match, regardless of outcome, the two men, sweaty and exhausted, would come to the middle of the ring and not just shake hands but hug. They understood something about each other, something they couldn't express with words, and it made their admiration, respect, and love all the more powerful.

Ryan lolled his chin toward the coffee table. A bottle cap and his wallet sat side by side. Had he paid for his beers? Had Andy? How much was in his wallet anyway? He blinked, tried to conjure the exact number of bills in his brown, cracked wallet, a series of changing numbers and moving decimals pinballing around his tired, achy mind.

Then he remembered. A memory so vivid it was as if it was happening again. Andy had stood in the living room, looking down at him. Flat on his back, Ryan had felt as if he was in a football game and had just been laid out trying to catch a pass across the middle, the kind of pain that had long provided moments in his life with remarkable clarity. His oldest friend pivoted around the room, hands on his hips. He looked down at Ryan.

"Dude, this is one sad apartment," Andy said. "It's time to grow up, man. You love that girl, right? You love that girl. Get on with your lives. Move in with her."

WEBN's Riverfest, Cincinnati's annual Labor Day celebration, was the largest fireworks display in the nation. On Sunday afternoon, late in the day when dusk was falling, Ryan and Ali drove south into downtown, as close to the river as they possibly could.

During the drive, Ali remained quiet, and her single word replies and utterances told Ryan all he needed to know about how disappointed she was in him. "Did you have to fight," she asked. "Did you?" He shrugged. Hadn't she known he was this way? Hadn't she known this since they first met? Whatever she once found captivating about his pugnacious, boyish energy no longer exuded the same charm. He knew it, sensed it the way he had in the past when a relationship was spiraling toward the end. Police officers in white gloves with orange batons waved cars away from the steel barriers that had been raised on the streets near the waterfront. He drummed his fingers on the steering wheel and steered into the parking garage on Third Street.

They parked, took the stairs down from the fifth floor and exited into the city. They hurried down the street in a sea of people. It was dusk, and the thick air was motionless under the heavy weight of the day. Garbage cans at the corners of the sidewalk overflowed with beer cans and food wrappers. The crowd, the sea of onlookers laughing as they rolled down the carless streets, pressed around them, people of every background, of every age, of every race, eager for one motive: celebration. Fireworks against the dark sky. The explosion of rock music along the waterfront. The entire city, tens of thousands, pressed together. The sidewalks weren't wide enough, the streets not large enough, to hold them all.

Ryan took Ali's hand and inched them forward. The city smelled of barbecue, every voice around them joyous. As they rolled toward the river into the gathering crowd, the city grew louder in rising civic glee. They pressed forward as close as they could until everyone was anchored in place. They tilted their chins toward the sky, and Ryan slipped his arms around Ali's waist, and she rested her head against his chest. Humid air made their skin sticky and slick.

She said, "I love fireworks. My first memory of this country is fireworks. Jerry and I always watched them on the Fourth."

She is two years old. Her father picks her up and carries her to the porch. They lived in an apartment then, of which she recalls little. She can see her brother walking in front of them and his tiny hands leaving their prints on the sliding door as he reaches for a door handle he is too short to grab. Cheap blinds are brushed aside, their clacking noise applauding. Her father's starched collar in her hands when he picked her up, and the smell of Old Spice, the aftershave he considered the most American. Their porch has the thin green carpeting found on mini golf courses. She and Jerry play out there. Her mother is already at the railing, looking up into the sky. Around them, all out on their small porches, decorated with rectangular flower boxes and lawn chairs and perhaps a small radio, people are outside with their families. The fireworks are coming. Independence Day. Her father holds her the entire time, never flinching or shifting his weight, even when she shrieks right in his ear at the first exploding color of red, the streaking sparks arching downward and vaporizing into a lovely boom of celebration. Then all the colors explode together over and over again, her mother pointed at the stream of sparks, Ali's hands clapped, and Jerry yelled, each time, "Dad!" as he jumped up and down, laughing while he covered his ears.

Ali said, "He loved it here. He once said that Cincinnati is a city of secret hills and peaceful parks."

Ryan nodded. If Jerry had said that to him, he would have noted that below his secret hills, it was all chaos, where people jostled each other, bustled about like mindless bees, buzzing through the madness of their daily lives.

Above, the fireworks exploded, a series of silent bursting stars of whites, blues, and reds, announcing the show would soon begin. The colors seemed to be bland, washed out, and without the thrilling rattle of the explosion something essential was absent. Glancing down, all he could see was the top of Ali's head, her thick black hair. Her face was turned upwards, and he didn't know if she was looking at him or the sky. From the massive speakers perched along the temporary, shiny towers of metal along the riverfront, an AC/DC song blasted out.

"After my brother died," she continued. "I went to Chicago. There was a card and comic convention. I took something that didn't belong to me. Three baseball jerseys. I don't know why I did it then, and I don't know why I did it now. But when I got home, I tried wearing one for a day, like putting on a new skin. Trying to get outside of myself, you know? After I got home I hung it up, and put it in the back of my closet.

"I went home, and I took them out of the closet, and I folded them up. They still had their creases. I refolded them a couple of times. Folded them, then grabbed the hem, snapped it out, and then fold them again. Like I'm OCD or something. Then, one of those times, I felt done with it. And I put them in a box, wrapped it up and mailed it back, anonymous. Does that sound completely crazy to you?"

"No. Like a purging."

"Cleansing, that might be more accurate. There's a point where you have to let go of all those shitty feelings of guilt and anger. Do you get that? You don't have to pretend you get it. I can explain it to myself, but I don't really understand it, do I?"

Ryan traced her ear with a finger. He didn't ask how she got the jerseys. He didn't ask who they belonged to. He could figure that out if he wanted to, and he didn't. Ali turned. She moved her hand up along his neck, stretching across his ear, touching his cheek. Pressing her lips against his ear, she kissed him.

"Let it go," she said. "You just can't be angry at the world all the time."

"Why not?"

The broadcaster, his voice booming through the speakers, announced the show would soon begin. He started to count down from ten. The crowd chanted with him, screaming out the numbers. They looked to the L&N, the ugly purple bridge the city had so much pride in, closed off for this: fireworks and loud music. The people erupted with screams, cheers, and sharp whistles.

Why not?

The thirty-minute spectacle started first with music. Guitars, hard rock, deafening. Then, three fireworks across the sky— red, blue, then white—and the cheering grew louder. On a large, darkened boat, a display of "WEBN" went up in flames, yellow and red flicking out like tongues. A rapid chain of shots fired into the air, the fireworks' tails whirled behind them, then they exploded in bright blues before turning green, then white, and then disappearing. Peonies sphered into the sky, then a quick blast of chrysanthemums, their visible trails of sparks elegantly disintegrating. Spiders with fast burning tails and palms bursting out their tendrils, mines and cakes, the steady blast of variety, thousands and thousands of shells, a kaleidoscope of compressed gas and chemicals. Everyone stood as one with their mouths held open, eyes wide and dilated, shoulders and necks and heads tilted in an awkward, immoveable position as each firework grew from tiny blips to massive streaks of colored flames that spread beatifically across the September sky. The grand finale made their ears ring. Hundreds of fireworks, like the cannons of a great warship, exploded above them and covered the bridge in tremendous plumes of smoke. The cheers and applause fed the noise until the explosions were so numerous their voices could not be heard. This moment seemed endless. When, finally, triumphantly, the last firework trailed off into the smoke, the cheering continued, loud and unstoppable, the city united in their celebration, the hollering becoming one voice, fists and middle fingers and peace signs thrown up as salutes to the celebration, to the music, to each other.

They stood still as the crowd, slow and thick with their celebratory mood, the long day now over, began to move away from the river. Drifts of residual smoke clung to the riverbank, floating around their heads. Ali unwrapped herself from him and took a step up the Serpentine Wall, her hairline slightly damp with sweat, and placed her hands on her hips. He stepped up next to her. She took his hand, but her face was turned toward the river. He touched the base of her neck, traced the bone and her smooth skin, and gently pushed his fingers into her dark hair. He dropped his hand to her lower back, and rested it against the curve of her spine. All the noise around them seemed to have faded to whispers.

She stepped back as if studying him. Then she turned away and climbed to the top of the wall. She took large steps, the muscles in her legs straining with the effort, and her flip flops batted against the concrete as she climbed. A small silver ring was visible along one of her toes, then vanished into shadows as she climbed higher, until she was high above him, as if he was looking up at her from the base of a ladder. She looked out at the river and the bridges, and the city threw light down on her like an offering, and he knew he could stand there looking up at Ali for a very long time.

The September heat, even in the shade, was brutal. The heat warnings had lasted for eight consecutive days, and the forecast refused to indicate a break from the triple-digit heat wave that was setting Cincinnati records. Meteorologists suggested drinking extra glasses of water, keeping fans on, avoiding being outdoors in the peak hours between noon and four, and minimizing outdoor exercise. Still, the heat claimed seven lives, six seniors and one overweight man who wasn't discovered dead in his Clifton apartment until the smell hit his neighbors, which they described to reporters as being like rotting tuna.

Ryan checked his watch; the sheriff was late. The locksmith, a young black man with reading glasses jutting out from his breast pocket, had arrived before him. Despite the heat, he sat in his truck smoking cigarettes with the windows open, the radio turned low to a country music station. Ryan wiped his brow and looked at Isaac Henderson's home.

All the windows remained dark and impenetrable. The lock on the iron-gate fence was gone. The front lawn was now buried in mounds of trash from driveway to fence. Squirrels hunted through the trash bags and scattered heaps of cardboard boxes, Styrofoam, stripped aluminum, broken stereos, and stained carpets that covered the entire front lawn. Under this sea of garbage, what could be seen of the lawn was muddy and yellow, and a hazy stench rose from the pile, its potency exacerbated by the heat.

The sheriff's patrol car rolled up slowly and parked on the opposite side of the street. The officer stepped out of the car. A black man with thick forearms, he carried weight in his neck and gut like an ex-athlete, the additional pounds unable to hide the ropy muscles in his arms. He carried the eviction papers in his hand loosely, as if he was out walking his dog. He waved to the locksmith, who tossed his cigarette into the street and pulled his toolbox from the floor of the passenger seat.

"Sheriff Mitchell?" Ryan asked.

"Mr. Riordan. ID, please."

Ryan handed him his driver's license, which Mitchell took, then scribbled down some information on a clipboard. He handed it back and said, "All right, fellas, let's go."

Mitchell lead. He pushed open the gate, and they kicked aside trash as they worked their way up the cracked sidewalk. The porch was remarkably clean: the paint was unchipped, and nothing covered the woodwork, not one dilapidated chair or a dirty ashtray.

"Sheriff's Department. Eviction notice," Mitchell said, rapping the door with the heel of his fist. The three men stood silent, the neighborhood deathly still. Mitchell knocked again, his chin tilted downward. He motioned to the locksmith. "Go ahead."

The locksmith worked fast, sliding his tools into first the lock, then the deadbolt, opening the door with a quick twist. He pushed, and the door halted. A thick chain prevented the door from being opened further.

"Unbelievable," Ryan muttered.

"You must be new," Mitchell said.

The locksmith silently removed a long claw like tool, its edges glimmering, and slipped its talons around the chain. He snapped it easily, then stepped back.

Mitchell pushed the door open and stepped in. "Sheriff's Department," he called. "Eviction notice." Ryan followed. In the unlit room, shapes began to form: a gray couch sagging under the weight of stacks of newspapers and magazines, bags of aluminum cans, an array of broken stereos and VCRs and DVD players, a high chair with three legs. Then the smell hit him.

"Fuck," Ryan coughed. He stepped back onto the porch. He looked at Mitchell, who still stood inside the doorway. "I'm okay."

"Don't worry. I haven't seen much worse than this."

Ryan entered. His vision adjusted. Large chunks of the wall were missing, huge unwieldy craters of drywall that looked as if they had been ripped loose with a pickax. Dark splatters, thick browns and yellows of mold and bacteria, covered the ruined carpet and crumbling walls. The light fixtures had been ripped out, leaving the ceiling with long veins of empty darkness, the electric wires dangling like nooses. The once indiscernible shapes became clear: mounds of trash higher than their waists, rotting food spilling from gashes in the plastic, and a whirl of flies spinning around the room. A small raccoon appeared from the middle of it all, stared at them, hissed, then scurried out the door.

"Eviction notice." Mitchell continued down the room and looked left down a hallway. He turned his head back to the kitchen and entered. Ryan stood with his back to the walkway, studying the living room, amazed by the sheer amount of garbage. He never heard the attack coming.

There was a flash, a metallic glint, and then something struck Ryan hard. His head snapped sideways. In his vision, the ceiling.

Someone shoved him hard, his vision blurry now, a nimbus of pain, and he tumbled against a couch. Newspapers, wet with mildew, crashed onto his head. A bag of trash exploded under his body, and something thick and liquid, like wet sand, enveloped him.

"I'll kill you! I'll kill you!"

Then, there was a loud crack. Nightstick on bone. The attacker howled. Ryan pushed his hands down into the filth to stand, blinking away the blood, and the slippery smell of waste hit him. He wretched, his vomit splashing down his sleeves and onto his hands, which were already covered in some black liquid, like bile. His ears buzzed, and painfully, he rolled over.

Mitchell had a man face down on the floor. The man's arms were behind him, cuffed, and he was screaming. Mitchell stood up and said, "You okay, buddy?"

Ryan didn't answer. Everything was hazy. The screaming, the blurs, the ringing; he shook his head to clear it all way, but this only created a shooting pain in his head and shoulders. A large hand gripped him under the arm and brought him to his feet.

"Let's get you outside," the locksmith said. Behind them, Isaac Henderson continued to scream.

The locksmith directed him to the curb and eased Ryan down to the street. A crowd—kids with popsicles melting down their hands, older women in house dresses, men in uniform coming off shift—had gathered on the opposite corner. Someone handed him a towel. He wiped his hands and forearms, then tried to wipe the blood from his eye. His stomach churned and he threw up again, his vomit spraying the street. He stripped off his shirt and finding a piece that was mildly clean, rubbed his face hard, then his neck, his hands, none of it removing the horrible stench from his skin. He threw the shirt in the street and stripped off his undershirt too. Knees up around his chin, Ryan hung his head. His cheek ached; he already could feel his face swelling, his right eye twitching closed.

The locksmith stood above him, then turned away and went back to the house. He returned carrying his large, steel toolbox, the muscles in his arms taut, walking with deliberate slowness. He unlocked his truck without setting it down. Once the large case was in the passenger seat, the locksmith closed his door, leaned against the engine, and removed a cigarette from his shirt pocket. He offered the exposed pack to Ryan, who refused. The locksmith took a deep drag from his cigarette and gazed at the house as if he was contemplating the final words in a long, meaningful argument.

A pair of Sheriff Department patrol cars appeared, and the officers entered the house two at a time. When Ryan heard footsteps coming from behind him, he looked up, and finally, he saw Isaac Henderson. Arms behind him, Mitchell pushing him forward, Henderson teetered down the sidewalk, his head held high and proud. His beard was trim and groomed, and he wore board shorts and unlaced basketball shoes. Who was he? What kind of person destroys his own home? Who lives in a place stuffed with garbage? He thought about the forms, the loan application, all the paperwork, and none of it really asked: Who is Isaac Henderson? The sheriff shoved Henderson into the back of the patrol car across the street, and when he was seated, leaning forward, he turned his face towards him. Ryan opened his mouth to speak and pain shot through his jaw. It didn't matter: Henderson couldn't hear him. Ryan looked down at his hands and tried to picture the people he had punched, had punched him—what, if anything, he could remember about the men he fought over the years. Nothing came to mind but dull memories of pain. Across the street, the patrol car roared to life and pulled away, and Henderson stared at Ryan until he was driven out of sight.

"How you feeling?"

Ryan looked up. Mitchell towered over him.

"What hit me?" Ryan asked.

"A Bowie knife with brass knuckles. I need a statement before you go to the hospital."

"I'm not sure what happened."

"Just tell it like it was. That's all."

The neighborhood buzzed with dissonant noise: loud chatter speckled with bursts of wild laughter, amplified sirens, honking horns from traffic, an applause of something metallic banging together, a rising crescendo of activity with no singular source. Everything in his vision haloed. Someone pulled Ryan up, and then he was sitting on the rear bumper of an ambulance. An EMT wiped down his hands and arms, removing the grime from his body with long even strokes of a damp towel, a smell of disinfectant creeping off Ryan's now shiny skin. He tried and failed to follow the medic's fingers up and down, side to side, a pulsating pain behind his eyes, pinching his neck. Another medic pressed an ice pack against his face, the cold plastic welcoming.

"You need to go to the ER, buddy," a medic said. "You probably have a concussion and you're gonna need stitches. That's a nasty gash you got there."

Ryan nodded. "I think I'm okay."

"No, you aren't. C'mon, get in the ambulance. I'll turn on the siren and everything."

Ryan looked down at his discarded shirt lying in the street, crumpled into a ball of sickly colors. If he could have, he would have stripped off all his clothes; somehow, he knew the stench of that house was never going to come off.

"I can't afford it," Ryan said. "Can't afford to get in an ambulance."

The EMT didn't argue. He stood tall and placed his hands on hips, staring down at Ryan like an exasperated school teacher. From somewhere behind him, Ryan heard, "I'll drive him."

He turned. The locksmith nodded like a bobblehead, then offered his hand to help Ryan up. With a hand on Ryan's back, the locksmith steered him toward his truck, held the door open, and reminded him to put on his seatbelt. He came around the front of the truck, hopped in, and lit a cigarette before turning the ignition.

"What's your name?" Ryan asked.

He blew out smoke. "Cary."

"Thanks, Cary."

"Hey, man, no problem. Those ambulance bills are crazy. If you get a good one, they'll talk to you first, see if they can get you in your car if someone else can drive you. But others, man, they don't give a shit. Smart of you to think of that." He grinned. "Maybe you didn't get punched in the head too hard after all!"

"Maybe not," Ryan said. He stared at Cary's face. In profile, he had a trim beard, gray spotting his chin, and an open expression with shrewd, merry eyes. He drove tapping his wedding ring against the steering wheel, commenting on the neighborhood with a point and a nod, Ryan listening without hearing, watching the man's face. *Cary the locksmith*, he thought. *I hope I can remember this.*

Ryan pressed the cold pack against his face and closed his eyes. He needed to call Ali. Or had he already? When he opened his eyes again, he was being led by Cary into the emergency room; could he have really fallen asleep in the truck? Everything about the next few hours seemed hazy, waiting to be seen, the various stages of distress the people around him were in—back pain, a bad headache, a family rushing in with a kid in a wheelchair—until it was his turn and someone was stitching up his face. By the time he had popped Celebrex and filled out the prescription form and stood finishing his discharge paperwork, Ali arrived.

"Hey," Ryan said. "How did you know I was here?"

"You called me, you idiot." Her fingers were cool against his head. "Jesus."

"I didn't fight anybody. I didn't."

She put her hand gently on the back of his neck. "I know."

"He's fine," the attending said. "Mild concussion. Nothing a good night's sleep won't take care of."

"Where's my car?" Ryan asked.

"I'm driving you home," Ali said.

"Home," he said dumbly. That's nice. It was also nice the way it felt like she carried him out of the emergency room and into the parking lot air, the humidity broken into a cool autumn night. He heard the firm smack of the car door closing, and when he rolled his head to the left, he saw her profile looking out onto the road, guiding them with watchful certainty through the night.

He didn't remember falling asleep again, but he did know that when he next felt bright and alert, it was the middle of the night, and he was flat on his back in Ali's bed, looking up at the ceiling and the shadows from the streetlights thrown in gray beams across the room. Across the room, Ali pulled a T-shirt over her head, giving him just a quick glimpse of her bare back, and then slid into bed next to him. She rested her hand on his bare chest, and he became aware of the numbness of his hands.

He turned his head toward her. He said, "I didn't fight anybody."

They were in the dark, his head ached, he was thirsty, and he could feel the fatigue all through his body. But he saw her. She was watching him, and he knew they would remember this moment together for a very long time. He never doubted that she loved him, but he had doubted that she would stay with him. But she was still here, looking after him, protecting him, steadfast when he was at his most vulnerable. *You see me, don't you?* He wasn't sure if he said this or just thought it. Headlights passed by the window, and there, bright and clear, Ali's face: black hair shaping her cheeks, brown eyes with the first traces of crow's feet in the corners, lean cheeks from her years of running, thought lines in her brow, a small jagged scar to the side of her nose from when she fell from a tree when she was a little girl, her lips slightly parted revealing white teeth, her smile a little lopsided. When Ali smiled—beautiful, that smile, that face, that person—she smiled with her entire body. Ali rested her hand on his chest, and it felt like she was the one that pumped his heart. "Of course," she said. "Of course."

ACKNOWLEDGEMENTS

Thank you to Mark Gottlieb of Trident Media Group, for your tireless encouragement and support, and Stephanie Beard of Turner Publishing, for championing my writing and her steadfast advocacy for all of my work.

Thank you to the editors who first discovered, read, and published these stories: Michael Koch, Caitlin Horrocks, David Lynn, Phong Nguyen, Alexander Weinstein, John Tait, Sophie Beck, Steven Church, James Scott, Cameron Finch, Erin Stalcup, and Kathleen J. Canavan.

Thank you to my friends who have read (many) drafts of my writing: Gordy Sauer, Jessica Rogen, Eve Jones, Keija Parssinen, Rachel Swearingen, Evelyn Somers, Tanya McQueen, and Alison Balaskovits. Thanks to the people who have supported a writing life with their friendship: Fred Venturini, Ted Mashtay, Valerie Cumming, Mike Croley, Bill Lychack, Adrian Matejka, Marc McKee, Anne Valente, Brad Babendir, Justin Eleazer, and the #CelticsWire crew. Thank you to my family—Kathy, Frank, Annie, and of course, my sister Robyn and my mother Kathy.

Finally, to my wife Liz, for her love, compassion, generosity, and partnership in this zigzag we call life.

ABOUT THE AUTHOR

Michael Nye is the author of two works of fiction: the story collection *Strategies Against Extinction* and the novel *All the Castles Burned*. His writing has appeared in *American Literary Review*, *Epoch*, *LitHub*, *The Millions*, *Kenyon Review*, *Normal School*, and *Notre Dame Review*. He is the editor of Story and lives with his family in Ohio.

CPSIA information can be obtained
at www.ICGtesting.com
Printed in the USA
BVHW030832210620
581884BV00020B/55

9 781684 425068